BOMBPROOF

Michael Robotham

SPHERE

First published in Australia and New Zealand in 2008 by
Sphere/Hachette Australia for Books Alive
This edition published in Great Britain in 2009 by Sphere
Reprinted by Sphere in 2010, 2011 (twice), 2013, 2014

A CIP catalogue record for this book
is available from the British Library.

ISBN 978-0-7515-4204-2

Typeset in Baskerville by M Rules
Printed and bound in Great Britain by
Clays Ltd, St Ives plc

Papers used by Sphere are from well-managed forests
and other responsible sources.

MIX
Paper from
responsible sources
FSC
www.fsc.org   FSC® C104740

Sphere
An imprint of
Little, Brown Book Group
100 Victoria Embankment
London EC4Y 0DY

An Hachette UK Company
www.hachette.co.uk

www.littlebrown.co.uk

This one is for my Dad

A Very Bad Day

Some days are diamonds. Some days are stones. John Denver used to sing that before he crashed a plane into Monterey Bay. It wasn't a diamond day for him.

Sami Macbeth's day has been nothing but stones. Emerging from Oxford Circus Underground, he blinks into the sunlight and coughs so hard it feels as if his sphincter is coming up through his lungs looking for clean air. His clothes are torn and bloody. His face streaked with sweat. His skin coated in dust.

Sami ducks beneath a makeshift barricade of crime-scene tape hanging from plastic bollards. People step aside and stare at him like he's some sort of ghost.

Six and a half pounds of TATP – the Mother of Satan – just blew a gaping hole in a packed carriage on the Central Line, peeling off the roof like a giant opening a big can of peaches.

It was horrible down there. Mayhem. One moment

Sami was standing near the train doors and the next he was lying on his back, flapping his arms and legs like an upturned beetle. Papers were blown through the air, glass showered down on him and the train shuddered to a halt. Things went quiet for a moment and completely dark. Then the screaming started.

People were hurt. Dying. God knows how many. Who was sitting in the other carriage next to Dessie? A guy in a Jesus T-shirt with his eyes closed, doing the nodding dog. Next to him was a suit with a briefcase. There was also a girl standing near the doors, wearing a short jacket. She had white headphones trailing from under her long hair.

Sami looks up and down Oxford Street. Traffic is at a standstill. Buses, vans, cars and cabs – nothing is moving. Someone hands him a bottle of water. He pours it over his head. Soot runs into his mouth and crunches between his teeth.

Crossing the road between two trucks, he forgets to lift his feet and trips over the gutter. A driver calls out. Sami doesn't answer. He turns down Argyll Street and crosses Great Marlborough, stepping round pedestrians. Moving quickly.

People are staring at each other. Shocked. Clueless. Sami hears snippets of their conversation: '. . . terror- ists . . .' '. . . a bomb . . .' '. . . underground . . .'

They're frightened. Sami is frightened. Dessie just blew himself to Kingdom fucking Come. He'll need a very short coffin – Y-shaped to fit his legs and his bollocks.

2

The rucksack slaps against Sami's back. He should ditch it and run. Take his chances. But what would Murphy do to Nadia?

It's like the platform announcer said: 'Please keep your bags with you at all times and report any unattended items or suspicious behaviour to a member of staff.'

Sami should call Murphy. Explain. What would he say? 'Hey, Mr Murphy, a funny thing happened on the way home. We accidentally blew up a train and Dessie lost his head and a little bit more . . .'

Sami doesn't have a mobile. Dessie wouldn't let him carry one. Now he notices a guy sending a text message. He's unshaven, wearing Levi's, slung slow, showing his arse-crack.

Sami asks if he can borrow the phone. The guy stares at him. 'Were you down there, man? Respect.' He hands Sami the phone. 'Take it. I can't get a signal.'

Sami punches in a number. Nothing happens.

'Too many people trying to make calls,' says the arse-crack guy. 'The network is overloaded.'

Sami hands him back the phone and keeps walking, crossing at the next intersection. He notices a black cab. Opens the door. Slips onto the back seat. Dumps the rucksack on the floor between his knees.

'You're joking, aren't you, mate?' says the driver. He motions to the road ahead. 'I haven't moved in forty fuckin' minutes.'

Sami catches sight of himself in the rear mirror. His

face is caked in dark soot except for two streaks of white, one on the tip of his nose and the other a line of perspiration running over his cheekbone and down his neck. It could be war paint. He's been into battle.

The driver is listening to the radio.

'Bomb went off,' he explains. 'There could be more of them.'

'More what?'

'Suicide bombers.' The driver looks at him. 'You must have been down there. You look like Al fuckin' Jolson.'

'Who's he?'

'You never heard of Al fuckin' Jolson?'

'No.'

'He was a white guy used to black up his face and sing like a nigger.'

'Why?'

'Fuck knows.'

The driver has his door propped open. He lights a cigarette and the roll of smoke seems to evaporate on the breeze.

'You got a phone?' asks Sami.

'Yeah.'

'Can I borrow it?'

'Won't do you any good. They shut down the network, or the whole thing has crashed. Every man and his dog is trying to call home.'

'Why would they shut down the network?'

'Stop them setting off any more bombs. That's how

4

the ragheads do it – use mobile phones. Call the number and boom. Makes no sense to me. Live and let live, I say. We should make a deal with the terrorists – we won't invade their fucked-up countries if they stop blowing us up.'

'Maybe it wasn't terrorists,' suggests Sami.

'Of course it was fuckin' terrorists,' replies the driver. 'You're not bleeding, are you? I don't want friggin' blood on the seats.'

'I don't think so.'

'You're covered in that black shit. Maybe you should just get out.'

'Couldn't I just sit here?'

'Does this cab look like a fuckin' backpacker's?'

Sami gets out. Swings the rucksack over one shoulder. Drops his head and keeps moving.

Turning out of Rupert Street into Shaftesbury Avenue, he almost runs into a big black rozzer standing on the corner, directing traffic. Really big, two-fifty pounds at least, made even larger by his vest, which is bristling with Old Bill gadgets.

Sami apologises. The rozzer tells him to slow down and watch where he's going. Then he clocks Sami's clothes and the rucksack.

'What you carrying, lad?'

'Nothing.'

'Looks pretty heavy to be nothing.'

'Dirty laundry.'

5

'Show me.'

'It's locked.'

'You always lock up your dirty laundry?'

'There's loads of perverts about,' says Sami. 'You can't be too careful.'

The rozzer is already reaching for the radio on his arm. He tells Sami to put the rucksack down and slowly step back.

Sami's insides are betraying him now. His hair is full of broken glass. His clothes are covered in shit. He doesn't need this. Not today. Not after what he's been through. At that moment, somewhere in Sami's subconscious, a camera shutter blinks and he can see a dozen years in prison. The shutter blinks again and this time he pictures his sister Nadia lying on a bed, her dress plastered to her body, a crack whore for Tony Murphy.

The black constable grabs hold of Sami's arm. Instinct kicks in. Sami drops his head into the rozzer's stomach, hearing the wind whistle out of his mouth and nose. He's running now, dodging pedestrians, leaping over a dog on a lead, bursting through a queue, knocking over a man carrying a sandwich board.

The Underground is closed. The steps deserted. There are transport police at the stairs. Across the street, between ambulances and fire engines, there are proper police officers keeping the crowds back. Sightseers. Rubbernecks.

Sami crashes into an outdoor table, spilling a bottle of

wine and upending a woman in mid-meal. A waiter gives him a gobful. He keeps running. The bag over one shoulder. Slapping against his back. He should stop and tighten the straps, clip the belt around his waist, redistribute the weight, but he's too scared to stop.

Run. That's what every sense tells him to do. Just run. Get away. Find somewhere quiet. Hide the rucksack. Steal a moment to think.

He ducks into an alley, leans his back against a wall. The rucksack props him up. He listens. Sirens. Stuck in traffic. Trying to outrun them on foot is a loser's game. They'll corner him and wait for reinforcements.

Sami has to go off the radar. Disappear. He has money now – the stash from the safe. But first he has to get out of the West End . . . out of London.

There's a church across the square. He can hide inside. Stash the rucksack in a dark corner. Say a prayer. It's a good plan.

He comes out of the alley and finds three policemen in front of him. One of them has a gun and is crouching, holding it in two hands, like he knows how to use it.

'Don't move,' he yells. 'Put the bag down.'

Sami looks behind him . . . looks ahead. Holds his fist in the air; his thumb cocked. Empty, but they don't know that.

'I got a fucking bomb,' he yells, not recognising his own voice. 'Get back or I'll flatten this place.'

The rozzers melt away. Sami runs past them. The one

with the gun is lying on the ground, on his elbows, trying to get a shot. Sami keeps moving, stepping from side to side.

A bomb. He told them he had a bomb. What a prize fuck-up. What a joke! Sami isn't just unlucky; he's a walking jinx, a Jonah, a one-man wrecking crew. He's trouble with a capital 'T' and that rhymes with 'D' and that stands for dead.

Three days ago he walked out of prison and swore he'd never go back. Thirty-six hours ago he was shagging Kate Tierney, the woman of his wet dreams, in a suite at the Savoy thinking life was looking up. Now he's carrying a rucksack that could send him to prison for the rest of his life through the West End of London and he's turned himself into the most wanted man in Britain.

This is how it happened.

Three Days Ago

1

On his last morning in prison Sami Macbeth woke early, brushed his teeth, folded his blankets in a neat pile and sat on the bed, waiting.

He told himself that everything he did was for the last time. It was the last time he would piss into a steel bowl; the last time he was strip-searched, or deloused, or would wake to the dawn chorus of farting, belching, swearing and coughing.

Unable to keep still, he rests his feet on his bunk and counts down through a hundred push-ups, breathing through his nose. He stands and looks into a shaving mirror, no longer surprised at seeing himself with short hair, although it's growing out quickly. He's put on weight. Most of it is probably muscle but he's not like those cons who spend every waking moment pumping weights and flexing in front of the mirror. Who are they trying to impress?

With two short fast steps, Sami leaps at the wall, planting his foot at chest height and spinning in a complete

11

somersault before landing on his feet. He does it again . . . and again.

A voice from below interrupts.

'Cut it out, cocksucker, I'm trying to sleep.'

'Almost done,' says Sami.

'Do it again and I'll kill your entire family.'

Sami's cell is on the first floor. No. 47. D-wing. It is eight feet wide and ten feet long, with brick walls and a cement floor. The only window, high on the wall, has tiny glass squares, some of them missing or broken. When he first arrived, in the middle of February, wind used to whistle through the gaps and the cell was freezing. Eventually, he filled the gaps with toilet paper, chewed into a pulp and wedged like putty into the holes.

He won't have to worry about another winter. By midday he's out of here. Not completely free, but as good as. Parole is a wonderful thing.

Sami yawns and rubs his eyes. He didn't sleep well. A fresh fish arrived yesterday and they put him in the cell next door. The kid tried to look relaxed and act tough but his eyes were big as saucers and he kept looking at people sideways like a bird in a cage.

The cons called him Baby Ray and he spent all night talking to Sami – too scared to go to sleep. First night jitters. Everyone has them. He told Sami he wouldn't be staying long, a short season, for one night only. He had a bail hearing the next day and his old man was going to pay whatever it took to get him out.

12

'Your old man must have deep pockets,' Sami said.

'I'm his only son.'

Baby Ray had a silver tongue, a sharp tongue, a tongue for every groove. He talked about the girls he'd shagged, the fights he'd won, the deals he'd done. Sami wasn't bothered. He was never going to sleep on his last night. He was going to count down the hours.

Baby Ray must have gone to breakfast or still be asleep. Sami's stomach rumbles. Normally, this is the only meal of the day he doesn't miss. You can't fuck up breakfast. You scramble eggs, you grill sausage, you heat up beans; nobody can fuck up breakfast.

Today he's not going. He doesn't want anything to go wrong. No shoving in the food queue, no fights, no bullying, nothing that could see him brought up on charges or see his parole revoked. Instead he sits on his bed, stares at the concrete wall and thinks of Nadia.

Nadia is his sister. She's nineteen. Beautiful.

They don't look like brother and sister. Nadia has long dark hair, brown eyes and golden brown skin. She's part Algerian. So is Sami, but he inherited his father's blue eyes and dirty blond hair.

Nadia was only seventeen when Sami was sent down. She was still at school. Now she's working as a secretary and going to college two nights a week. She's renting a flat and driving her own car – one of those Smart cars that look like it comes with a Happy Meal.

13

Sami hasn't seen her since Christmas. He only transferred back to the Scrubs a fortnight ago from Leicester nick, which was a long way for Nadia to travel, even with a rail warrant.

Someone drove her to see him. Waited outside. Her boyfriend. She wouldn't tell Sami his name. He had a sports car and drove with the top down, mussing up her hair.

When everyone has gone to breakfast, Sami leaves his cell to use his last phone card. He calls Nadia. No answer. It's been three days. She knows he's getting out today.

He goes back to his cell. Sits. Waits. Watches the clock.

Time has special meaning to him now. He has studied it closely and mastered the art of imagining it passing. For two years, eight months and twenty-three days he has become an expert in how much a minute takes out of an hour and how much an hour takes out of a day. How fast a fingernail grows. How long it takes for his fringe to cover his eyes.

He has missed two birthdays, two Christmases, two New Years and countless opportunities for meaningless one-night stands with single London girls who have a thing for guitar players. He'll have to play catch-up.

At 11.30 Mr Dean, the senior screw on D-wing delivers Sami's belongings in a pillowcase.

Mr Dean waits for him to get changed into a pair of jeans, a shirt, a leather bomber jacket and trainers. Sami

14

has to hand back his prison kit which Mr Dean checks off on a list. Afterwards he walks in front of the warder to the reception centre, carrying his personal effects in his arms. They don't consist of much: a wristwatch, a transistor radio, three photographs – two of Nadia – a bundle of letters, a mobile phone with a flat battery and a plastic bag containing thirty-two pounds and seventy-five pence. Sami has to count the money and sign for it in three places.

As he walks along the landing and down the metal stairs, some of the other cons are calling out to him.

'Hey, Sparkles, when you get out get yourself laid for me.'

'Get shit-faced,' someone else yells.

At three minutes past noon, Sami walks out of the small, hinged door in the much larger gates of Wormwood Scrubs Prison. It's been raining, but the shower has passed. Puddles fill the depressions, reflecting blue sky. Bluer now he's outside. He raises his face and blinks at the sky. Takes a deep breath. He knows it's a cliché about freedom smelling sweeter, but it's a cliché for a reason.

He keeps walking across the cobblestones, away from the gates. There's no sign of Nadia. She could be running late. London traffic. There's a car parked opposite in a bus zone, a big black four-wheel drive Lexus with the darkest legal tint.

As Sami walks past a window glides down.

'Are you Sami Macbeth?' asks a squeaky voice coming

15

from a head so round and smooth it looks like it should be bobbing on the end of a string. Maybe that explains his voice, thinks Sami.

There are three other guys in the car all wearing dark suits like they're auditioning for a Guy Ritchie film. They're not friends of Nadia's and they're not from the local mini-cab firm.

'Are you fucking deaf?' asks the guy with the balloon-shaped head.

Sami scratches his cheek. Tries to stay calm. 'Why do you want Macbeth?'

'You him or not?'

'No, mate,' says Sami, swinging his bag over his shoulder. 'Macbeth kicked off at breakfast this morning. Got into a row with some bloke and threw a mug of tea in his face. They're keeping him in.'

'For how long?'

Sami motions over his shoulder. 'Knock on the door. Maybe they'll tell you.'

Then he gives a little skip as he walks away, telling himself not to look back. What do these guys want with him? Where's Nadia?

Down the street he finds a bus stop. Sits down. Waits some more.

A bus pulls up. The poster on the side shows a woman in a bikini lying on a pool chair. Golden skin. Clear eyes. Sami is so busy looking at the girl he forgets to get on the bus. The doors close. The bus pulls away.

He waits. Another bus comes. The driver doesn't look at him.

'Where you going?'

'Station.'

'Which one?'

'Nearest.'

'Two quid.'

Sami takes a window seat. Looks at the playing fields. Nadia must have had to work. She'll have left a note at the flat. They'll celebrate later. Order a curry. Watch a DVD.

Ever since their mum died, Sami and Nadia have looked after each other. And even before then, he'd kept Nadia out of harm's way when any of their father's lecherous friends took a liking to her.

She wanted to leave school at sixteen. Sami made her stay. He did courier jobs, drove a van. At night he played gigs. He wasn't cock deep in cash but he had enough to keep the wolf from the door.

Sami had often wondered what that saying meant. What sort of wolf – the fairytale kind, like in Little Red Riding Hood or the Three Little Pigs, or the human kind?

It wasn't always happy families. Sami and Nadia's fights were legendary. That's the thing about Nadia. She's not some sort of innocent butter-wouldn't-melt-in-her-mouth angel. She's had her moments. Skipping school. Underage drinking. Sneaking into nightclubs when she was only fifteen.

Nadia also had some black days. It was a family disease. A school counsellor wanted to send her to a psycho-whatsit, but Sami wouldn't let them. He also had to fight Social over letting her live with him. He went to court. Won. Didn't rub it in. You don't give them any excuses.

For a long time Nadia had no idea she was beautiful. Blokes would have licked shit off a stick for her, but she didn't care. After a while she began to realise.

She had a few modelling shots taken when she was sixteen, glossy professional ones, soft focus around the edges. She touted her portfolio around some of the modelling agencies but they said she didn't have the look they were after, you know, the anorexic don't-let-me-near-the-fridge heroin chic look.

She did have something going for her. The photographers knew it. One of the agents knew it. Nadia had that vulnerable, big eyes, full lips, just-been-shagged look that directors love. Porn directors.

Sweet but not so innocent Nadia.

Sami saved her from the wolves.

That's what big brothers are for.

2

Vincent Ruiz's worst dream has always included an orange sledge and an ice-covered pond with a hole at its centre. A child is pulled from within, blue lips, blue skin. He is to blame.

His second worst dream features a man called Ray Garza, who is like the ghost of Christmas past showing Ruiz his past failings. Garza's face has sharp features, bone beneath skin, with a scar across his neck where someone once tried to slice open his throat but didn't cut deep enough. Hopefully they were more successful at cutting their own throat because you'd want to die quickly if you crossed Ray Garza.

Garza is now a pillar of society, a member of the establishment, rich beyond counting. He is invited to dine at Downing Street, given gongs by Her Maj and gets mentioned in newspaper diaries as a philanthropist and patron of the arts.

Yet every time Ruiz sees a photograph of him at some charity function, or film premiere, he remembers Jane

Lanfranchi. It was twenty-two years ago. She was only sixteen. A wannabe beauty queen.

Garza was going to make her a page-three sizzler, the next Sam Fox. That's before he sodomized her and chewed her cheek open to the bone.

Such a beautiful face, destroyed. Such a sweet girl, traumatised. Ruiz promised Jane that he'd protect her. He promised that if she were brave enough to take the stand and tell the truth, he'd put Garza in prison. It was a promise he couldn't keep.

Jane Lanfranchi committed suicide two days before the trial, unable to look at her face in the mirror. The charges were dismissed. Garza went free. He smiled at Ruiz on the steps of the court. His crooked mouth lined up when he grinned and his acne-scarred cheeks looked like lunar craters.

Ruiz has always been a pragmatist. There are bad people in the world – rapists, murderers, psychopaths – many of them nameless, faceless men, who are never caught. The difference this time was that he knew Ray Garza's name, knew where he lived, knew what he'd done, but could never prove it.

One of Ruiz's mates, a psychologist called Joe O'Loughlin, once told him that some dreams solve problems while others reflect our emotions. Carl Jung believed that 'big dreams' were so powerful they helped shape our lives.

Ruiz thought this was bollocks, but didn't say so.

20

History showed that whenever he disagreed with Joe O'Loughlin, he ended up looking stupid. Ruiz knows why he had the dream. It happens every year. Just before his birthday. He's sixty-two today. In a couple of hours the first post will arrive. There'll be a birthday card from his son Michael and daughter Claire. Twins. His ex-wife Miranda will send him something funny about him being only as old as the woman he's feeling.

There'll be another card, one from Ray Garza. He sends one every year – a goading, vindictive, poisonous reminder of Jane Lanfranchi, of broken promises, of failure.

Ruiz looks at the clock beside his bed. It's gone six. He doesn't feel rested or rejuvenated. One of the annoying legacies of old age is the copious passing of water and learning the odours of various vegetables and beverages.

Pain is the other legacy, a permanent ache in his left leg, which is shorter than his right and heavily scarred. A bullet did the damage. High velocity. Hollow pointed. Painkillers were harder to recover from. Even now, as he lies in bed, it feels as though ants are eating away at his scarred flesh.

The pain always wakes him slowly. He has to lie very still, feeling his heart racing and sweat pooling in his navel. The hangover is entirely expected and nothing to do with pain management. Ruiz drank half a bottle of Scotch last night and almost fell asleep on the sofa, too cold to get comfortable and too drunk to go to bed.

Now it's morning. His birthday. He wants it to be over.

Ruiz gets out of bed at seven. Runs a cold tap in the bathroom. Fills his cupped hands. Buries his face in the water. He dresses slowly, methodically, as though working to a plan. Socks, trousers, shirt, shoes. There is order in his life. He might be retired but he has his routines. He goes downstairs and puts on a pot of coffee.

Sixty-two. When you reach such an age, you don't so much stop counting birthdays as *lose* count of them. Does that make him old or is he still middle-aged?

Most people can remember their childhoods with great clarity and later in life entire decades disappear into the ether. Ruiz is different. For him there has never been such a thing as forgetting. Nothing is hazy or vague or frayed at the edges. He hoards memories like a miser counts gold – names, dates, places, witnesses, suspects and victims.

He doesn't see things photographically. Instead he makes connections, spinning them together like a spider weaving a web, threading one strand into the next. That's why he can reach back and pluck details of criminal cases from five, ten, fifteen years ago and remember them as if they happened only yesterday. He can conjure up crime scenes, recreate conversations and hear the same lies.

He looks out the window. It's raining. Water ripples across the Thames, which is slick with leaves and debris.

He has lived by the river for twenty-five years and it's still a mystery to him.

Maybe the post won't arrive if it's raining. The postman will stay at the sorting office. Keep dry. In which case the card from Ray Garza will come tomorrow. He'll have another night of waiting. Dreaming.

Darcy comes downstairs when the coffee is done. She must be able to smell it. She's dressed for college, in dance trousers, trainers, a sweater and sleeveless ski jacket.

'Happy birthday, old man.'

'Piss off.'

'Don't you like birthdays?'

'I don't like teenagers.'

'But we're the future.'

'God help us.'

Darcy isn't his daughter or his granddaughter. She's a lodger. It's a long story. Her mother is dead and her father has known her for less time than Ruiz. She's eighteen and studying at the Royal Ballet School.

She sits on a chair, crosses her legs and holds her coffee with both hands on the mug. She can bend like a reed and move without making a sound.

'I'm going to bake you a cake,' she announces.

'You don't have to do that.'

'What sort do you want? Do you like chocolate? Everyone likes chocolate. How old are you?'

'Sixty-two.'

'That's old.'

23

'You don't count the years, you count the mileage.'

'What does that mean?'

'It doesn't matter.'

She has found a piece of fruit. Breakfast. There's nothing of her.

'Are you ever going to get married again?' she asks.

'Never.'

'Why not?'

'It's an expensive way to get my laundry done.'

Darcy doesn't find him funny.

'How many times have you been married?'

'Haven't you got classes to go to, stretches to do, pirouettes?'

'You're embarrassed?'

'No.'

'Well, tell me. I'm interested.'

'My first wife died of cancer and my second wife left me for an Argentine polo player.'

'There were more?'

'My third wife doesn't seem to remember that we're divorced.'

'You mean she's a friend with benefits.'

'A what?'

'A friend who lets you sleep with her.'

'Christ! How old are you?'

Darcy doesn't answer. She sips her coffee. Ruiz starts thinking about sleeping with Miranda. It's a nice idea. She's still a fine looking woman and if memory serves they used to tear up the sheets. The sex was so good even the neighbours had a cigarette afterwards.

They divorced five years ago but stay in touch. And the intervening period hasn't been benefit-free. They had a steamy weekend in Scotland when one of her nephews got married, and had another brief fling when Ruiz got stabbed in Amsterdam and Miranda looked after him for a couple of days.

Friends with benefits – the idea could grow on him.

'What are you smiling about?' asks Darcy.

'Nothing.'

A metal clang echoes from the front hall. The post. Ruiz feels hollow inside. Darcy springs up and fetches the envelopes, counting out the birthday cards and putting them on the table.

'Aren't you going to open them?'

'Later.'

'Oh, come on.'

Michael has sent a postcard from Bermuda. He's sailing charter yachts. Claire's card has a portrait of a bulldog, all jowls and slobber. She's going to call and arrange lunch. She has a boyfriend now – a barrister, who knows all the scurrilous gossip and rumour. Ruiz suspects he's a Tory.

Miranda's card has a cartoon of a naked woman wearing an astronaut's helmet. The pay-off line is: 'Very funny, Scotty, now beam down my clothes.'

There is another envelope. Square. White.

'This one now,' says Darcy, handing it to him.

Ruiz slides his thumb under the flap. Tears it open. The front has a photograph of a kitten playing with a ball of wool.

'Many happy returns,' it says. Ray Garza has signed his initials and written a postscript.

She's still the best fuck I ever had.

Ruiz closes the card. His hands are shaking.

'Who is it from?' asks Darcy.

'Moriarty.'

26

3

Sami Macbeth got sent down for the Hampstead jewellery robbery, which isn't the whole story. He got sent down because a mate with a van ran across six lanes of motorway and got cleaned up by a German lorry carrying eighteen tons of pig iron.

Andy Palmer wasn't even a proper mate. He was a man with a van who used to take their gear to gigs; the amps, leads, mikes and drums. He was a roadie. A muppet. A hanger-on. Andy couldn't play an instrument, he could barely drive, but he loved bands and he loved live music.

This particular Saturday afternoon he and Sami were heading to Oxford to set up for a gig. They stopped at a motorway service area because Andy had turned one on the night before and needed one of those high-energy caffeine drinks and Tic Tacs. Sami waited in the van, listening to Nirvana and doing his Kurt Cobain impersonation.

A police car pulled up alongside the van. One of the officers nodded to Sami. Sami's eyes were closed, but his head was rocking back and forth.

Just then Andy came out of the automatic doors, sucking on a can of Red Bull. He spied the police car next to the van and took off, legging it past the pumps and sliding down the embankment. He sprinted across three lanes of westbound motorway and barely broke stride as he hurtled the crash barrier.

By then the rozzers were chasing him but Andy didn't stop. He sidestepped a BMW, dodged a caravan, slid between a transit van and an Audi station wagon and just beat a dual rig with a soft top that swerved to avoid him.

The rozzers were still stuck on the central reserve, trying to make the traffic slow down. Andy thought he was away. Six lanes. He'd crossed them all. Sad fucker didn't bank on the motorway exit, which is why a German truck driver turned him into a speed bump six times over. Bump. Bump. Bump. Bump. Bump. Bump.

Sami watched it happen. Nirvana was still playing. The guitars were screaming just like the truck tyres.

What Sami didn't know was that Andy Palmer had a bit of extra kit in the van. Tucked into one of the amplifiers was a diamond the size of a quail's egg and a dozen emeralds, all of them linked together.

The necklace belonged to a rich widow in Hampstead whose hubby used to be a diamond dealer in Antwerp. She wasn't some doddery old dear who put baubles in a pillowcase. She had a state-of-the-art, dog's-bollocks safe, imported from America, with motion sensors and alarms.

It was fireproof, earthquake proof, bomb proof, but for some reason it wasn't Andy Palmer proof.

Sami found this hard to believe. The same Andy Palmer who couldn't find his arse with both hands, had broken into the most sophisticated safe in the world. It was beyond comprehension – a mystery for the ages.

Sami's lawyer could see the funny side of it. His client was sitting in a van playing air guitar when he got nicked for the biggest jewellery robbery of the decade. Meanwhile Andy Palmer – the world's most unlikely safebreaker – became a skid-mark on a motorway off-ramp.

The trial was a farce. The arresting officer testified that Sami had been pursued on foot for a quarter of a mile before being crash tackled and apprehended. The fat fucker must have weighed two-fifty pounds. He couldn't have run down a traffic cone.

The CPS offered Sami a deal. If he pleaded guilty to possession they'd drop the robbery charge. Sami's lawyer thought it was a good offer. Sami's lawyer had a villa in Tuscany and plans for the long weekend.

'You do believe I'm innocent, don't you?' Sami asked him.

'Mr Macbeth, I'd still believe in Santa Claus if he hadn't stopped leaving me presents.'

'Can't you plead it down?'

'What would you like – pissing in a phone box?'

'Can you do that?'

'I'm being sarcastic, Mr Macbeth. Take the deal.'

29

'I didn't steal anything.'

'Possessing stolen property is a serious offence.'

'I didn't possess the stuff. I didn't even know it was in the van.'

'Then it's another shining example of you being in the wrong place at the wrong time. Take the deal.'

The courtroom was Victorian, huge, high-ceilinged and panelled with wood. The wigged judge told Sami to stand. Then he started talking about how society had to be protected from miscreants like the accused.

He can't mean me, thought Sami.

Nadia was crying in the public gallery.

Five years. Sami felt numb. They led him downstairs, handcuffed to a policeman. Outside there was a coach waiting to take him to jail. He had a number. He was in the computer. He was part of the vast human cargo system, silent and unseen, shuffling men around Britain, from one prison to the next. First it was Wormwood Scrubs, then Parklea, then Leicester before going back to the Scrubs.

Sami was scared that first night. He knew all the stories about prison bullying and the gangs; the prison sisters, the bikers, the sadistic screws.

But a funny thing happened on the way to the exercise yard. Sami was minding his own business, trying not to make eye contact with anyone, when a big fucker approached and offered him a cigarette.

The guy called him 'Sparkles'. It became Sami's nickname.

Sami had a rep. The cons thought he was a jewel thief. Not just any jewel thief, but the man who had broken into the biggest, baddest safe in the world. He had peeled it like a banana, stripped it like an engine, opened it like a tin of sardines.

And that's how Sami managed nearly three years inside without getting any aggro or becoming someone's bitch. Other newbies were worried about lights out or bending over for the soap, but not Sami; he was treated as an equal by geezers who would normally have kicked his body around the yard for the fun of it.

In spite of his newfound reputation, Sami learned there was nothing fraternal about the criminal fraternity. The only thing that mattered was the fear you engendered or the respect you were given. Either you were a ruthless fucker or you had a skill.

Sami unwittingly, accidentally, fraudulently, had a skill. He was a cat burglar, a safe breaker, a master craftsman, one of the elite.

Even so, he made sure he played down this talent. He did his time as quiet as possible. Kept away from the sex cases and nonces. Didn't associate with any of the serious heavies or complete nutjobs. Ninety five per cent of all cons are complete morons with IQs that match their shoe sizes, which is why they're always getting caught.

Now Sami is a free man. He's going home. 'Sparkles' is

deader than Andy Palmer. And no matter what else happens in his life, he's never going back inside. You can bank on it.

A bus ride. Two trains. Even the Tube smells good after the Scrubs. Sami walks out of the Underground and looks for the familiar. Nothing much has changed about Brixton, as far as Sami can tell. It's still full of two-up two-down terraces, in narrow streets that are grim and grey and devoid of colour. The corner shops are bolted with steel shutters, padlocked and alarmed, with razor wire on the rooftops.

Middle-class mortgage slaves who couldn't afford Balham and Clapham have tarted up some streets, planting flower boxes and painting terraces in pastel colours so that local teenagers with spray cans have a better canvas.

Ton-of-Brix is not a place you fall in love with, it's a place you survive. That's what his father used to say, which is ironic since he's dead now.

When he gets to Nadia's flat, Sami checks his reflection in a neighbour's window, wishing he could have cut his hair. A woman answers when he knocks. She is mid-thirties with a pie-plate face. Sami looks past her, expecting to see Nadia.

'Who are you?'

'I live here,' she says. 'Who are you?'

Sami looks at the number on the door.

'Where's Nadia?'

'Who?'

'My sister.'

32

'How would I know?' She tries to close the door. Sami spots cardboard packing crates and bulging plastic bags in the hallway behind her. She's just moved in.

'The woman who was here – did she leave a forwarding address?'

'No.'

'Did she say where she was going?'

She tries to stop Sami looking past her.

'I had some stuff here,' he says. 'Clothes, CDs, a TV.'

'Place was empty.'

'I had a guitar.'

'Ain't seen no guitar.'

'A Gibson Fender.'

'Who's he?'

Sami can hear Oprah in the background. He pushes past the woman into the living room. She's not happy. Screaming. Hurling abuse. Says she's going to call the police, the landlord, the social . . .

'That's my TV,' says Sami.

'Prove it!'

'How do I do that?'

'I bought it off the landlord,' she says, defensively. 'It was confiscated. Unpaid rent.'

Sami looks at her hands, which are twisted with arthritis. He's on shaky ground. Two hours out of prison and he's already breached parole.

Nadia has lost the flat. She wouldn't move without telling him. She'd leave word.

33

4

Ruiz settles onto a tube from Baron's Court. He never drives into Central London these days – not since the congestion charge. He's not opposed to road tolls or traffic fines as long as someone else is paying them.

The train moves through tunnels that pop his ears, before emerging into the light and disappearing again.

Peak-hour is over. The men in suits are in their offices. Not all wear suits these days. Some wear jeans and chinos. What do they do, wonders Ruiz? Sit in front of screens. It seems a poor substitute for hunting and gathering.

There's no romance in office work. No thrill of the chase. Ruiz was at a rugby dinner a few weeks back, sitting at a table with fifteen men. Successful professionals. A newcomer among them was asked what he did for a living. He said he made concrete blocks.

The conversation petered out. Nobody knew what to say. Then Ruiz pointed out that this guy was the only person at the table who actually *made* something. The rest of them shuffled paper, traded futures, negotiated deals, added value and took their margins. They didn't build anything, or save anyone, or make a mark on the world other than on a balance sheet.

Ruiz felt guilty about being too critical. There was no romance in police work either. That's why he retired – jumped before he was pushed or became an exhibit in the Black Museum.

At Regent's Park he emerges from below ground and walks to Harley Street. Today is his annual medical. It normally falls on either side of his birthday, but this year the dates have aligned.

He sits in the waiting room. Picks up a magazine. It's one of those celebrity rags full of paparazzi photographs and 'at-home-with' specials where TV stars announce how happy they are together and you know they'll be divorced within six months.

Ruiz is about to toss it back onto the coffee table when he notices a shot of Ray Garza, smiling at the cameras from the red carpet at Covent Garden. He is hosting a charity performance by the National Opera in aid of spina bifida. There are more shots over the page. Garza is mingling with the great and the good. The cast. The artistic director. The Arts Minister. Celebrities.

The media nicknamed him 'the Chairman' years ago and the name has stuck. It's almost like Garza plays up to it, dressing in charcoal grey suits, bright ties, and never being photographed without a cigar in his fist, unlit.

Three years after Jane Lanfranchi died, Garza married a society girl with a double-barrelled surname whose father had inherited a pile in Wiltshire but had to sell it to the Government in lieu of death duties. Garza rescued the old man when the ónly thing he had left was a few hereditary peerages that he was trying to flog off to rich Americans. Garza took over one of the titles: the Earl of Ipswich. It must look impressive on a business card.

Garza wasn't always a wealthy man. He started out as a soldier – an officer, who specialised in logistics and transport. As such, he understood supply and demand and the importance of being able to move quickly.

A lot of legends have grown up around the Chairman. Not all of them are true – but what's not in dispute is how he made his first million. Garza helped liberate Kuwait in the first Gulf War and was on hand when the Iraqis were pushed back across the border.

The world saw smoking convoys of vehicles, charred wreckage of luxury cars that had been looted from Kuwait and bombed by Allied planes as they fled across the desert. But that was only some of the stuff. Hundreds of luxury cars were abandoned. Untouched. Mercedes, BMWs, Jaguars and Bentleys were left sitting in the desert, the keys still in them.

There was more. Convoys of trucks full of computers, washing machines, air conditioning units and Mont Blanc pens. The Iraqis looted everything that wasn't bolted down and the Kuwaitis didn't want the stuff back. Oil drilling equipment, earthmovers, yachts, helicopters, private jets – Garza found a way of shipping them out of Kuwait.

He finished the job the Iraqis started. He looted Kuwait, stealing from rich oil sheiks, who were so relieved to have their country back they didn't give a shit about a few missing cars or boats or planes.

Nobody raised an eyebrow. Nobody turned a hair. The only hint of scandal came when a UK Sunday paper did an exposé about an armour-plated Mercedes, specially built for the Kuwaiti Minister for Trade, which somehow finished up under the hammer at a car auction in Croydon.

For Ray Garza it was just the beginning. He left the army and soon he was moving massive shipments of hardware out of countries in the midst of war, famine or caught up in Africa's perverse interpretation of 'democracy'.

Questions were asked in Parliament. MI6 took an interest. Nothing stuck. Whenever Garza looked shaky he managed to walk away. Witnesses disappeared. Cast iron cases crumbled. One Spanish middleman jumped off Waterloo Bridge with bricks in his pockets. A junior accountant changed his testimony, spent six months inside and that same year bought a sixty foot yacht.

Meanwhile, Garza launched himself on society. He transformed himself into a patron of the arts, a media darling, the orchestrator of a thousand publicity stunts involving pretty girls in short skirts.

Garza suddenly had a finger in every pie. They were La Maison pies. River Café Pies. Savoy Grill pies. They were the dog's bollocks and the bee's knees of pies. He was dining at the head table, supping with the great and the good and the morally bankrupt.

His chequered past, the question marks over his business dealings, nothing seemed to matter. Not even the distant scandal of a rape allegation and a troubled teenager who threw herself off a tower block in Hackney.

A receptionist interrupts. Ruiz looks up from the magazine. Dr Reines will see him now. He tosses the rag aside and stares at the newsprint on his fingers, wanting to wash it off.

The doctor asks him to sit on the examination table. Takes him through the normal checks. Blood pressure, cholesterol, finger up the bum . . . Having his prostate checked always reminds Ruiz of a joke about knowing you're in trouble if your doctor checks your prostate and has both his hands on your shoulders.

Doctor Reines is telling him horror stories about fat-choked arteries and how people his age are dropping like flies. Then comes the lecture about him exercising more: walking or swimming – six laps of a pool or two miles on foot.

He listens to Ruiz's heart. It's strong. A champion's heart. A thoroughbred. Everything else about his body is turning to shit, but his heart is going strong.

Dr Reines asks after Ruiz's mother.

'How is her Alzheimer's?'

'She has good days and bad.'

'Does she still think I'm Josef Mengele?'

'She thinks all doctors are Josef Mengele.'

Ruiz's mother, Daj, doesn't live in the present any more. Most of the time she's reliving the war, escaping from the Gestapo and SS, surviving the concentration camps.

Daj met Mengele once. He was standing on a ramp in dress uniform and polished black boots. He wore white cotton gloves and held a cane, directing a sea of exhausted and starving women and children either left or right.

A handsome man, Daj said. Cold. He looked like a gypsy with dark hair, dark eyes and tawny skin. 'Perhaps that's why he hated us so much,' she said. 'He was purging the world of the things he hated about himself.'

Ruiz leaves the doctor's surgery and takes a bus to Victoria, before walking along Vauxhall Bridge Road. He has another appointment, another annual check-up.

Every year on his birthday, he has a beer with an old mate from the Met, his former second-in-command at the Serious Crime Group, Colin 'Bones' McGee.

McGee was a rising star when Ruiz first met him – one of the university graduates they fast-tracked through training and nudged upstairs after the Flying Squad got disbanded. He topped his class at Hendon, made

Detective Sergeant at thirty and Detective Inspector at thirty-five. Then his wings fell off.

It was 2002 – a sting operation involving twelve million quids worth of cocaine found in a shipping container in Rotterdam. McGee took the decision to leave the container on board and let the ship sail for Felixstowe. He ran the surveillance operation.

Can you see what's coming? The drugs vanished. Not a trace. Maybe the haul got tossed into the North Sea. Maybe it was never on board. It was all supposition and it didn't wash with McGee's bosses. That's when he got the nickname Bones because his career was dead and buried.

Since then Bones has been treading water with the Specialist Crime Directorate, tracking assets and chasing paper trails. It's a dead end job because no serious player will ever hold assets in their own names. They hide behind shelf companies and dodgy corporations based in the Bahamas and the Caymans.

Ruiz doesn't particularly like Bones. Never has. He was always a little too ambitious. Too grasping. But when he left the job, Ruiz handed over his old files – including the Lanfranchi case. He asked Bones to keep an eye on it . . . just in case.

They meet at a pub on Vauxhall Bridge Road. Union Jacks hang from the rafters.

Bones is at a table drinking single malt. He's lost his boyish innocence, thinks Ruiz – a receding hairline will do it every time – but he still dresses sharply in grey trousers, Italian loafers and a jacket. His copper-coloured hair – dyed most likely – is combed straight back on his scalp.

'How's it hanging, Vincent?'

'I'm good, Colin.'

They swap small talk. Retirements. Promotions. Prostate cancer. There's twenty years between them – almost a generation – but the job doesn't change, only the rules.

Eventually the talk gets around to Ray Garza. It's been years since there was any news on the Lanfranchi case. At past meetings, Bones has made shit up to keep Ruiz happy and Ruiz knew it, but this year he has something fresh, something new, something hot off the press.

'Ray Garza's boy got busted two nights ago after a high speed pursuit. They found eight kilos of cocaine in the boot of his Porsche and a semi-automatic, which he waved around at the coppers. Took a shot.'

Ruiz ponders the information. Garza's son – Ray Jnr – how old is he now? Out of school. Nineteen. Twenty tops.

'It's a commercial quantity,' says Bones. 'The kid's going down.'

'Where is he now?'

'Spent last night in the Scrubs. He's in court today.'

Bones continues talking, spinning a story about the Specialist Crime Directorate offering Ray Jnr a deal if he turns on the old man. It's not going to happen, thinks Ruiz. Junior won't bite the hand that feeds him – not unless he has bigger ambitions. But it still warms his heart to think of Ray Garza losing sleep over his precious boy.

Ray Jnr wasn't even born when his father raped Jane Lanfranchi and chewed open her cheek. Ruiz always thought Garza should have had a daughter. That way he could have worried when she turned sixteen and went out at night. Wondered about where she was and whom she was with. Hopefully, he's worried sick now.

'What about the Lanfranchi case?' he asks.

Bones shrugs.

'Any similar rapes?'

'Nope.'

'Any missing women with links to Garza?'

'Can't you forget the fucking Lanfranchi case for once?' says Bones. 'It's old news. Ancient bloody history.'

Ruiz ignores him. 'Garza likes the wholesome girl-next-door types. Suburban princesses. He thinks they're hiding their true natures.'

Bones shakes his head. 'You're fucking obsessed. I'd get more sense talking to the wall.'

'And less whisky,' says Ruiz swallowing the last of his Guinness.

There's a moment of friction. Bones wants to tell him to fuck off, but something about Ruiz's silences has always unnerved him.

'I'm just giving my opinion, Vince. You don't have to

42

take it,' he mutters, speaking slowly like he's talking to a child. 'There's a bail hearing today. Police are going to oppose because Ray Jnr took a shot at a copper.'

'He'll walk.'

'Yeah. Maybe. But it's going cost Daddy big time.'

'Where's Garza now?'

'He flew in from Geneva this morning. Smart money says he's going to be in court. Media haven't got wind of this yet, but the storm's coming.'

Ruiz takes another sip of beer. Maybe today won't be such an anticlimax after all.

5

Sami has called Nadia's friends, her workmates, and talked to her old neighbours. Nobody has seen her. She hasn't been at work for three days. Didn't call in sick. Didn't hand in her notice.

Next Sami calls the local hospitals and drops in to Brixton police station to lodge a missing persons report.

The desk sergeant is a doughnut short of being fat and has a torn piece of tissue paper, encrusted with blood, stuck to his neck.

'How long has she been missing?' he asks.

'Since the weekend.'

'Did you fight with her?'

'No.'

'Who was the last person to see her?'

'I don't know.'

'What was she wearing?'

'I don't know.'

'Do you have realistic fears for her safety?'

'I don't know. Yeah. Maybe.'

44

The sergeant presses his right hand into his lower back and grimaces as if relieving himself of lower back pain. 'Are you sure you even have a sister?'

Sami has to fill in a form. Tick boxes. Old Bill isn't going to raise a sweat looking for Nadia. He needs another plan.

Uncle Harry will know where she is. He promised to keep an eye on Nadia when Sami got put away. He's not really Sami's uncle: more of a family friend from the days when Sami's old man was still alive and running a bookmaking operation out of an upstairs room in Harry's boozer.

Going even further back, Harry used to be a professional boxer, whose fighting nickname was 'Homicide' on account of him killing a guy in one of his early fights. Sami has never met anyone who'd seen one of Harry's fights, but in his heyday he fought at Crystal Palace on the same card as Henry Cooper.

The White Swan is tucked behind Waterloo Station not far from the Old Vic Theatre. Sami pushes open the pub door and peers into the gloom. There are punters inside who act as though someone has opened the lid of their coffin.

Same faces. Same smells.

'You been away?' one of them asks.

'Something like that,' says Sami.

'It's your shout.'

'I'll buy you a pint if you can remember my name.'

45

The drunk looks at him hard. Looks at his empty glass. 'Rumpelstiltskin.'

'Close.'

Harry Galanto turns the corner and lets out a bellow. 'My boy! My boy!'

He squeezes through a gap in the bar and throws his arms around Sami in a bear hug, a beer hug, a cross between the two.

Harry has gone up a few weight divisions since he hung up the gloves. His stomach is like a different person, but he refuses to wear trousers any bigger than a forty-four waist. This has the effect of squeezing everything upwards until his gut spills over his belt in a doughy tsunami.

Harry dusts off a stool. Goes back behind the bar. Pours Sami a pint. It's his first alcohol in two years. He upends the glass. It's good.

'Have you seen Nadia?' he asks.

Harry grimaces slightly. 'She dropped by Tuesday.'

It's not the whole story.

'She was supposed to do a shift,' says Harry. 'She's been working behind the bar a few nights.'

'Yeah, she told me. What happened?'

'I told her not to bother.'

'Why?'

Harry eyes him sorrowfully. 'I didn't like some of the clientele she was attracting.'

'Like who?'

'Toby Streak.'

Sami feels his face twitch. 'What was the Streak doing here?'

'Sniffing round Nadia like she was on heat.'

'They were together?'

Harry nods and pours another pint. The beer has reached Sami's bloodstream. He wants more. Needs it badly. Suddenly, he wants to be one of the boozed up shit-kickers in the bar, living the simple life, drunk by midday and a kebab at closing time. Instead he has to deal with the implications and possible consequences of Nadia being hooked up with Toby Streak.

Sami doesn't know Streak well but he's aware of his reputation. He's a pimp and a small-time coke dealer, but these are just sidelines. His main action is running a lover-boy scam out of nightclubs and bars, picking up girls and showing them a good time.

Flash car, flash clothes, just the right patter. He wines them and dines them; buys them baubles, takes them to stay at expensive hotels. He treats them like film stars or supermodels and then introduces them to the snorting stuff.

And once he's swept them off their pretty little size-seven feet, he says, 'Do you love me?' And they say, 'Yeah.' And he says, 'How much do you love me.' And they say, 'Completely.'

'Would you do anything for me?'

'Anything,' they say.

47

And that's when he opens the door and invites another man or another girl into the room.

They do it for Toby. They do it for the cocaine. And soon they do it for the camera. Girl on girl. Threesomes. Straight sex and then more.

'If you love me you'll do it,' he tells them. 'If you love me you'll have your nipples pierced. If you love me you'll have a boob job. If you love me you'll have a "tramp stamp" tattooed on your back. If you love me you'll let these three men fuck you every which way . . .'

That's what Toby Streak does. That's how he operates. He finds girls, grooms them and sells them on.

Sami feels the vomit rise. He swallows hard. It's not the alcohol rushing around his bloodstream. It's the image of Nadia and Toby Streak. The foul taste in his mouth won't go away.

6

Ray Garza Jnr doesn't look much like his old man, thinks Ruiz, as he watches him being led into the dock. He looks more like a foppish public schoolboy, who can't flick the fringe out of his eyes because each of his hands is cuffed to a policeman.

Maybe he has the makings of a moustache on his top lip. Maybe he's been playing with a black crayon downstairs. Only his eyes betray his breeding. He's got that Garza don't-fuck-with-me glare.

Ruiz takes a seat in the public gallery. The cold wooden benches are designed to give you piles.

The prosecutor opposes bail, claiming that Ray Jnr is a flight risk. He talks about the seriousness of the charges, the discharging of a firearm and a high-speed pursuit that put lives at risk.

Meanwhile Ray Junior's silk is acting like he's heard it all before. He's bored. When are they going to get some new material or change the record? He's not saying any of this, but you can see it in his body language. Then it's his turn. He takes to his feet. Shoulders back. Launches into a booming defence of his young client, who is going to vigorously defend the charges and who disputes completely the police account of what happened.

It's a bravura performance, including a description of how earlier on in the evening in question, young Ray had been confronted by hooligans who had taken offence at the vehicle he was driving and made threats against 'his person'.

'When later that evening a vehicle came up behind Mr Garza at such speed on the motorway, he thought he was being chased and feared for his life.'

'The vehicle in question had a flashing light,' points out the judge.

'Absolutely, your honour,' replies the silk. 'And very similar lights are available at pound shops and only a month ago one was used by bogus policemen to hijack a high-performance vehicle in Manchester.'

The judge doesn't respond. The silk is in full flow.

'It will be our submission, your honour, that the police illegally searched my client's vehicle. Anything recovered is inadmissible in criminal proceedings.'

The judge has heard enough.

'This is a bail hearing, Mr Cleary. Save your argument for the trial.'

'Of course, your honour, I just wanted it clearly noted that my client will be pleading not guilty.'

'It's duly noted.'

Mr Cleary's next speech is almost as florid as the first one. Ray Jnr is portrayed as a model citizen, a promising young businessman and a credit to his schooling and his family.

'My client's father is a well-respected business figure and a patron of the arts. He is prepared to put up a substantial surety and to personally guarantee his son's appearance at any future court proceedings.

'The only witnesses in this case are the police officers involved so it's not a question of protecting their interests . . .'

Ruiz is watching the door as Garza Snr enters. He comes alone, wearing an expensive suit and a cashmere overcoat draped over his forearm.

Ruiz watches him descend three steps. Turn right. Find a seat. He glances into the body of the court, at the judge, the bench, the dock – surveying everything as if he's putting a value on it.

Finally his eyes rest on Ruiz. They don't change. Nothing about him suggests that he's surprised or anxious. This is what people mean when they talk about the stillness on the surface of the pond.

The judge is making his decision. A lot of words say very little.

Ray Jnr is granted bail: two million pounds and conditions. He has to surrender his passport and to report every day to Bow Street Police Station.

Ray Jnr hasn't said a word. Hasn't looked at his father.

There are problems, thinks Ruiz. Maybe Bones was right. The boy might be Ray Garza's blind spot.

Outside the Old Bailey, Ruiz waits under the arches. How does someone pay two million pounds in bail, he wonders. Do they write a cheque? Organise a bank transfer? Maybe Garza is so well respected now, they'll accept an IOU.

A black Mercedes is parked outside, the driver waiting. An hour passes. Garza emerges. Garza Jnr is behind him. They're still not talking.

'The wrong Garza was in the dock today,' says Ruiz, stepping from the shadows.

Ray Snr stops and turns. 'Many happy returns, Vincent. Did you get my card?'

'I haven't opened it.'

'I'm sure you have dozens waiting. How is retirement treating you?'

'Fine.'

'You were never really cut out to be a detective, were you? It must have been like climbing to the top of the ladder and finding it leaning against the wrong window.'

'The view doesn't change.'

Ray Snr smiles. 'That's where you're wrong. It's much better from where I am.'

Ray Jnr has gone to the car. He leaves the door open.

'I admire you, Vincent.'

'How so?'

'Most people choose the path that gains them the

52

greatest reward for the least amount of effort. It's a law of nature. You defied it. You could have made decent money. You could have had a reasonable life. Instead you chose to make a difference. You have issues, Vincent, an obsessive nature. Maybe your old man was a violent fucker, smacked you round; bruised you on the inside. Now you're damaged goods.'

'That's a fascinating story,' says Ruiz. 'Ever think about adapting it for the stage?'

Ray Jnr leans out the car door. 'Come on. Ditch the drunk. I'm hungry.'

His father laughs. 'He thinks you're a tramp, Vincent.'

'Is that right. Talking out of your arse must be hereditary.' Ruiz glances at the car. 'I'm sure they'll find a way of stopping that in prison.'

Garza slides his overcoat onto his shoulders, wearing it like a cape. He smiles, showing his incisors.

'Voltaire said that madness was thinking of too many things in succession too quickly or to think of one thing obsessively. Get a life, Vincent. Before it's too late.'

'Yeah, well, a philosopher called Jagger once said, "Anything worth doing is worth overdoing".'

'You're a Stones fan. I should have known.'

7

Sami has been sitting on the same beer for nearly an hour. It feels like it cost him his left testicle. Five quid. It's fucking outrageous!

The place is called the Rockpool, which is pretty apt considering they let slime like Toby Streak hang out here. He's not around yet, it's early days, but he's expected, according to the bartender. It took another fiver for the information. Extortion.

The dance floor is starting to fill. It's all yuppie music and rag trade types, wannabe models, wannabe wannabes and mega-rich girls with shit-paying jobs on *Tatler* and *Vogue*.

Sami knew the bouncer on the door, a Neanderthal called Albert, who used to do security at some of Sami's gigs. The queue stretched down the alley, most of them men. The good-looking birds were ushered inside.

It's a numbers game. Women won't go to a club where drunk blokes on the pull outnumber them and drunk blokes won't go to a club where there are no women.

54

Sami keeps scanning the room, looking for Nadia. He should never have left her. Never have allowed an incompetent lawyer to talk him into pleading guilty.

He keeps glancing at the door every time it opens, waiting for Streak to arrive. He knows what he looks like. They've met once before but he doubts if Streak will remember. It was at a party in Notting Hill full of music producers, sound engineers and managers. Sami had been invited to meet a top manager, one of those guys who turns run-of-the-mill pub singers into the next Robbie Williams.

Streak was there. He came in the back door, grabbed a Bollinger and acted like he was a proper guest, the life and soul, and everyone's best friend just because he was bringing their toot. But once they had their stuff they wanted him to fuck off – use the tradesman's entrance please.

That's the thing with pimps and coke dealers. They hang out at celebrity parties and backstage at rock concerts, thinking they're bosom buddies with celebrities but they're nothing but delivery boys.

Sami didn't sign with the manager or get a recording deal that night, but he did shag a cute-looking waitress from Rotherhithe who had a thing for doing it in the shower.

The club is heaving. Young babes and blokes with city jobs are bouncing up and down on the dance floor. Streak should be here by now.

There he is – on the stairs. He's wearing a Paul Smith suit and drinking a cocktail. He's with a girl. It's not Nadia. She's blonde, young, with an innocent face and an athletic body. She presses it against Streak, rubbing her tits against his chest.

Streak is treating her like she doesn't exist – gazing over the top of her head – perhaps looking for someone prettier.

Sami watches him for a while. Every so often someone approaches. A nod, a wink, a palm against palm, and then they wander off. A few minutes later, Streak sends the girl after them. She must be carrying the stuff. Where? There's no room in that dress for anything else but her tits.

She comes back again. Steak gives her a little something as a reward. She queues for a cubicle – the lines are longer outside than inside – and she comes back all dreamy and grateful, nibbling on his earlobe.

Sami waits for a while. Gets the lay of the land. A black girl in a short denim skirt sits on a stool next to him. Her handbag swings against her rump and her braided hair click-clacks like marbles in a sack.

'You look lonely,' she says.

'You look expensive,' replies Sami.

She gets the hump and walks off, swinging her hips.

Finally, Sami approaches Streak. Says hello. Watches his reaction. He doesn't remember him. Sami wants to reach out and squeeze his throat until his eyes pop out.

56

Instead he negotiates a score. He glances at the girl. She throws her shoulders back so her tits lift higher. So does the hem of her dress. My God, those legs! She's seventeen if she's a day.

'Outside in the alley,' says Streak, yelling over the music. 'Zoe will meet you there.'

Sami turns away and pushes through bodies on the dance floor. The music seems to die suddenly as the fire door closes. He can hear himself think.

A few minutes later, Zoe joins him. Her eyes check him out as if she's trying to decide if he's a player. Suddenly, she puts her arms around his neck and kisses him. The small silver foil wrap slides between his lips. Her tongue caresses his. His hard-on is instantaneous. He's been inside for nearly three years. It's criminal to press a body like that against him.

'You know someone called Nadia?' he asks.

Zoe frowns. 'Nah.'

She's lying.

'She used to hang out with Streak.'

Zoe glances toward the fire door.

'Nadia is my sister. I'm looking for her.'

Zoe steps back. She's wearing a handbag the size of a cigarette packet. She pulls a lipstick from inside.

'She used to hang out with Toby. He dumped her.'

'When?'

She shrugs. 'I have to get back inside. He's waiting.'

'Don't go. Stay here.'

'Hey, you're sweet and you're horny, but Toby is going to look after me.'

'Toby is going to pimp you the first chance he gets.'

Zoe doesn't believe him. She turns to go. Sami grabs her arm.

'Ow! You're hurting me.'

'I don't want to. Just stay here.'

'Toby's going to miss me.'

'That's the idea.'

Zoe doesn't say a dicky bird, but Sami knows she's worried. She's rocking from foot to foot like she's got to pee.

Sami doesn't regard himself as a violent type but sometimes the shortest answer to the hardest question is a smack in the head. He reaches into his pocket. Fingers a roll of ten pence pieces wrapped in brown paper.

He watches the door. Waits.

Sure enough, Toby comes looking. He peers out the door. Clocks Zoe. Sees Sami. He has this quizzical look on his face but it doesn't last. Sami sinks a fist into his stomach and then bounces his face off the doorjamb at a hundred miles an hour. Wrenches it back. Does it again.

Cartilage crunches. It's a gusher. Blood all over his nice suit.

Streak falls backwards. Zoe has her hand over her mouth. Her pretty legs are shaking.

Sami steps back. Breathing hard. Trembling.

'I'm looking for my sister.'

Toby spits blood onto the cobblestones. 'Nothing to do with me.'

'I haven't told you her name.'

'Yeah, well, I got a lot of jealous boyfriends looking for me. It's a nervous reaction.'

'What have you got to be nervous about?'

He raises his eyes to look at Sami for the first time.

'What's her name?'

'Nadia.'

'I'll have to check my phone.' He reaches into his jacket pocket. A flash of brightness. A blade opens.

Sami launches a kick before Streak can straighten his arm. The sprung steel blade spins out of his fingers and bounces off the wall.

A second kick connects with his stomach. Sami takes a four step run up and kicks him again.

Zoe lets out a sob. Sami tells her to go home. Watch *Sesame Street*. Learn something.

'Give him back his gear.'

She pulls a dozen small packets of silver foil from her handbag and another half dozen from her knickers. Tosses them at Streak. Some of them float in a puddle, silver on black, catching the light.

Zoe disappears through the fire door. Sami jams a rubbish bin across the frame to stop them being disturbed.

'Now it's just you and me, Toby. Your nose is broken. Maybe they can set it straight again. I could try. I could mess it up a bit more. They say every beautiful face needs a blemish. Where's Nadia?'

Toby is sitting in a puddle. 'I don't fucking know,' he sniffles. 'I ain't seen her.'

'Since when?'

'Days.'

'What did you do?'

'Nothing.'

'Did you give her drugs?'

'She's a consenting adult.'

Louder this time: 'Did you give her drugs?'

'Nothing serious,' whines Toby. 'She wanted to party.'

'What did you give her?'

'She's eighteen.'

'Where is she?'

'Like I said, I ain't seen her.'

Sami takes off his jacket, rolls up his sleeve. Picks up the knife, cleans the blade on the front of his jeans.

'What are you doing?' asks Toby.

'Take off your pants.'

'Why?'

'I've been nearly three years in prison Toby. You get a taste for certain things.'

'You're kidding me, right.'

Sami unbuckles his belt. Toby's eyes pop. Suddenly, he's scuffling backwards through a puddle like a crab on polished marble. Sami steps past him, wraps a forearm around his neck.

Toby sobs, 'No fucking way, man. No way.'

'Where is she?'

'I swear I don't know.'

'You're lying.'

'OK. OK.'

'What did you do?'

'I just passed her on.'

'What do you mean?'

'Tony Murphy wanted her.'

Sami tries to get his head around this. Tony Murphy doesn't know Nadia. What's he got to do with any of this?

'We came to an arrangement,' sniffles Toby.

'What sort of arrangement.'

'I sold her to him.'

61

8

Sami jogs out of the alley and back onto the street. He walks fast, trying to be inconspicuous. He can hear sirens starting to wail. Zoe must have called the police.

Sami curses himself. He wasn't exactly subtle. If Toby Streak lodges a complaint, he's screwed. Parole revoked. Go straight to jail. Do not pass go . . .

He comes out of St Martins Lane into Charing Cross Road. Buys a copy of *The Times* from a news stand and hails a cab, keeping his face covered. The cab drops him at Waterloo Station. He walks towards Elephant and Castle and into Camberwell Road.

Toby Streak sits in a police car, holding a towel over his face. Two uniforms are interviewing Zoe, quizzing her about a fake ID. Neither of them seems too broken up about Toby.

'What took you so fucking long?' he complains.

'Just you mind your language, sir.'

They finish talking to Zoe. Tell her to go home. Toby's next.

'Do you want to file a complaint, sir?'

'Will it do any good?' he asks. His nose is blocked completely.

'That depends on the quality of your information and if we feel it warrants further investigation.'

Toby knows what that means. They're going to write this one off as a small time drug deal gone sour. He's not going to report Sami.

As soon as the uniforms leave, he opens his mobile. Punches in a number.

'Is that Mr Murphy?'

'This better be important, son.'

'That person you wanted to meet. He might be calling on you.'

Sami stands across the road from the bail hostel on Camberwell Road. There is a sign on the door: rules for residents. One of them is not to break the curfew.

It's 3.00 a.m. There is a light on. He presses a buzzer. A large woman swings open the door, black as paint with a square, hard-boned face. She stands in the doorway, unsmiling, as though waiting for his excuse.

'I've been looking for my sister. She's missing.'

'Not good enough.'

'I'm worried about her.'

'I don't want to hear your lies, honey. You break the rules, you go back to prison.'

'I'm not lying. It's my first day out.'

63

She steps back, opens the door wider. Sami has to detour to get around her hips. She's wearing a uniform – a light blue shirt with double pockets and dark blue trousers that stretch so tightly across her rump he can see the outline of her knickers. My God, she's wearing a G-string. A nightstick and a can of mace swing from her belt.

Sami follows her to the office. She turns down the TV. Moves a jumbo packet of crisps. Signs him in. Next she hands him two stiff bed sheets, a grey blanket, a towel and a bar of soap.

'The laundry is in the basement. Detergent is extra. Don't go leaving shit in your pockets when you use the machines. Two been fixed in the last month.'

She takes a swig of soft drink and wipes her hand across her mouth. 'You been doing something you ain't supposed to?'

'Nope.'

'Don't believe you.' Her hand shoots out and grabs Sami's wrist. Turns it over. His knuckles are torn and bleeding. She shakes her head. 'You're just aching to get back inside, ain't you, honey? Maybe you like the sex in there.'

She hoists herself out of her chair and gives him a tour, keeping her voice down because other 'residents' are sleeping.

'No eating in the common room. No smoking in the common room. No drinking. No drugs. No women . . .'

'And they leave you here to tempt us,' says Sami.

64

'You trying to be funny, skinny boy?'

'No, I'm just saying you're a fit-looking woman.'

'You trying to tell me you're not gay, honey? Well you don't have the hammer and you don't have the nail to impress me.'

She turns off the lights as she leaves each room. They climb the stairs to the first floor.

'No damaging property, no touching the CCTV cameras, no loud music – you wearing an electronic tag?'

'No.'

'Don't let anyone talk you into wearing theirs.'

'I won't. How many people are here?'

'Thirty.' They stop outside a door. 'This is your room. Don't lose the key.'

She waddles away, almost brushing each side of the hall with her hips. Sami closes the door. Locks it. Walks to the window. It overlooks a walled courtyard with empty flowerbeds that look silver under the security lights.

The room has a single bed, a lone chair, a wardrobe and a bedside table with a lamp, an ashtray and a Bible. A laminated copy of the House Rules is pinned to the back of the door.

Sami lies on the bed and feels himself slipping into a dark envelope of depression. He thinks about Nadia and about Tony Murphy and about the four guys who came looking for him earlier outside the Scrubs. Freedom wasn't supposed to be like this.

9

Under normal circumstances – better circumstances –
Sami Macbeth might never have heard of a gangster
like Tony Murphy, but there are two things you have in
abundance when you're pacing an exercise yard: time
and prison gossip.

Most of the stories are bullshit. Every con will tell that
you he's innocent of the crime he was convicted of and
then brag about the ones he got away with.

According to the skinny on Tony Murphy, he came
from one of those big Irish families (seven brothers and
sisters – the girls as mad as the boys) who seem to live
everywhere except Ireland. Murphy grew up in Kilburn,
North London, and began stealing cars to order when he
was barely old enough to see over the steering wheel.

From car rackets he branched out to running escort
agencies, nightclubs and casinos (illegal and otherwise),
including a floating Chinese junk in Manchester that he
shipped from Hong Kong. His latest passion was a
restaurant on the river near the Millennium Bridge –

one of those up-market nosheries where the chef is a daytime TV star who can make a four course meal out of a bag of spuds and a Bisto cube.

The place has booths along the walls and linen table-cloths. The maître d' gives Sami the hairy eyeball.

'Do you have a reservation, sir?'

'I'm here to see Mr Murphy.'

'Do you have an appointment?'

'No.'

'Mr Murphy doesn't like being disturbed while he's dining.'

'Maybe you could pass him a note,' says Sami. He borrows a piece of paper and writes Nadia's name, draws a sad face on it, folding it twice before handing it to the maître d'. Then he watches him weave between the tables, up three stairs, pausing at a table overlooking the main seating area.

He hands the note to a fat man whose head seems to be stitched onto an oversized tweed jacket. A hard man turned to lard.

Murphy reads the note and sways back, sucking down an oyster from the shell. Juice dribbles over his chins. He wipes it away with a napkin. Waves Sami over.

Sami tells himself to relax. It's a busy restaurant. Nothing's going to happen.

Murphy's luncheon companion is a head taller, with ruddy cheeks discoloured by broken veins beneath his skin. This guy is walking proof of man's simian ancestry – flared

67

nostrils, torso like a wardrobe, arms reaching his knees. He doesn't say a word.

Murphy and Sami make the introductions.

'What can I do for you, son?' asks the fat man, edging the blade of a knife beneath the flesh of another oyster.

Sami has to be careful here. It's a balancing act. Tony Murphy is not the sort of man you threaten or yank about. It's also not a good idea to crawl up his rectum and set up house. He has to be respectful. Considered. Polite.

'Toby Streak says you might know where my sister is.'

'What's your sister's name?'

'Nadia Macbeth.'

'What makes you think I know where she is?'

'Toby said he sold her to you.'

Murphy puts down his fork. Wipes his mouth. Folds his napkin. Places it on his side plate.

'Slavery was abolished in 1841, son. People don't get bought and sold any more. Didn't they teach you that at school?'

'Toby Streak seemed pretty confident, Mr Murphy.'

'What makes you think that?'

'I had my boot on his balls, sir. Figuratively speaking.'

'Well, if we're speaking figuratively, in my experience drugsters like Toby Streak can be coerced into saying almost anything.'

'Toby still seemed pretty sure.'

Murphy's voice drops an octave.

'Let me give you a piece of advice, Mr Macbeth. You don't want to be making unsupported allegations against people. There are laws about that sort of thing. Defamation. Slander.'

'I'm not here to cause any trouble,' says Sami. 'I just want my sister.'

'How old is she?'

'Eighteen.'

'Old enough to make up her own mind.' Murphy summons the waiter. Asks for another glass. Pours a wine for Sami.

'I appreciate your candour, Mr Macbeth. I can also see you got courage. You got balls as big as the Ritz to waltz in here and accuse me of wrongdoing. This makes me think that either you're a very loving brother or you're so dumb you couldn't piss straight with a hard-on.'

'I'm a loving brother.'

'That's good. Now let's talk about you.'

Murphy sucks down another oyster. He offers one to Sami, who'd rather eat cold snot.

'I heard about you, Mr Macbeth. I hear you're a talent.'

'Me? No.'

Murphy drizzles lemon juice on an oyster and gives the pepper mill a twist. 'Dessie has given me the skinny on the Hampstead job. Very impressive.'

Dessie must be the other guy at the table. Dessie Fraser. 'The Dobermann'. Sami remembers a story about Dessie, who used to be in the army, stationed in Northern Ireland. He was there when the IRA killed Earl Mountbatten by planting a bomb on his boat in County Sligo. Two more bombs went off that day, but nobody remembers them because old man Mountbatten made all the headlines.

One of them was detonated beside a road in County Down just as a Bedford drove by with Dessie Fraser and a load of Paras in back. A second bomb was timed to go off as people tried to help the wounded. A dozen soldiers died. Dessie survived.

A week later, dressed in uniform, Dessie walked into a notorious IRA bar in the Newry and ordered a beer. Waited. Not for long. He left three people near death, tore the place up and the COs needed teargas to get him out. Dessie was dishonourably discharged. Prematurely ejected. Returned to civilian life even less civilised than before he signed up.

Clearly he doesn't bear a grudge against Paddies, thinks Sami, glancing at Murphy.

'Don't believe everything you've heard about me, Mr Murphy. If I was so talented, I wouldn't have got caught.'

'You were unlucky,' says Murphy.

Tell me about it, thinks Sami.

'Modest, too, I like that in a young man, Mr Macbeth. You're not some cocky little gobshite who thinks he's seen it all. And you're not a flash prick like Toby Streak, who buys himself a sports car and rubs the law's nose in his success. You're old school. A skilled technician. An artist. I like surrounding myself with talented people; people who use their god-given skills. You know what I'm saying, son?'

The answer is no, but Sami doesn't utter it out loud.

'You're a quiet achiever. That's why none of us had ever heard of you until the Hampstead job. You kept a low profile. Used your discretion.'

What the fuck is he talking about, thinks Sami.

'I could use someone gifted like you,' says Murphy. 'Someone who thinks on his feet, someone flexible, someone who can open things.'

'You got the wrong guy,' says Sami, feeling the conversation has taken a wrong turn. 'I just want to find my sister and get my shit together in one pile.'

Murphy slathers butter on one half of a torn bread roll.

'You work alone, I understand that, but I could open up whole new horizons.'

'It's not that,' says Sami. 'I'm going to concentrate on my music.'

'Come again?'

'I play guitar. I'm a musician.'

Murphy has stopped chewing. 'You taking the piss, son?'

Sami realises his mistake. 'No, no, I'm just thinking, given what's happened, that it might be best to change my career. I thought I might concentrate on my music, you know.'

71

Murphy gives him the pointy finger. 'You're planning something, aren't you? The big score.'

'No, sir.'

'Nobody fucking retires in this business unless they're planning a see-you-later job.'

'It's not about money.'

'It's always about fucking money. You want to contemplate retirement – you do it while you're tossing champagne bottles off the back of your yacht or sipping sangria in a Spanish villa.'

'I'm not planning anything,' says Sami.

Murphy looks at him dubiously, wondering if he's lost his bottle, or worse, gone over to the other side.

'How old are you, son?'

'Twenty-seven.'

'How much have you got in your pocket?'

Sami shrugs.

'You're potless, aren't you?' Murphy pushes back his chair. 'Poverty isn't freedom. Look at the poor fuckers out there.' He points to a bus queue over the road. People are shivering in the rain. 'Most of 'em ain't got a pot to piss in. They're shell-shocked, exhausted, they're tired of scraping away week after week, year after year, making the giro stretch till next pension day, living on overdrafts and plastic. Meanwhile, the politicians keep telling them they've never had it so good and they're too stupid to know they're being lied to. Only scraps ever fall from the top table, son. Toast crumbs and bacon rind. So when you hear a politician start talking about trickle down economics and how everyone benefits from the good times, that's because they're pissing on you from a great height.'

Dessie chuckles.

'Do you ever think about the future, Sami?' Murphy asks.

All the time, thinks Sami.

'What are you gonna do?'

'Start a band. Get some gigs. Look after Nadia.'

'Work with me, son. And I'll make sure you've got a tidy little stack before you walk away. I'll even throw you a farewell party.'

'What about Nadia?'

'I'll see what I can do to find her. I got contacts. I'll lean a little on Toby Streak. Get the real story.'

This is crazy, thinks Sami. He's two days out of prison – innocent as the day he was born – and Tony Murphy wants him to join the firm. His guts are churning.

'I just want to find Nadia,' he says.

'Like I said, I'll help you find her.'

'Do you know where she is?'

'Not without asking.'

Sami looks hard at Murphy's face, searching for a clue that he knows more. Out of the corner of his eyes he sees Dessie's right eyebrow go up a quarter of an inch. He doesn't understand what it means but he knows enough to sense trouble.

'It's nothing personal, Tony. I'm not interested.'

There's a moment. A heartbeat. Murphy's face has turned to stone. 'Don't fucking call me Tony, you little prick.'

'I apologise. No offence meant, Mr Murphy.'

'Listen, you dainty little poof, you come in here, interrupt my meal, make outrageous allegations and then piss on my offer to help like I'm some up-his-own-arse charity worker.'

'No, sir.'

'You consider what I have to say, son. And don't leave it too long.'

Somehow Sami finds his feet, makes it through the restaurant, down the stairs, outside. He walks along the river past a group of Japanese tourists who are following a yellow umbrella like it's a religious artefact.

10

Tony Murphy belches quietly, getting a second taste of his rabbit poached in red wine with mashed potato and truffle oil. His gout is acting up – his right toe swollen – but the pain is preferable to the controlled diet his doctor recommended. No pâté. No port. Bollocks to that!

Murphy sighs and lets out a stream of urine into the porcelain. Sami Macbeth is exercising his mind. The kid didn't come round. That's the problem with the new breed. Most of them are soft pricks and idiots, who grow up thinking they're entitled. Gimme a freebie; gimme a discount; gimme a spot of unsecured credit – they're a gimme fucking army who don't know the meaning of good honest criminal graft.

Life would be a lot simpler without families. Sami Macbeth wouldn't have to worry about his sister and Ray Garza wouldn't have to worry about his idiot offspring.

Ray Jnr started all this. The kid took liberties. Took something that didn't belong to him.

Murphy should have known better than to help the

boy out but he thought it might be useful having the Chairman's son in his debt. Big mistake. Huge fucking mistake. Next thing the kid is riding round town like some outlaw baddie, dealing cocaine and drag-racing rozzers.

He was always a fuck-up. That's why Ray Snr packed him off to boarding school at twelve. Thought it might improve his prospects mixing with a lot of chinless trout in straw boaters and blazers.

Education is never wasted on the young they say and Ray Jnr didn't waste his. By his second year he was running an SP operation out of the junior common room and selling contraband – cigarettes, dope, girlie magazines, you name it. In year ten he smuggled two hookers into the senior dorm as part of a 'use it or lose it' weekend for spotty virgins.

The Eton version of a court martial followed. It wasn't the last time. Ray Jnr went to three more posh schools in the next two years and was asked to leave each of them. His old man paid the damages, apologised to the parents and made donations to the building funds.

At one point he employed a brace of security specialists, ex-Paras, to keep an eye on Ray Jnr and make sure he didn't dig a tunnel under the fence. Made no difference. The kid was a chip off the old block, an entrepreneur, a mover and a shaker without the brains or the guile of his father.

Eventually, Garza's missus suggested he let Ray Jnr

leave school and bring him into the business where Daddy could keep an eye on him. They gave him a junior management position. Put him on a salary. Began showing him the ropes.

Unfortunately, the only ropes Ray Jnr was interested in were wrapped around a young lovely's wrist and knotted to the bedpost while he snorted cocaine off her gym-sculptured stomach.

Ray Jnr didn't have an A-level to his name but he wasn't a complete moron. He knew Daddy was worth millions and the trust fund kicked in when he turned twenty-five. All he had to do was wait.

Consequently, he stopped showing up for work and hung out with his hooray buddies, partying hard. He liked the ladies. He liked the clothes. He liked the flash sports car Daddy bought him for his eighteenth.

The Chairman must have been tearing his hair out, so he tried something different. Tough love. He cut the kid's allowance. Figured he'd bring Ray Jnr to heel. It didn't quite work out that way.

Ray Jnr went into business for himself, dealing coke and Gary Abletts to his trust fund buddies and posh mates. He had all the right connections and enough chutzpah to think he was a class act, when in reality he had about as much sophistication as a coat-hanger abortion.

Ray Jnr was dealing to the top end of the market, the quality street gang, the crème de la crème and didn't notice he was treading on some big hairy fucking toes. The Albanians and the Turks didn't give a shit if he was Ray Garza's boy. To them he was simply a young punk muscling in on their primo uno turf.

That's when Ray Jnr came to Murphy. Couldn't go to his old man. There was too much yuppie Mafioso shit going down and he wanted protection. Security.

Murphy offered him advice. Said he'd make some calls.

Ray Jnr was scared. He wanted a piece for his personal protection. Murphy promised to sort him out in a few days, but the kid took something from him. Something he shouldn't have. Something nobody could know about.

Maybe things would have worked out if Ray Jnr had kept his head down and let things cool off with the Albanians and the Turks. Instead he got clocked doing over a ton on the M40. The rozzers gave chase. Ray Jnr burned them off. An hour later they found his Porsche parked up outside a pub in Hammersmith. They wanted to search inside. Ray Jnr told them to fuck off. Rozzers just love it when you talk dirty to them. Their eyes must have lit up when they found eight kilos of cocaine under the spare wheel.

Ray Jnr went off his head. Pulled the semi-automatic out of his belt. According to Ray the shooter went off accidentally. According to the charge sheet it was attempted murder.

The rest is history, as they say, except Ray Garza wants

to rewrite the whole episode and get his boy off. Only this is a rap he can't bribe or beg or blag his way out of. And history is going to get rewritten a dozen different ways when the boffins in the ballistics lab test the gun Ray Jnr was waving around. It's all about scratch markings on the chamber of the gun. Telltale signs. Damning evidence.

The kid got bail yesterday. Daddy forked out two mill and Ray Jnr was probably straight down to his clubster mates, bragging about how he toughed out his first night in the Scrubs. How he ran the joint like King Rat.

The cack-handed moron has no idea of the chain of events he's set in motion or how much shit is gathering on the fan. It's a mess and Murphy has to clean it up before someone hits the switch.

He shakes. Shakes again. Zips his fly. Washes his hands.

Dessie is waiting outside the door, standing guard like a loyal Labrador with less intelligence.

Murphy has a plan, but he needs Macbeth.

'What do you want me to do?' asks Dessie.

'Persuade him.'

'And if he does the job?'

'Get rid of him.'

Murphy goes back to the table and orders a crème caramel for dessert, which isn't on the menu, but the chef will do it by special request. So he should, thinks Murphy. 'I own the poncy arsehole.'

11

Sami has an appointment. It's part of the deal with his early release – a once-a-month pow wow with a probation service supervisor.

He's late. Missed his turn. He sits on a plastic chair in the waiting room, staring at a potted plant that seems to be surviving without light or leaves.

'Hello, Mr Macbeth,' she says. 'Can I call you Sami?'

It's a woman, Miranda Wallace. Well-preserved. Mid-forties. Dressed in a grey suit with a pink ribbon pinned to her lapel. She calls herself Ms, which makes Sami think she could be gay but she's too hot for that.

They sit in her office with the door open. Paperwork comes first. Twenty questions. Notes. Finally, she leans back and pushes her fringe from over her left eye.

'How do you feel about being out?'

'Good.'

'Have you had any trouble adjusting?'

'No.'

'What plans do you have?'

'I want to be a rock god.'

'That's an ambition rather than a plan. Perhaps you should find a more realistic goal.'

'I play guitar.'

'That's a good life skill.'

She makes it sound like needlework.

Sami starts telling her how he used to be in a band, playing gigs and occasionally supporting indie bands from the States who have one hit song and think they're going to fill Wembley Arena.

'What sort of music?' she asks.

'Rock infused with blues,' says Sami. 'Solid wall of sound stuff full of attitude.'

'Live fast, die young.'

'Leave a pretty corpse.'

'Sounds great,' she says.

Sami's surprised. Maybe she's an old rock chick. 'When was the last time you went to see a band?' he asks.

'I saw REM at Wembley Stadium in the summer.'

He's impressed.

They talk music a bit more and then she steers him on to his future plans. She wants to know about his accommodation arrangements and his employment prospects.

One of the conditions of Sami's probation is that he looks for work.

'That's what I'm going to do,' he explains. 'Once I find Nadia, I'll get my Fender, call up the old band, rustle up a gig or two and get some money in the jam jar.'

'It's not exactly steady work,' says Ms Wallace. 'Who's Nadia?'

'My sister.'

Sami starts telling her about going to Nadia's gaff and finding someone else living there. She hasn't been to work. Isn't answering her mobile. He doesn't know how much he should tell her about what happened last night with Toby Streak or about his meeting with Tony Murphy. He could be back inside before his feet touch the ground.

Ms Wallace asks the questions. She wants to know if Nadia is the sort to go missing or take off without leaving a note.

'Never,' says Sami. 'We're tight, you know. We look after each other.'

Next thing Sami is telling her about their mother dying and how he won custody of Nadia. One thing leads to another and soon he's recounting the whole sorry saga of Andy Palmer becoming a speed bump and Sami pleading guilty to possession.

She doesn't say much. Sits. Listens. Maybe she hears stories like this all the time, thinks Sami, but it doesn't stop him spilling his guts. His whole life story comes tumbling out – how his father was a Scottish merchant seaman and his mother a French Algerian refugee when they met in Montpellier and eloped.

She was a Moslem but didn't wear the veil. She never mentioned her family. Didn't call them. Didn't write. It

82

was as though when she married she ceased to have a history or a bloodline.

Sami's father quit the boats and worked in an abattoir in Glasgow, while running an SP operation on the side. He did everything at a hundred miles an hour, full bore – drinking, singing, fighting and fucking. Women loved him.

Sami's mother could tolerate his drinking and turn a blind eye to the bookmaking, but she hated the 'whores', as she called them.

'What happened to your father?' asks Ms Wallace.

'He drowned.'

'I'm sorry.'

'He was drunk.'

The parole officer is watching him intently, but whatever she's really thinking is hovering around the edges of her sentences.

'I'm not going back inside,' Sami tells her, his voice shaking. 'I just want to find Nadia. Make sure she's OK. I'll get a job, I promise. I'll pay the rent. It's not the whole future but it's a plan.'

'Who was the last person to see Nadia?' she asks.

'A tossbag called Toby Streak.'

'You've talked to him?'

Sami grimaces slightly. 'Yeah.'

'Did he know anything?'

'He mentioned an arrangement with Tony Murphy.'

'Do you know this Murphy?'

'I never met him until today.'

'What does he do?'

'He owns a restaurant, clubs . . . stuff like that.'

'Nightclubs.'

'Strip clubs.'

'Under the terms of your parole I'm sure you are aware that you're not supposed to be mixing with criminals or their associates.'

'I know, I know, but it's about Nadia.'

'If you have concerns for her safety you should take them to the police.'

'I've been to the police. They don't care.'

Ms Wallace seems conflicted. She's caught between her professional duty and her innate sense of concern.

'What did this Mr Murphy have to say?' she asks.

'He said he didn't know where Nadia was.'

'But you don't believe him.'

Sami shrugs. He's not going to tell her about Murphy's offer. He's said too much already.

Ms Wallace lets her gaze shift over Sami and her fingertips drum on the blotter. Sami can see in her eyes that she's already made assumptions about him. He's just another low-life fuck-up, who'll be back inside within a year.

Sami stands to leave. 'Will that be all?'

'Do you have somewhere else to be?' she asks.

'I have to find my sister.'

'Do you have a photograph of her?'

'Why?'

'I might know someone who could help you.'

Sami reaches into his pocket and pulls out a weathered Polaroid taken at Nadia's sixteenth birthday party. She's wearing a party hat and is draping streamers over Sami's head.

Ms Wallace studies the image and then writes a phone number on a piece of paper.

'If you don't hear from your sister you should give this man a call. His name is Vincent Ruiz and he owes me a big favour.'

'Why?'

'I was married to him for three years.'

12

Friday afternoon. Quarter to six. Ruiz presses the door-bell. Watches Miranda appear behind the frosted glass.

The door opens. She smiles. Kisses both his cheeks.

'I brought flowers,' he says.

'So I can see. Are the neighbours missing any?'

'That's cruel.'

Miranda leads him down the hall to the kitchen. Ruiz walks four paces behind. She looks great. She always does. Not just for a woman of her age but for any woman. Any age.

She fills a vase and arranges the flowers. Her cargo pants hang loose on her hips and her blouse is cut just low enough to show him what he used to have access to and is now off-limits. Another downside of divorce.

Miranda is a probation officer. That's how they met. Ruiz was working a case involving a boatload of stolen Levi's back in the late-eighties when 901s were the hottest ticket on the high street. Ruiz was married. Happily so, except for the cancer that was eating away at Laura from the inside.

He flirted a little with Miranda, became friends and then lost touch with her for a decade. By then Laura was dead and Jessie, his second wife, a suppressed memory.

He and Miranda were married for three years. They've been divorced for two. She's the sort of ex-wife blokes dream about. Low maintenance. Friendly. She's even tried to set him up on dates. Unmitigated disasters.

When they were married, Ruiz could never fully reconcile himself to the fact that Miranda worked as a parole officer. He didn't like the idea that low-life scrotes and toerags were sitting in her office wondering what underwear she was wearing. He half suspected – but never told Miranda – that half the reason she had such a good retention rate was because her parolees lusted after her.

Miranda was always careful. She dressed down. Minimal make-up. Nothing provocative.

'You want tea or coffee?' she asks.

'Got anything stronger?'

'Nope.'

'Is it proper tea?'

'Camomile.'

'Tastes of nothing, smells like potpourri.'

'It's very good for you.'

Ruiz produces a bottle of red wine from behind his back. 'So is this. It's full of antioxidants. Good for the heart. Ask the French. Sarkozy lives on this stuff and bags himself a pop star and a supermodel. What do we get? Gordon Brown. I rest my case.'

Ruiz finds a corkscrew and Miranda gets two glasses. The garden flat is nice. Homely. Ruiz likes the way it smells. He also likes the fact it's full of reminders and souvenirs of their marriage. The rug in front of the fireplace is from a holiday they took in Cornwall and the painting above the dining table was bought from a sidewalk artist in Florence.

Miranda sets out two balloon glasses and fills a bowl with roasted cashews. She's self-sufficient. Classy. Never asked him for a thing when they divorced except for the souvenirs. And all she asks of him now is that he returns her phone calls and lets her stay involved with Michael and Claire – the twins. Laura's kids, not hers. They still need a mother, she says, and she's happy to fill the role.

She sits down on the far end of the sofa. Curls her legs. Ruiz stares at her earlobes. He could nuzzle them for a few hundred years and never get bored.

'You called,' he says, trying to change the subject.

'What did the doctor say?' she asks.

'Is that why you asked me round?'

'Not entirely.' She sips her wine. 'But since you're here.'

'He said nothing.'

'What did you say?'

'Nothing.'

'It must have been very quiet.' Her eyes are dancing. 'Did he tell you to exercise?'

'I told him I was going to exercise by being a pallbearer for all my friends who exercise.'

'What about your weight?'

'What about it?'

'You've put on a few pounds.'

'No I haven't.'

'Stop trying to hold your stomach in.'

Ruiz relaxes. 'It looks good on me. You're too skinny.'

'I'm the same size as when you married me.'

'That's why I divorced you.'

Miranda gives him a hurt look. Ruiz wants to take the comment back. She has this way of acting that makes him believe that several women are living inside her and only one of them divorced him. The rest are still undecided.

Ruiz takes a sip of wine and a handful of cashews. Miranda has stopped talking and grown pensive, one tooth biting into her bottom lip.

'You all right?'

She nods and starts telling him about her new parolee, Sami Macbeth, released after nearly three years in prison. Tells him the story of his sister going missing.

Ruiz is thinking runaway. This Nadia is probably having the time of her life. She's found herself a boyfriend, doesn't want to associate with a jailbird brother.

Miranda hands him a photograph – a prison mugshot that must have come from Macbeth's file.

89

'What was this guy in for?'

'Possession of stolen goods.'

'First timer.'

She nods.

'What makes him think his sister is in trouble?'

Miranda tells him how Nadia abandoned her flat. She hasn't turned up for work or at college. Isn't answering her phone.

'When was the last time he heard from her?'

'A week ago.'

'This Nadia have a boyfriend?'

'According to Sami she had started seeing a guy called Toby Streak.'

Ruiz doesn't know the name. 'What does Streak have to say?'

'Says that he and Nadia parted company. Last time he saw her she was with Tony Murphy.'

Now there's a name that does ring a bell. Dozens of them, pealing from the rooftops.

Miranda senses as much.

'It's not good news, is it?'

Nothing about Murphy is good news, thinks Ruiz. 'What do you want me to do?'

'I thought you might ask around – make a few calls, you're good at that sort of thing.'

'What sort of thing?'

'Finding girls.'

'I'm a bit long in the tooth.'

'As a favour,' she says, rubbing her stockinged foot against his ankle. 'I feel good about this guy. I don't think he's a bad egg. He wants to straighten himself out.'

Ruiz has to fight the urge not to run his hand up her leg to her thigh. After another glass of wine he's beginning to settle in for the evening – something Miranda recognises.

'Off you go, big man,' she says.

'Why?'

'It's Friday night. I'm going out,' she says.

'Who with?'

'None of your business.'

She gives him a hug. Ruiz runs his hands down the small of her back and squeezes her backside.

'What was that for?' she purrs into his mouth.

'Old time's sake.'

'Stop calling yourself old,' she says.

'It's all right for you. You still look great.'

'It just takes me twice as long to look half as good.'

Ruiz smells her hair and turns away, walking up the stairs, onto the street. How is it, he wonders, that something so soft can make him so hard.

13

When Sami was in Wormwood Scrubs he received a letter from a girl called Kate Tierney. Kate used to hang around the band – not like a groupie, but as part of the entourage.

She was dating the drummer, Shortie, a good-looking bastard who treated her like shit. What is it about drummers? Ringo Starr falls out of the ugly tree, hits every branch, yet still manages to pull birds like Patti Boyd and Barbara Bach, a Bond girl for fuck's sake.

Sami used to lust after Kate from afar, or at least from the front of the stage. She was always upfront, in the mosh-pit, eyes closed, swaying to the music.

She was only eighteen when he first met her. When that particular band broke up, she drifted away. Over the next few years he bumped into her once or twice before losing touch.

Then Sami got sent down for a stretch. Three months in, he gets a letter from Kate Tierney. Perfumed. Little blue flowers around the border. Sami lay back in his cell and imagined the same little blue flowers on the edges of her knickers.

After that she wrote to him twice a week. Told him about her life. Her folks had been rich until her old man invested in junk bonds and blew the lot. Kate went from a private school in Surrey to a comprehensive in Hackney.

Sami had no idea why Kate decided to write to him. Maybe she felt sorry for him. Maybe she'd secretly fancied him for years. Maybe the reason was more fundamental and deep seated.

He asked her to send him a photograph. She sent one of her wearing a silk teddy, sitting astride a rocking horse. That's when he realised it was about lust. He was now a bad boy. An outlaw. Some girls think they deserve guys like that.

Kate Tierney studied hotel management and got a job working at the Savoy. She started in reception and worked her way up to night manager.

Sami calls her at work. Tells her he needs somewhere to stay. He's spent all afternoon and evening looking for Nadia. Visiting her friends, talking to her workmates. He's not going back to the bail hostel.

Kate thinks about it. Puts him on hold. Sami can hear her talking in a posh voice to one of the guests, telling Mr Somersby to have a nice evening and enjoy the opera.

Then she's back on the phone, whispering about the

tradesman's entrance in a side street near Embankment Gardens. He has to wait till ten. Call her when he's outside.

Sami does as she says.

The fire door opens. Kate looks great. She's dressed like an airline stewardess only sexier, in a black pencil skirt and a fitted black blazer. Armani. Her eyes are made up to look huge and her hair is piled up on her head, making her neck look even longer.

'You can stay, but you have to be out by six,' she whispers, waving him inside. The door shuts.

She takes him upstairs in a service lift. Unlocks a suite with a master key. The place is bigger than most of the houses Sami has lived in.

'Don't take anything from the mini-bar. I have to go. I'll come see you later.'

Sami has a shower. He's so whacked out he almost falls asleep under the water, which is spilling out of this big silver head the size of a dinner plate.

Afterwards, he puts on one of those soft white robes and crawls onto the bed. He needs to think. Needs to sleep. His eyes close. He dreams.

It's about Kate Tierney and it's not unlike a lot of the dreams he's had about her in the past two and a bit years. She's cupping his balls in her right hand and taking him in her mouth. She looks up his chest, into his eyes, and then rubs her tongue along the length of him, popping him into her mouth, sucking hard enough to almost bring him off. Just when he's about to blow, she pinches him hard just below the head of his penis.

That's when he wakes up and looks down. Sees her tousled blonde hair. She crawls up the bed, straddling his chest, rocking her hips back and forth.

She eases back, squats over him, takes him inside. He can see their reflection in the mirror. Sami looks twice to make sure it's him. Surely he must be in heaven. He's lying on Egyptian cotton sheets in one of the most expensive hotel suites in London, being screwed by a girl he's fantasised about for more nights than he can remember. Kate Tierney. No longer a wet dream. A reality.

Later, as they're lying in bed, they talk about old times, about the past couple of years. She wants to know all about prison, the nitty gritty, the violence, the gangs. Kate seems to get off on all those men being in the one place. Sexually frustrated men. Unfulfilled. Violent.

Sami doesn't need much time to recover. Kate gets on all fours and says, 'Show me how they do it in prison.'

Prison sex normally involves a left hand and a bartered copy of Big Jugs magazine but Sami thinks her version is a lot more interesting.

They cuddle afterwards. It's nice. They know stuff about each other. Sami remembers the details of her letters. He knows about her brothers and her father losing his job and how they always spend Christmas in Scotland with relatives. She wrote about ordinary run-of-the-mill stuff, but Sami loved reading about it. It made him feel normal or at least that one day his life could be normal.

At six the next morning he's out of the Savoy the way he came in, smelling of sex and tasting Kate on his lips. Sami buys a coffee from a kiosk near Embankment Tube. Sits on a bench in Victoria Gardens. Makes his plans for the day. The wind comes off the river and tugs at the coats of commuters leaving the station.

Tony Murphy denied any knowledge of Nadia, but he could have been lying. Toby Streak was too frightened to be telling lies. So what does he do next?

He takes a crumpled piece of paper from his pocket and smooths it on his knee. The name and number are written in pencil. Vincent Ruiz. Sounds foreign.

Sami looks at his watch. It's gone seven. He flips open his phone and punches the number. Gets an answering machine.

'Hello, ah, this is Sami Macbeth. You don't know me. I'm, ah, looking for my sister, Nadia. Ms Wallace, my probation officer, said you might be able to help me. You can call me on this number . . . if you're interested.'

Sami can't think of anything else to say. He hangs up and buys another coffee. Contemplates a doughnut. Suddenly, his mobile beeps and he glances at the screen. It's Nadia's number. His heart flip-flops in his chest like a landed fish. Hot coffee spills over his fingertips. He opens the handset.

Two words and an address, that's all she sends him.

Meet me, is the message. It's not an explanation. Not an apology.

The address is in the East End. Sami hits redial. Waits. The number rings out. Why is she playing games with him?

14

Sami emerges from Whitechapel Underground and studies a map on the wall beside the ticket office. He played
his first pub gig not far from here – in the basement of
the White Hart, with a band called Raw Liver.

The venue was so small and PA so large, it was noisier
than the Blitz according to the locals, who called the
police and tried to have the gig stopped. That's what
young bands do – make bold statements, argued Sami.
Raw Liver seemed to be saying, 'We might not be as good
as the Stones, but we're louder.'

He walks the last half-mile to the address. The place
looks like a fortress with barbed wire on the rooftops,
metal shutters, broken windows and a graffiti paintjob.

Sami is feeling double uneasy. This reeks of a set-up.
Why is Nadia's mobile still turned off? He looks at the
message again . . . tries to read between the words.

Most of the flats don't have numbers. Some of them
don't have doors. Sami finds the right one by a process
of elimination. Second floor, third one along, with a

patched plywood door and 'Fuck off' scrawled across it.

Sami knocks. Nobody answers. He tries again and then calls through the remnants of the mailbox.

Someone is coming.

A black rasta opens the door, with beads clacking. Levi's sit low on his hips and his tight-fitting red T-shirt has a picture of Bob Marley in full voice.

'What's up, mon?' he asks.

'I'm looking for Nadia.'

'What took you so long? She been waiting,' he says in a singsong voice.

'Who are you?'

'Puffa.'

Sami walks through the kitchen. The sink is overflowing with takeaway tins and garbage. No way Nadia is living in a place like this. There's a chicken sticking out of the plughole. Why in fuck's name did someone try to shove a chicken down the drain?

Next comes the lounge or maybe it's a bedroom. The floor is littered with punctured cans, pipes, cones, tin foil, burnt spoons, needles, tourniquets, half-filled bottles of water and wedges of lemon. It's a drug den, a crack house.

The room is dark. There are two bodies sleeping on beanbags and two more curled up on a mattress. Sami listens to make sure they're breathing. You got to be careful around junkies. They get paranoid. Psychotic.

Puffa has disappeared. He was here a moment ago. Sami moves along a corridor past another filthy room. Empty. Reeking. He opens the next door with his elbow. The smell hits him first. It's like something died weeks ago and nobody bothered giving it a decent burial.

Puffa is near the window.

The curtains open. The brightness is like an explosion.

Sami spots the baseball bat but sees it too late. He tries to duck and the bat bounces off the top of his head. Pain explodes and his brain washes from one side of his skull to the other.

The next blow almost breaks across his back. He drops to his knees in a world of hurt and tries to crawl away but the bat keeps hitting him, bouncing off his neck, his shoulders, his lower back . . .

Sami is doubled over and vomiting. Fingers lace in his hair and slam his head forward onto a raised knee. His bottom lip bursts against his teeth. Blood leaks into his mouth.

He doesn't want to fight. He doesn't want to get up. He just wants the beating to stop.

Someone drags him up. Sits him in a chair. Hits him again. Sami's head flies off at a different angle. The room goes dark. Drops away. Disappears.

Sometime later he sees a blurred light and the air swims for a moment before things come into focus. Nadia is curled at his feet, resting her head on his lap. She's wearing only jeans and a bra.

100

Sami wants to stroke her hair but his arms are tied behind his back. Bound to a chair. Blood and saliva stain his shirt.

Nadia turns her head. 'I'm so sorry, baby,' she whispers, stroking his cheek. Weightless and brittle, her eyes are black rimmed and cavernous.

Sami's mouth is taped. He can't answer.

He scans the room, looking for a way out. It has a wardrobe, a soiled mattress and two armchairs worn thin by squirming arses. A dirty brown blanket lies curled on the floor. Everything is brown – brown walls, brown carpet, brown furniture.

The door opens. Nadia stands. She smiles at Puffa, who sways into the room like he's on a catwalk. No way this emaciated crackhead beat Sami up. He must have had help.

Nadia becomes someone different. She wraps her arms around Puffa's neck. Squeezes her thighs around his leg.

'Have you got something for baby?' she purrs. 'Baby needs her medicine.'

Puffa grins with a gob full of gold.

'First you got to dance for me, princess. Show me how much you want it.'

Nadia hesitates. 'Don't make me do it now.'

'What's wrong?'

'Not in front of my brother.'

Puffa shakes his head. His dreadlocks swing. 'How bad you want to ride the dragon?'

'Please.'

'Come on, princess, just one dance. Show Sami how much you love the dragon.'

Nadia is about to cry. She pleads with him again.

'First you dance,' he says.

And she does, holding her arms above her head, rolling her hips in long slow circles. Her eyes are closed. Tears of shame glisten on her cheeks.

Puffa isn't watching her. He's looking at Sami. He pushes his face close.

'Do you know what crack is, mon?' He holds up a small yellow stone between his thumb and forefinger. 'It's the devil's sputum.'

Sami can feel his face burning and his skin crawling. He wants to cry. He wants to go home. He doesn't want to play any more. Puffa sits cross-legged in front of Sami, so he can watch what he's doing. Nadia is watching too, as she dances. Pale. Beautiful. Ugly.

Puffa burns a cigarette and collects the ash, putting it in a makeshift pipe fashioned from a mini whisky bottle, chewing gum, a rubber band and foil. He flattens the ash in the pipe and nestles the crack on top.

He signals Nadia. She drops to her knees like a dog begging for food or waiting for a scrap to fall from the table. She's hooked. Taken. Spoken for.

Sami wants to yell at her. He raises his feet a few inches from the floor and stamps them down, making the chair jump.

Nadia turns. Sami pleads with his eyes.

'I need to do this,' she says.

Sami stamps his feet again.

Puffa laughs. 'She doesn't love you any more, mon. She loves the rock. She loves the rockman.'

Sami tries to launch himself out of the chair. The bindings hold him back.

'Cool it bro, you got to chill,' says Puffa, as he holds the pipe towards Nadia and turns the lighter upside down. A bubbling crackling sound fills the room and smoke as white as cotton wool is trapped in the glass.

Nadia inhales. Her cheeks puff out. Her eyes shut. Her head lolls back. She tries to hold the smoke in her mouth and then swallow it bit by bit, holding it in her lungs for a minute or more until it seems as though she might pass out if she doesn't exhale.

Nadia looks at Sami and smiles. It's not her normal, beautiful, radiant smile. It's a chemical reaction. Opiate-induced. Her pupils are dilated. Her hands are twitching. She's blissful. Ecstatic. She's gone now. In another place.

Puffa chuckles. 'Don't she just love the dragon.'

Sami's head is spinning. The pain makes it hard to frame questions, let alone answers. He can see the pulse beating in Nadia's neck and the flaring of her nostrils.

She's started to come down. It's not like falling off a cliff. It's like the walls of paradise are nothing but stucco façades and behind them lie ugliness, anxiety, despair . . .

'The devil does it every time,' says Puffa. 'He tricks

103

you. Makes you believe you're in heaven, but when you've signed up, when you've taken the pledge, when you've hocked your soul, he shows you the gates of hell and says, "Don't believe the brochures, mon".'

Nadia is clawing at the skin on her forearms and whimpering like a frightened child in the biggest, darkest haunted house imaginable.

Sami looks at Puffa. Pleads with his eyes. He has to give her something. Make her better.

Puffa takes a tablet from his pocket. 'It's Valium,' he explains. 'It will help her come down.'

Puffa peels the wrapper off a chocolate bar and takes a bite. His eyes have a liquid sheen as he looks at Nadia proudly, as though his work here is done.

After ten minutes, she's calm.

'I need another pipe,' she says.

'Ain't got no more rock.'

'But I need some, baby.'

'Maybe I dropped some on the floor.'

Nadia doesn't hesitate. She's on all fours, looking for crumbs of crack on the stained rug or between the floorboards, trying to force the wooden planks apart with her fingernails. She's not Sami's sister any more. Not the one he remembers. She's a ghost. She's a crack whore.

The air pressure changes slightly. A door has opened and someone is standing behind Sami. Puffa isn't smiling any more. He opens his mouth to say something, but no words come out because a fist is squeezing his throat trying to narrow his neck size.

Puffa is scrabbling on his toes, but he can't get traction. Whoever has hold of his throat is 'walking' him outside. Meanwhile, Nadia has stopped looking for crack and is curled up in the corner, rocking gently, trying to make herself small.

Sami calls out but the gag muffles his voice. He wants Nadia to untie him. They can get away. He bounces on the chair and almost topples backwards.

Someone moves behind him and a voice whispers, pronouncing every syllable in a Scottish accent.

'You're taking a wee trip, Mr Macbeth. It's not the same sort of trip as your sister. Don't resist and you won't get hurt.'

Sami catches a whiff of the cologne and remembers smelling it before at Tony Murphy's restaurant. Dessie Fraser was wearing aftershave. Maybe he was the one who bounced the bat off Sami's head.

Oddly enough Sami feels relieved. Safer. Drugsters like Puffa see monsters in their Rice Krispies. At least Dessie is a professional. If he'd wanted to kill Sami he'd be dead already, despatched, gonski.

Sami takes a journey in a car boot. The darkness is oddly reassuring. He can feel the sides of the boot and smell the nylon carpet and spare wheel.

Nadia would have hated a ride like this. She would have panicked at the darkness and the enclosed space.

Even after thirteen years she still has nightmares. She hates wet nights. Swollen rivers. Drunk drivers. Narrow bridges. Nadia was in the front seat of the car. Sami in the back – just turned fifteen. Their father had been drinking at a casino in Brighton and had left them sleeping in the car. He woke them at 2.00 a.m., drunk, but determined to drive back to a cottage they were renting for the holidays.

The car demolished a crash barrier on the approach to a bridge, landing upside down in the water. The windows were open. It sank within seconds.

Douglas Macbeth was pinned by one leg behind the steering wheel, but he twisted his body so he could hold Nadia, pushing her face into the shrinking bubble of air. Sami tried to open the rear doors, but they were locked. Finally, he pulled one open. Grabbed Nadia. Scissored his legs to the surface.

They fought the current as it dragged them away, unable to go back. Swallowing water. Spluttering. Sucking air.

Sami no longer has nightmares about it; no longer has phantom phone calls from his father at three in the morning.

Douglas Macbeth was a coward and Sami feared him the way children fear all cowards, because they prey on the weak and make excuses about why they do it.

Some nights Douglas Macbeth would get so drunk that Sami would try to avoid him or give him one-word answers but his father would pull Sami onto his lap and tickle him mercilessly; tickle him until tears ran down his cheeks. Not tears of laughter. Douglas would use Sami's giggles to mask the moment that he drove his thumbs deep beneath his son's armpits, leaving bruises so deep they took a week to show and would always be hidden beneath his school uniform.

When the current dragged Sami and Nadia away that night, sweeping them down the swollen river, Sami didn't want to go back. He wanted to keep floating away. He wanted to forget he had a father.

Nadia couldn't forget. She clung to Sami for six hours before they were rescued. Clung to him on the way to the hospital. Wouldn't let him leave her side, even when they cut off her clothes and stitched the gash on her hip.

And for years after that she would crawl onto Sami's bed at night and curl asleep at his feet like a tabby cat, with one hand reaching across the bedclothes, making sure that he was still there.

The car stops. A roller door opens. Sami waits, listening. He doesn't want the boot to open. He wants to stay in the dark.

15

Saturday morning, Ruiz gets out of the shower, turns on his mobile and listens to his messages. The last one is from Sami Macbeth, who sounds tired and worried. He's still looking for his sister.

Ruiz makes himself breakfast. Looks at the headlines. Listens to the message again. Nadia is eighteen – old enough to disappear, old enough to find herself. Maybe he should flick past this one and find something better to do.

Only he can't think of anything better. That's one of the problems with being retired – he doesn't get any holidays. Every day is the same. Leisure. Leisure. Leisure. All play and no work.

He puts in a call to a prison psychologist and gets the skinny on Macbeth, who boasted a clean rap sheet until he got picked up for possession of stolen jewellery. He has a 150-point IQ, three A-levels and about as much common sense as a pork chop.

Next Ruiz calls Fiona Taylor, an old pal from his days

on vice. She began her career as a parking warden, putting tickets under wiper blades, and then spent ten years in uniform before they gave her sergeant's stripes. Now she's a Chief Inspector, which isn't surprising given her talent, but a minor miracle in the Metropolitan Police Service where the glass ceiling is bulletproof.

Blonde, muscular and unmarried, Fiona has the sort of aggressive posture that leads some men to think she's gay. In reality she's a challenge and well worth the effort, thinks Ruiz, who had a brief fling with her a decade ago before he hooked up with Miranda.

'I thought you were dead,' she says warmly.

'Not even in the departure lounge.'

'I'm glad to hear it.'

They swap small talk about family and mutual friends. He asks about work. The less said the better.

'What do you need?' she asks, knowing he's called for a reason.

'I want to bounce a name off you. Toby Streak.'

'I remember him. Why are you interested?'

'A favour for a friend.'

Fiona is typing on a keyboard. 'He's a pimp and dealer. I busted him ten years ago for statutory rape and he did a deal with the girl's father.'

'Paid him off?'

'You might very well think that; I couldn't possibly comment.' She's doing her Francis Urquhart impersonation.

Ruiz plays along. 'What *can* you comment upon?'

'Streak's main angle is a lover-boy scam, finding fresh meat for the pornsters.'

'Does he work for anyone in particular?'

'Freelance mainly. He started as a DJ working raves in the mid-nineties. He used to pick out the prettiest girls dancing around the cowpats and invite them to Ibiza for the summer. They'd begin by wearing bikinis and dancing in cages at the clubs. Then came the modelling shots, the promises of recording deals, the screen auditions . . . you know the rest.'

Ruiz asks about a last known address. Fiona checks the computer. Gives him the details of a flat off Abbey Road in St John's Wood.

Fiona is busy. She has to go.

'One more thing,' says Ruiz. 'Tony Murphy – is he still in the market for girls?'

'He still has a couple of clubs, but he doesn't have to recruit. The girls come to him.'

'Why's that?'

'His clientele are known to shower occasionally.'

'He's gone upmarket?'

'Right to the top.'

It's midday Saturday. The sun is shining. Toby Streak will still be asleep. Ruiz quite fancies a trip to Abbey Road. He might walk the famous crossing and relive a Beatles moment; even go barefoot like Paul.

Streak lives in a luxury block of flats with an intercom and security cameras. Business must be good. Ruiz tries the neighbours on the intercom and one of them buzzes him through the main door. He catches the lift to the fourth floor and hammers on the door until Toby stumbles from a bedroom and peers through a security peephole.

Ruiz gives him a spiel about reading the gas meter. Flashes a library card. Works every time.

'It's Saturday,' says the voice behind the door.

'I could come back Monday, but you won't have any gas by then. They'll have turned it off. Your meter hasn't been read for six months. Won't take a second.'

A deadbolt slides back. In the same instant Ruiz kicks the door open, hitting Streak in the head. Toby lets out a cry and falls to his knees, clutching his already bandaged nose. As he tries to scramble away on his hands and knees, Ruiz follows him down the hallway. Flicks a boot into his elbows. Toby falls on his face and Ruiz pins him to the floor, massaging his ear with his right heel.

A girl peers from the bedroom. She's young – maybe too young – wrapped in a sheet.

'You Nadia Macbeth?'

She shakes her head.

'Put your clothes on. I'll give you the cab fare home.'

She looks at Toby. Ruiz leans a little harder on his head.

'Go home, babe,' he says, trying to act cool with his face pressed into the hall runner.

111

The girl slips on a dress, wads up her underwear and shoes and steps over Streak, almost flying down the stairs.

'I'm looking for Nadia Macbeth,' says Ruiz.

'You and everyone else,' Toby sniffles. 'Can I get up now?' The plaster across his nose makes him sound like a cartoon character.

Ruiz lifts his foot. Toby climbs to his feet and slumps into a chair, tentatively touching his nose.

'If you've broken it again . . .' He doesn't finish the statement.

'Who broke it the first time?'

'That cunt Macbeth.'

Ruiz glances around the flat. The décor is a cross between bachelor chic and a seventies brothel.

'Let's start at the beginning,' he says, pulling up a chair.

It's not difficult to get the story out of Toby. He's an expert at telling it now. Tony Murphy paid him a thousand quid to hook Nadia Macbeth in a lover-boy scam.

'It wasn't worth the fucking aggravation,' says Toby, acting like a victim in all this.

'Why did Murphy want her?'

'Fuck knows.'

'But it had to be this particular girl?'

'Yeah.'

'You ever provided girls for Murphy before?'

'No.'

'Why this time?'

112

He shrugs. 'He said it had to be done quick – in three days. Sweep her off her feet. Deliver her.'

'Where?'

'Place off the Whitechapel Road.' He tilts his head back, trying to stop his nose bleeding. 'You won't tell Murphy I told you, will ya?'

'That's the least of your problems, Toby.'

16

'Sorry about the transport, son,' says Tony Murphy, brushing dust off Sami's shoulders. 'It's the best Dessie could come up with at short notice.'

They're standing in a concrete car park with numbered bays and reserved signs. Sami can hear a crowd cheering from somewhere outside. Maybe it's a football match.

Murphy's face is full of chubby bonhomie. He's playing the jolly fat man, dressed in a lightweight woollen suit with his pork pie hat at a jaunty angle.

'You remember Dessie.'

'He bounced a few things off me earlier,' replies Sami, flexing his left shoulder, which still aches. The swelling above his eye feels like a golf ball beneath his skin and he can taste blood in his mouth. He fingers his front teeth, counting them.

'He's a very capable individual, Dessie. He managed to find your sister.'

'He beat the crap out of me.'

114

'On the contrary, he saved your life. Those drugsters can be very fucking dangerous. You were lucky Dessie was there.'

Sami shakes his head in wonder. What sort of parallel universe has he been transported to?

'Where's Nadia?'

'In safe hands.'

Mr Murphy leads the way. Sami is to follow. A lift opens. It takes them upwards and they emerge into a carpeted room furnished with comfortable chairs facing a large picture window. A corporate box, but it's not a football match. They're at the dogs.

A moment later a bell sounds and gates open. Half a dozen loose-limbed greyhounds scramble into full stride and hurtle around the first bend, chasing a fake rabbit. Accelerating down the straight, the dogs fight to stay upright on the corners as the crowd roars. Sami watches, mesmerised. This isn't sport – it's an arcane spectacle, like seeing lions fight elephants at the Colosseum.

Murphy isn't taking any notice. He's on the phone arguing with his wife about where they should put the marquee. She must be throwing a party.

Sami smells the food. Curries. Two tables on either side of the viewing window are lined with stainless steel tureens. Samosas, onion bhajis, chicken korma, beef vindaloo, butter chicken, pilau rice, chapatis and naan bread.

Dessie is already tucking in. He must have worked up an appetite swinging that bat.

The race has finished. The rabbit won. A dog came second. Extra Chum for him tonight.

'Terrible thing crack,' says Tony Murphy, offering Sami a plate. 'It's a cocaine derivative. Not physically addictive like heroin. Psychologically addictive. Once your mind has been there it wants to go back again and again.'

Sami watches him spoon korma onto rice. 'People get all paranoid when they come down. Twitchy. Scared. It's so bad that some of them start taking heroin, which is the beginning of the end. Know what I'm saying? Once you're needled up and rattling, you're truly fucked.'

He takes a mouthful of naan bread and takes a seat. Sami stares at his plate of food, no longer hungry.

'I've never punted the stuff,' says Murphy. 'It's not a moral thing with me, just too much aggravation getting webbed up in shit like that. I did try it once though and I can understand the attraction. Do a pipe and get a blowjob at the same time. You'll believe you're in heaven.'

Sami weighs the fork in his hand. He wants to drive it through Murphy's throat.

'Are you a drug taker, son?'

Sami shakes his head.

'Very wise decision. It gives you an advantage. Power. You take your sister, Nadia. From what I hear that little moppet would suck off an Alsatian to get her next fix. It's a shame.'

Sami sees the red mist. He launches himself across the

116

room but seems to stop in mid-air and crash to the floor. On his knees, Sami takes a boot in the stomach and a punch to the kidneys. A socket of pain races up his spine and explodes like fireworks in his head.

Dessie grabs his collar. Sits him in a chair. Murphy takes another mouthful of chicken korma as though nothing has happened.

'You're not the complete package, son,' he says, picking a grain of rice from his shirt. 'Some parts are still missing.'

Sami's mouth is opening and closing like a guppy.

'This plan of yours to retire, I don't think it's a good one. You can't just walk away from the life you chose; the life that chose you. You're too good at what you do, son.'

Murphy loads his fork with Indian pickle and rice.

'Young bloke like you should use his talent wisely. Make a decent score. Know what I'm saying?'

Sami can breathe again. The pain is easing.

'You got savvy, son. You know what savvy means?'

'I'm not sure.'

'You're bright. You learn fast. You know your way around. Am I right?'

Sami feels like he's being led by the dick and there's nothing he can do about it.

'Let's face it, son, you're too young to retire. You're in your prime. You've come of age. You got that hungry look in your eyes.'

'That's cause I haven't eaten,' explains Sami.

'I'm speaking metaphorically, son. Work with me here.'

Sami sucks on a wobbly tooth and feels perspiration prickle along the skin beneath his hairline. Mr Murphy is getting to the point.

'That's why you're going to do this small favour for me. A single job and then you can walk away. And I promise you nobody is gonna give you any grief. You'll be out.'

'What about Nadia?'

'I'm going to look after your little sis. Get her straightened out. Clean.'

'Can I see her?'

'When the job is done.'

'What do I have to do?'

'I want you to open a safe for me. It's more of a strong room than a safe. Locks and metal bars. No funny combination whats-its. Someone of your experience will do it in his sleep. Blindfolded. One hand tied behind his back.'

'I can't do it,' says Sami.

Murphy stops chewing.

'You saying you can't open the safe?'

'Yes.'

'Why not?'

At this point Sami knows he's on shaky ground. He doesn't have the first fucking clue how to open a strong room. He's not a safecracker or a safe blower. 'Sparkles' is a figment of the imagination, an invention, a lie.

'What if I told you that I didn't do the Hampstead job?' he says.

118

'I don't understand.'

'I wasn't there. It was a guy called Andy Palmer. Or maybe it was someone else. I was just sitting in a van.'

Murphy laughs. 'Pull the other leg, son, it plays "Land of Hope and Glory".' Then his face grows hard. He gives Sami the pointy finger. 'Enough pissing about, son. You do this job and you have a future, simple as that.'

'I'm out of practice.'

'Nonsense. It's like riding a bike.'

'No offence, Mr Murphy, but it's nothing like riding a bike.'

'I'm speaking figuratively, son.'

'Yes, sir.'

Sami looks at Dessie and back to Murphy. He can't see a way out of this. He needs time to think. Time to come up with a plan.

'What sort of strong room?' he asks.

'Big fucker.'

'I need the make and model, the specs. I don't try to open a safe unless I know everything about it – the type, location, tensile strength of the steel. Manufacturer. How old it is?'

'I can get you that.'

'I don't have any tools.'

'What do you need?'

Sami is winging it now. 'It's very technical equipment.'

'Just tell me what you need.'

'Depends on the job.'

119

Sami starts talking about diamond tipped drills, fibre-optic cameras and stethoscopes. He doesn't know about half the stuff he's asking for, but hopefully neither does Murphy.

'I'm going to need explosives,' he says.

'Why?'

'A failsafe, just in case the door won't open.'

Murphy clips the end from a cigar and draws on a flame, puffing out clouds of smoke.

'Give Dessie a list.'

'What's in this strong room?' asks Sami.

'That ain't none of your business, son.'

'If I'm going to open it, I should know what's inside. Safety reasons, you know.'

'I am looking after your safety,' says Murphy. 'I'm giving you deniability.'

'Deniability?'

'Yeah. It's like the old song goes, "You don't put your dick in the blender if you're running short on swizzle sticks".'

'I don't know that one,' says Sami.

'I could get Dessie here to sing it for you, but he's not a fan of karaoke.' Murphy spits a fleck of tobacco leaf onto the floor. 'He's also not partial to smart-mouth sarky toerags who ask too many questions.'

Sami keeps his mouth shut.

'Right, that's decided,' says Murphy. 'We'll get you the specs. Dessie, here, will get you the equipment. You do the job tomorrow.'

'What do you mean tomorrow?' says Sami. 'I need more time to prepare . . . to practise.'

'Got no time.'

A bell clangs. The dogs are off again. Murphy turns to the window to watch. 'Another thing, son, I don't want you even thinking you might tip off Old Bill about these discussions. That's why you're going to stay with Dessie until tomorrow, understand?

'And if you did go shooting off your mouth at some later date, I got a dozen people, including a member of parliament, who'll put me three hundred miles from here, watching Man City play Everton.

'The CCTV cameras will tell 'em the same thing. Ever heard of body doubles, son? Saddam had used dozens of 'em – fat fuckers with moustaches who strutted around firing shots in the air. So did Adolf. Now I don't like the Krauts as a rule but they've had some pretty good ideas, Mercedes, BMWs. Gassing them Jews was right out of order, mind you, but some of the kikes I know wouldn't give you the steam off their piss unless they were charging usage. I shit you not.

'So don't you go blabbing about our little enterprise, before or afterwards. Understand? Or I'll have Dessie here hold open your smart mouth with a spout while I piss down your throat.'

17

The address is off Whitechapel Road – three streets back from the river. Jack the Ripper territory but nowadays it could be in Bangladesh or Mogadishu or Mecca. There are headscarves and Halal butchers, Halal bakers and Halal greengrocers. How do you get Halal fruit and veg, wonders Ruiz, as he parks the car on vacant ground beside a mosque.

A gaggle of teenagers in hoodies and low-slung jeans slink out of the shadows – every one of them a genetic time bomb. They begin checking out the Merc and regarding Ruiz with hate and envy.

The ringleader looks no older than twelve. Fearless. Freckled. Hostile.

'This is our fucking turf. You can't park here without our say so.'

'Is that right? I didn't see any signs. Must be getting old.'

'It's gonna cost you.'

'How much?'

The kid looks at his gang. 'A fiver.' And then adds, 'for a half hour.'

Ruiz takes out a tenner. 'You got change?'

The kid looks at it greedily. 'You can stay an hour.'

Ruiz balls up the ten quid note and looks at the gang. One of them is a mixed race kid, small and whippet thin. Built to run. Ruiz points to him. Motions him forward. Gives him the tenner.

'Whoever catches you, gets the money. Otherwise, you get to keep it.'

The kid takes off, darting across the allotment, leaping a fence, dodging rubbish bins and parked cars. He's flying down the street with the others in pursuit, screaming abuse.

Ruiz's mobile vibrates against his heart. Fiona Taylor sounds concerned.

'Funny thing happened after I talked to you. I typed Tony Murphy's name into the PNC and pulled up his file.'

'How many pages did it come to?'

'Oh, it's long, but I'm more interested in the pages I'm *not* allowed to see.'

'What do you mean?'

'There's a lock on some of the information. I don't have the security clearance to access it.'

Ruiz can hear her tapping a pencil on the edge of her desk. She's thinking. 'It could be special ops.'

'A surveillance operation?'

'MI5 or maybe MI6.'

'Murphy isn't in that league.'

'Maybe not, but it might be worth treading softly on this one,' she warns.

'I'm very light on my feet. You should see me dance.'

'A ballroom king – now I've heard everything.'

She hangs up and Ruiz contemplates why a club owner like Tony Murphy would warrant so much secrecy. There were rumours years ago that he laundered money for the IRA, but not even Murphy would be crazy enough to swim with those sharks.

Ruiz starts looking for the block of flats where Toby Streak said he dropped Nadia Macbeth. What he finds is a graffiti-stained pile of shit with scorch marks around the balconies and plywood nailed over most of the windows. A black guy with dreadlocks opens the door and blinks at the brightness, whacked out on something.

'You know what time it is, mon?'

'Four o'clock.'

'People are sleeping.'

'It's the afternoon.'

'Time is relative. That's what Mr Einstein say.'

'He also said only two things are infinite – the universe and human stupidity – and he wasn't completely sure about the universe.'

The rasta scratches his arse. Ruiz looks past him. The hallway is littered with junk mail, bills and final demands.

'I'm looking for someone.'

'You a copper?'

'Do I look like one?'

'You fat enough.'

'I'll polish my boot on your arse.'

'That would be police brutality, mon.'

'Not if my foot slipped. I'm looking for someone. Her name's Nadia Macbeth.'

'You want a girl. Why didn't you say so? Follow Puffa.'

He motions Ruiz inside and down the hall. The carpet sticks to his feet. Puffa leads him into a semi-dark room strewn with burnt spoons, bent cans, water bottles and foil wrappers. He kicks a mound of blankets. A white face emerges, with sunken cheeks and chemical green eyes. He calls her Treka.

'So what do you think? Talk to Puffa. We can negotiate.'

'I'm only interested in Nadia Macbeth.'

'Nobody here called Nadia.'

Treka crawls back under the blanket.

Ruiz brushes past Puffa and begins searching the flat. He talks to a kid who looks about twenty, but is probably younger. He's eating cereal straight from the box and staring at a corner where the TV used to be.

'You ever heard of Nadia Macbeth?' he asks.

'I heard of Macbeth. Studied it at school. It's one of them Shakespeare plays about three witches and a dude who wants to be king.'

'You must have been listening.'

125

Ruiz takes out his mobile and looks at the list of recent messages, before hitting a button to return a call. The sound of a phone ringing fills the room. Puffa looks at the ceiling pretending he can't hear it. The handset is vibrating in his pocket.

'Aren't you going to answer that?' asks Ruiz.

'Not just now,' says Puffa.'

'I think you should.'

Puffa pulls out the handset. Flips it open. 'Hello?' he asks nervously.

'Hello,' answers Ruiz.

'Can I help you?'

'Yes you can. Every time you open your mouth it's like a fart in a colander. From now on you're going to answer my questions honestly or I'm going to set fire to your dreads.'

Puffa's eyes go wide and he puts both hands on his head.

'How did you get this mobile?'

'Dude left it here.'

'What was his name?'

Puffa shrugs.

Ruiz points to the kid with the cereal box. 'What was the name of that play you studied?'

'Macbeth.'

He looks at Puffa. 'That's a clue.'

Puffa starts bleating about having memory problems. 'I smoke too much grass, mon. I forget things, you know.'

126

Ruiz gathers the occupants of the flat into one room. There are six of them – junkies, hookers and runaways, all of them whacked out on something, sweating or ill. He takes Puffa through the story again, marvelling at how he can tie himself into knots and harangue himself for telling lies, before starting a completely new explanation about how he came by Sami Macbeth's mobile.

Eventually, Puffa gets so tangled up in his lies that he starts telling bits of the truth. Someone paid him five hundred quid to get a girl hooked on crack. He had to start her on the brown, he explains, because she wouldn't co-operate but soon she rode the dragon and didn't want to stop.

'Who gave you the money?'

'Big white dude. Smelled like he fell in a tub of aftershave.'

'Give you a name?'

'Nope.'

'You didn't ask or you didn't care?'

'He wasn't a great talker.'

'How did you get the mobile?'

Puffa starts telling a lie. Stops. Starts again.

'Guy left it behind. He come looking for his sister. The big mon gave him a hiding and took him away.'

'What about Nadia.'

'Her too.'

'Are you sure that's how it happened?'

Puffa nods. 'If you want me to say it didn't happen, that's OK. Tell me what you want to hear.'

'The truth.'

'The truth is relative, mon.'

Ruiz slaps him around the head.

'Ow, that hurt!'

'Pain is relative, too.'

Ruiz keeps quizzing him, but the story doesn't change. The others are next to clueless. 'Anyone got anything to add?'

They shake their heads.

Ruiz puts a fatherly arm around Puffa's shoulders, flicking his beaded dreadlocks with his thumb.

'You got a passport, Puffa?'

'No, mon.'

'I'd get one if I were you. Maybe consider relocating. See the islands. Meet the distant cousins.'

Puffa frowns. 'Why's that, mon?'

'After I find the girl you got hooked on crack, I'm going to come back and turn your balls into worry beads.'

18

Tony Murphy has four mobiles on the table in front of him. He chooses one. Punches in a number.

'I thought we were going to talk tonight,' says a voice on the other end.

'I'm calling now. Is this line OK?'

'Yeah.'

'Where's the stuff now?'

'Same as before, but only till Monday. Should have gone to the lab yesterday.'

'Tell me about this strong room.'

'It's not really a room. It's more like an industrial wardrobe.'

'What's an industrial wardrobe?'

'It's like an ordinary wardrobe only it's made of steel.'

'Any locks?'

'Three of them: one internal and two padlocks.'

'Motion sensors or alarms?'

'It's the Old Bailey, not the Bank of England.'

Murphy doesn't appreciate his sarcasm. 'I need the make and a serial number.'

'You want fries with that?'

'Don't be a comedian. Brummies aren't funny.'

'What about Jasper Carrott?'

'My armpit is funnier than Jasper Carrott.'

They discuss the details. Decide the timetable. Murphy can get a floor plan and the location of the security cameras.

'What about our cover story?'

'I'm working on it. You just have to worry about the strong room.'

'It's under control.'

'I don't want a mess.'

'In. Out. I got an expert who's slicker than a butcher's prick.'

19

Sami spends the night on a bunk bed in a warehouse just off the south circular. The place is full of air-conditioning units, still in boxes. Some bright spark entrepreneur bought up four thousand of the systems from Taiwan figuring global warming was a sales opportunity. That was before the wettest, coldest summer in a century.

Bankruptcy resulted, allowing Tony Murphy to snap up the entire stock for a tenner each. It was the perfect example of stupidity and capitalism working in perfect harmony.

Sami didn't sleep. He spent the night thinking about Nadia and feeling sorry for himself. Bad luck is supposed to float around and fall randomly on people – a little here, a little there. It's been raining on Sami his whole life. Dumping on him. Now he's swimming in an ocean of shit (front crawl, not backstroke) and he doesn't know which shore to head for.

He still can't rid himself of the images of Nadia dancing for crack and crawling on her hands and knees, trying to prise apart the floorboards. His last glimpse of her was crouching in a corner, shivering, terrified, humiliated, unable to speak.

When Sami rescued her from the sunken car she was like that, struck dumb. For months Nadia didn't say a word. The psychologist said it was post-traumatic stress. Sami imagined the screams were trapped inside his sister's head, echoing so loudly that Nadia couldn't hear the sound of her own voice.

Sami took her to a place he knew – an underpass near Clapham Junction where the express trains roared overhead and created a wall of sound that nobody could shout over. He hired a portable generator and set up a microphone and the band's biggest PA amp beneath the underpass. They waited for the next train and he told Nadia she had to open her mouth and let the scream out. The train was roaring over their heads in a thunderous roll.

It took five more trains before it happened. Nadia squeaked, then she cried, then she screamed into the microphone, throwing back her head and howling as tears squeezed from her eyes. Sami always wondered what the passengers on the train must have made of the voice they heard booming from the underpass, drowning out the drumming wheels and rushing wind. Nadia had rediscovered her voice; heard it over the screams in her head; let it come pouring out in a rage of tears, snot and regret.

Sami pauses and listens. A vehicle has pulled up outside. The roller door opens and a white van pulls inside. Dessie is sitting up front next to a driver who's wearing dark sunglasses and looks like a hod carrier. Certain details about him seem familiar – the pallid skin and balloon-shaped head.

Then Sami remembers. It's the same geezer who spoke to him outside Wormwood Scrubs on the day he was released.

Sami imagines he's going to be huge, but when he steps out of the van he only comes up to Sami's chest. He calls himself Sinbad and doesn't bother shaking hands. Instead he cracks his knuckles and flexes tattooed forearms which are thicker than his legs.

The van has ladders on top and a logo on the side: *Elevation Solutions: Lift Repairs and Maintenance.*

Dessie tosses Sami a peaked cap, work boots and a blue boilersuit, nothing too new or clean. They're supposed to be repairmen. Professionals.

Inside the van there are ropes, pulleys and tools. Underneath a tarp is some extra gear: a fuck-off drill on a frame, a stethoscope and a fibre-optic camera still in the box.

Dessie hands Sami a brown manila A4 envelope. Sami has a feeling it isn't a permission slip. Opening the flap, he pulls out the specs for a strong room along with floor plans of a building showing the lift shafts, security doors and CCTV cameras.

Sami takes a seat and begins studying them, trying to look like he knows what he's doing, which couldn't be further from the truth.

'Got to get moving. Job's been called in,' says Sinbad.

'What job?'

'Broken lift.'

'I need longer.'

'No time.'

Sami dresses in the boilersuit and work boots that are a size and a half too big.

'I don't think I can go. These don't fit,' he tells Dessie.

'They're not supposed to, dickweed. We don't want you leaving any wee footprints that match your shoe size.'

'Good thinking,' says Sami, marvelling at the logic.

Sinbad hands him a canister.

'What's this?'

'Mate of mine knocked it up. It's called TATP.'

'What's that mean?'

'Triacetone tri-oxymoron,' says Sinbad, 'or something like that. You got to treat it real gentle or, you know what . . .'

'What?'

'It goes off.'

'You mean it goes bad?'

'No, it blows up, moron. The ragheads call it the Mother of Satan.'

'I said I wanted plastic explosives.'

'Tescos was fresh out.'

134

Sami takes the container from Sinbad. Holds it at arm's length. Sweat prickles on his forehead. This is crazy. He could get a twenty-year sentence for possessing even half this shit and now he's nursing a homemade bomb.

'Check the gear,' says Dessie. 'Make sure we got everything.'

Sami makes a show of flicking switches and holding up the fibre-optic camera, blowing on the lens. One half of his brain says, 'How hard can it be to open a strong room? Andy Palmer managed it.' The other half of his brain says, 'Who am I kidding?'

Dessie is counting out the latex gloves and balaclavas. He loads the gear into a zip-up holdall and tosses an empty rucksack in the back of the van.

'If anything goes wrong; if we get separated, call this number,' he tells Sami.

'I don't have a phone.'

'Use a call box.'

Dessie turns off his own phone. Mobiles can be traced.

He gives Sinbad the nod. They're ready. The roller door opens and the van pulls out into bright daylight.

Sami sits in the middle, next to Sinbad, whose feet barely reach the pedals. Nobody is saying much. There's not a lot to say. Sami decides to read the instructions for the fibre-optic camera.

'I thought you knew how to use this shit,' says Dessie.

'Different brand,' explains Sami. 'This one's Japanese.'

He shows him the box. Dessie blinks at the writing. It says *Made in Germany*. He can't read.

Sami met guys doing bird who were illiterate. Some of them used to bring their letters to him to read or ask him to write back to their wives and girlfriends. It could be heartbreaking because the news from home wasn't always positive.

A con called Phil Bucket (everyone called him Lunchbucket) got a letter from his missus one day and as Sami read the first line to himself he realised it was a Dear John letter. She was giving Phil the flick. Filing for divorce.

Sami looked at the expectation on Phil's face and couldn't do it. Phil had six years to go. If he took the news badly he might shoot the messenger and break a few of Sami's bones. So Sami made up a different letter – one that said everything was great at home and the kids were missing him.

Then he sat Phil down and they wrote a letter back. 'Tell me how you feel about Nancy,' he asked him.

'She's a good bird.'

'What's she like?'

'Well she's let herself go a bit, I guess, put on a few pounds.'

'But you love her, right?'

'You trying to be funny?'

'No.'

'You think I'm a soft prick?'

'No, Phil, not at all,' Sami stammered. 'I just think you

should tell Nancy how you feel about her. Let her know how much she means to you.'

'Why?'

'She deserves it, doesn't she? She's raising your kids on her own. You're not round to help.'

Phil thought about this. Mulled it over. 'She makes a cracking sherry trifle with those little sponge squares and custard.'

'I was thinking of something a little more romantic.'

'Like what?'

'How about we say this, "Dear Nancy, I think about you all the time. At night when I lie in bed I remember how nice it is to just hold you and hear you sleeping. A man like me doesn't deserve a woman like you".'

'You can't say that – she might leave me.'

'Trust me, Phil. She'll love it. Then you'll say, "I know you're paying for my mistakes, Nancy, but one day I'll make it up to you and the kids. I'm gonna show you how much you mean to me. How much I miss you. Don't give up on me, Nancy. Keep a candle burning for me in the window and I'll keep one burning in my heart."'

The letter did the trick. Nancy wrote back saying she'd changed her mind about the divorce. Mission accomplished. Body intact.

They're in central London. It's Sunday morning. The streets are full of tourists and tour buses. Rubbernecks. Sightseers. The city never sleeps.

They cross Blackfriars Bridge and turn right up

Ludgate Hill towards St Paul's Cathedral and left into Ave Maria Lane. They must be close to the Old Bailey, thinks Sami. The last time he was in this part of London he was being sentenced for the Hampstead job but he couldn't see much from the back of a prison van.

Sinbad pulls up at a large set of security gates flanked by spiked fences. A yellow sign declares: *Warning: No Unauthorised Admittance*. Beneath it are symbols for security cameras, dogs and armed guards.

'Why are we stopping?' asks Sami.

'We're here,' replies Dessie.

Sinbad is talking to a uniformed guard behind a grille. Hands him paperwork. A motor whirs and the metal gate slides open. The van swings into a parking area below the building and pulls up at a fire door. Dessie jumps out and begins unloading the tools and ropes onto a trolley. He's wearing surgical gloves beneath heavy-duty cloth gloves. Sami has trouble getting his fingers into the latex because one rogue finger always gets caught on the outside.

'Come on, dickweed.'

'Don't wait for me.'

Dessie gives him a clip behind the head. A security guard is watching him from a control booth that looks like a bomb shelter. Dessie gives him a wave, indicating everything is fine.

'Keep your head down. Don't look at the ready-eyes.'

Sami has to fight the urge to look up and wave at the

CCTV cameras, which are aimed at the doors and stair-wells. What would happen if the rozzers caught them now, he wonders. He could explain about Nadia, say he was acting under duress.

Dessie props open the fire door and they wheel the stuff inside. Meanwhile, Sinbad climbs behind the wheel of the van and spins back up the ramp.

'Where's he going?' asks Sami, feeling twitchy.

'Relax. He's going to wait for us outside.'

'But what if . . .'

'We don't want the van trapped down here.'

Wheeling the trolley along a basement corridor, they reach three lifts, including the broken one. Dessie sets up a red and yellow safety triangle and prises the doors open, peering up the darkened shaft.

'What are we supposed to be doing?'

'Fixing it.'

'Do you know how to fix a lift?'

'Does it fucking matter?'

Dessie separates the gear and wheels the trolley into the adjacent lift. He presses 5. The doors close. Sami watches the numbers light up as they rise between the floors. He can see himself reflected in a mirror. It's like he's going to a fancy dress party.

The doors slide open. Dessie straightens and pushes the trolley into a large open-plan office with smaller pri-vate offices and conference rooms running down both sides.

As they wheel the trolley along a corridor, Dessie pushes each door open, making sure they're empty. Most of the desks face away from the windows and the office walls are lined with shelves full of box files and bound volumes. Sami can see manila folders with red ribbons looped around cardboard wheels, like they're legal files.

The last office has an annexe. Half of it is filled with files. The other half has a metal door. It's the strong room.

'You get started. I'll be back,' says Dessie.

'Where are you going?'

'I'm going to lay down some tarps and bang a few cables, just in case they come looking.'

Suddenly Sami is alone. He looks at the strong room. Taps the door. Tries the handle, just in case someone forgot to lock it. No, he couldn't be that lucky. Not Sami Macbeth.

Then he glances over his shoulder at the nearest office. There's one of those really smart phones with a command unit sitting on a desk. It's most likely '9' to get an outside line.

He should call the police.

And say what?

The truth.

Yeah, like that worked last time.

What would Tony Murphy do if Sami grassed him up? Kill Nadia. Then he'd find a way of killing Sami. Slowly. Painfully. Sami considers his other options but whichever way he looks at the problem he's fucked seven different ways and it isn't even lunchtime.

Putting the stethoscope in his ears, he places the end against the metal door. Listens. Nothing.

'I'm sorry, sir, but we did all we could. In the end, we just couldn't save her.'

Dessie reappears. 'Who are you talking to?'

'Nobody.'

'So what do you think?'

Sami scratches his chin and tries to look crestfallen. 'Can't open this fucker.'

'Why not?'

'Too hard.'

'Tony said you opened a safe that was ten times harder. This should be a piece of cake.'

Sami tries to be decisive. 'They call it a strong room for a reason – 'cause it's strong. If they called it a weak room anyone could open it.'

Dessie isn't in the mood for sarcasm. He puts his face up close. Nose to nose. Bacon breath on the exhale. In the same instant he wraps the stethoscope around Sami's neck and pulls it tight. Lifts him off the floor. Watches his eyes bulge.

'You taking the piss? You taking the mickey?'

Sami doesn't have the oxygen to answer.

This is Dessie Fraser in full Dobermann mode. He slams Sami's head against the door, punctuating each of his statements with violent compelling exclamation marks.

141

'It's got locks! It's got a handle! Open the fucking door.'

Dessie lets him go. Straightens his cap.

'How long will it take?'

Sami rubs his neck. 'Give me fifteen.'

'You got ten.'

'Just tell me one thing,' he risks. 'What's inside?'

'Exhibits.'

He makes it sound like a science project.

'What sort of exhibits?'

'Courtroom exhibits. Exhibit A, exhibit B, that sort of shit.'

Oh, this is priceless, thinks Sami. They're inside the Old Bailey. The Central Criminal Court. The last time he was here he was wrongly convicted of carrying tools to commit a felony and being in possession of stolen goods. Now he's carrying almost identical tools and is supposed to rob the place.

Dessie has gone back to his pretend lift repairs. Sami looks at the drill and considers how long it would take to get through the door. If this were a movie, it would take about four minutes. You can multiply that by about a hundred in real life.

Then his eyes rest on the canister Sinbad gave him. Maybe he could wedge a little of the stuff near the hinges and set off a small explosion, just enough to lift the door off its frame.

That's one possibility. He considers the others. It's a short consultation.

Sami looks through the nearby offices, searching wastepaper bins and mini-fridges until he finds two plastic water bottles. Emptying them, he unscrews the metal container. Inside is a white powder, granulated like sugar. He gently pours a small amount into each bottle. It doesn't look like enough. He adds some more.

He puts one bottle at the base of the strong room door, beneath the lower hinge, and the second bottle balancing on top. Taking a length of electrical cord, he strips away the plastic coating from each end.

Among the gear that Sinbad had provided him are two small light bulbs. Sami shatters the glass and gently places the filaments into the powder in each bottle. He attaches a wire to the base of the bulbs and re-screws the bottle lids, before trailing the electric cord across the floor – ten, twenty, thirty feet . . . he should have asked for something longer. If he had a long enough wire he could be on a different floor or in another building or out of the county.

Dessie has come back.

'You want to do the honours?' Sami asks him.

'Why?'

'No reason.'

'Why are we standing way back here?'

'This is a job you can only fuck up once.'

Sami shoves two bare wires into a power socket and flicks the switch. He's hoping for a dull *kerplunk* as the hinges pop off. Instead he blows the door through the next wall, bringing half the ceiling down.

Brick and plaster dust fill the air. Every window in the vicinity has been blown out and the sprinklers have triggered. They'd be getting wet if the pipes weren't so twisted by the force of the blast that instead of spraying downwards the water is jetting off at crazy angles.

Dessie pushes a lump of plasterboard off himself. He looks like someone has painted his face white.

'Where's the safe?' he asks.

'It was here a minute ago,' says Sami.

They pull aside a desk and broken ceiling panels, looking for the strong room. Dessie wraps his arms around a buckled filing cabinet and tosses it to one side.

Sami's ears are ringing from the blast.

'Maybe we should get out of here,' he suggests.

Dessie doesn't answer.

'Well, if you don't need me, I'll catch up with you later.'

Dessie smacks him in the side of the head. 'Shut the fuck up and keep looking.'

20

For a moment Sami considers whether he could have blown the strong room through the floor. Instead he finds a cistern and a sink from the bathroom above.

Dessie tosses them aside like he's moving empty boxes. He discovers the strong room door behind a collapsed wall, which is still smoking from the blast.

Kicking away the last of the debris, he finds the room and starts going through drawers, pulling out exhibits and evidence bags, looking at the labels. There are guns, bags of drugs, knives and artefacts.

He picks up a semi-automatic – checks the label. Puts it in a rucksack. Then he grabs bags of white powder. Cocaine. Sami gets a look at one of the labels. *Court 4. Exhibit 1a. Raymond Peter Garza.*

One moment his heart is racing, the next it stops completely. It's a mistake. Insanity. No way they're doing a job for Ray Garza.

A sprinkler has been spraying down Sami's back, soaking his overalls. His face is coated in brick dust and the ringing in his ears turns out to be the fire alarms.

Dessie screams at him above the noise. 'Pack up the gear. Leave nothing behind.'

Sami tosses the drill, the camera and the canister of TATP into the holdall. He has to drag a shelf to one side to lift the bag. Suddenly he spies a lump of cash the size of a house-brick, wrapped in plastic cling film.

It has to be fifty grand. Maybe more.

Dessie looks at him. Looks at the cash. Grins. In a heartbeat Sami has gone from being a fuck-up to having golden bollocks. Dessie takes the money and tucks it into the rucksack.

Sami is still trying to get his head around the Garza connection. If he weren't so scared already, even the mention of Garza's name would make his throat close and scrotum tighten. Some criminals get their reputations for being violent bastards, but Ray Garza is notorious for being a completely ruthless fucker. The Keyser Söze of the British underworld.

Tony Murphy might rip off mug punters, horny businessman and foreign tourists, but Ray Garza ransacks entire countries. Diamond mines in Angola, nickel mines in Botswana, platinum mines in Zimbabwe. According to the press reports he's Mugabe's favourite Englishman – a pretty elite club.

Occasionally in prison Sami heard blokes brag about having worked for Garza. They said he was a genius, a visionary, top of the food chain, but most wouldn't talk about him or even mention his name.

Then some dumb moke would shoot his mouth off, saying Garza was a pussy or a wanker. From that moment you knew the poor bastard would spend the rest of his life looking over his shoulder, paranoid that Garza would find out. Every car backfiring, every set of headlights in the rear mirror, every bit of bad luck, every fuck-up and he'd be wondering if it was Garza. He might as well have bought a shovel and started digging his own grave.

Dessie is still stuffing evidence bags into the rucksack. The sirens are getting closer.

'We should go,' says Sami.

'Wait. I'm not finished.'

'No time. Let's split.'

'I said wait.'

Next minute they're legging it down the corridor. Dessie has the rucksack. Sami is trying to carry the holdall, which is bashing against his knees.

The lifts aren't working. They've managed to break all three of them. Either that or the fire alarms have cut the power. They head for the stairwell. A security guy comes charging out the door, puffing hard, hand on a nightstick.

'Thank God you're here,' says Dessie, pointing down the hall.

'What happened?'

'Some sort of explosion.'

He looks at their bags. 'What were you doing?'

'Fixing the lift,' answers Dessie. 'We smelled a bit of gas earlier. Must have been a leak. Blast brought the roof down.'

The guard looks at Sami for verification.

'Anyone hurt?'

Sami shakes his head.

'We could have been killed,' says Dessie. 'Health and Safety are gonna hear about this.'

The guard tells them to evacuate. They're supposed to wait for him on the ground floor. Next minute they're alone, swinging down the stairwell between the landings. Lugging the bags.

They reach the ground floor fire exit. Dessie pushes open the door, looks both ways. A fire engine is blocking the alley. Firemen are jogging towards them.

Dessie and Sami stroll past them, heads down, avoiding the ready-eyes. They turn left and left again, crossing a parking area. Following a railing fence they reach a gate leading up to a set of stairs. The gate is locked. They climb over, tossing the bags to each other.

There are more fire engines and police cars in Newgate Street. Dessie holds Sami back. Their blue boilersuits are streaked with plaster and soaked through. Dessie's hair looks like he's gone prematurely grey.

Waiting for another police car to pass, they leg it down Newgate Street and duck into Bishops Court and Fleet Passage, avoiding the major roads. Dessie seems to know where he's going.

'We got to get out of these clothes,' he says, peeling off his gloves. He spies a narrow alley with industrial bins on wheels. *Commercial waste only.* Crouching between two bins, Dessie begins unbuttoning his sodden boilersuit. He opens his rucksack. Shoves the overalls inside.

'Why not just ditch it?' asks Sami.

'Yeah, and let forensics have a field day.'

Sami copies Dessie. His jeans and shirt are wet, but they're clean. The boilersuit is packed away. He keeps the cap on his head.

Dessie hoists the rucksack onto his back. Checks the lane. Makes a decision. He jogs round the corner and down some stairs to Old Seacoal Lane and slows to a brisk walk, heading towards Farringdon Street.

Pedestrians give way to traffic. Buses, black cabs, cars and vans are banked up in every direction. Gridlock has choked Fleet Street, Ludgate Hill and Holborn Circus.

Dessie peers left and right, looking for something.

'What's wrong?'

'Sinbad isn't here.'

'Maybe this is the wrong corner.'

'I know the fucking corner.'

'He could be lost.'

'He's not lost.'

Dessie turns on his mobile. Calls Sinbad. Sami can only hear one side of their conversation, which mostly consists of cursing and Dessie calling Sinbad a yellow mongrel and a gutless prick.

149

The gist of their exchange is that a policeman moved Sinbad on, so he drove the van around the block, but each time he came back the rozzer was still standing there. It smelt like fish. Then he heard the explosion and got spooked.

'Where are you now?' asks Dessie. 'What do you mean you've gone home? We're fucking waiting.'

Dessie hurls the mobile onto the concrete shattering it into a dozen pieces.

'Is he coming?' asks Sami.

'No he's not fucking coming.'

Sami ponders this for a moment. Clearly the criminal code doesn't have the same 'never leave a man behind' philosophy as the SAS.

'So what do we do?' he asks.

'We leg it.'

Two police cars are heading down Farringdon Street towards them, negotiating the traffic by nudging other vehicles aside with duelling sirens. Sami and Dessie are too exposed. They have to stay off the main thorough-fares. Find somewhere to hide. Lie low.

'We could catch the tube,' suggests Sami.

'I don't catch trains,' replies Dessie.

'Why not?'

'I just don't.'

'We're running a bit low on choices for you to be taking a personal stand.'

Dessie grunts. Sami takes it as a yes.

150

They cross the road, walking between cars, not making eye contact with the drivers. They duck down St Bride Street and meet Shoe Lane. Dodging puddles and recycling bins, they weave left and right in narrow lanes, not talking, not looking back.

Sami could pass as a backpacker but Dessie looks like a German hiker with his trousers tucked into his boots. He keeps muttering under his breath about Sinbad.

He stops. 'Will you fucking keep up for fuck's sake.'

'This bag is heavy.'

'Don't be such a faggot.'

'I'm carrying the stuff that goes boom. I don't fancy being pavement art.'

Dessie takes the holdall and slings it over his shoulder. He gives Sami the rucksack with the drugs, the money and the semi-automatic. Happy days.

Sami makes another suggestion. 'We should think about splitting up. They'll be looking for two of us. We'll be less conspicuous if we travel alone.'

Dessie looks at him dubiously. 'I'm not taking my eyes off you, dickweed.'

'At least let's walk on opposite sides of the street.'

Dessie agrees. Sami crosses over and jogs past an Oxfam shop, a wine warehouse and a travel agency with billboards propped on the pavement. For thirty-eight quid he could fly to Milan. Five hundred gets him a week in Barbados. That's where he wants to be now – sipping pina coladas in the Caribbean while some island lovely who looks like Beyoncé rubs coconut oil into his chest with her breasts.

Moving at a half-jog, Sami weaves through Plough Place, Fetter Lane, and Norwich Street. Dessie is close. Puffing hard. His head looks like a turtle's popping out of its shell.

Many of the buildings have brass plaques announcing law offices and legal chambers. Sami's brief had a place around here. He was a QC. Mr Quick Cash.

The red, blue and white Underground sign is ahead, just visible above the roof of a flower barrow. Chancery Lane Station. They disappear down the stairs into the cool and dark. It's a hole to hide in. It's a way out.

21

Bones McGee is staring at the debris. The exhibits room at the Old Bailey has been demolished. The roof has partially collapsed and a sink from the bathroom above is lying in the middle of sodden plasterboard and broken ceiling panels.

Water has done most of the damage. It's still leaking down the walls and dripping from twisted pipes.

His stomach is churning. He let Tony Murphy call in one favour and look at the result. Murphy promised him a surgical strike. Quick. Clean. Nothing left behind. Instead some moron blew out every window on the fifth floor and brought down half the ceiling.

CID is calling it a terrorist bombing. Al Qaeda has been mentioned. Three Pakistani brothers are due to go on trial next week for plotting to bring down a British Airways flight out of Qatar. All the evidence was in the strong room.

Bones picks his way through the wreckage and finds a quiet corner. He calls Tony Murphy.

'What the fuck did you do?'

'Calm down, Bones, what's wrong?'

'You said you had an expert.'

'I did.'

'Well, I'm looking at a fucking bomb site.'

'You know what they say about making an omelette, Bones.'

'Yeah, well your boy just blew up the egg factory.'

Sami and Dessie are standing on the westbound platform of the Central line. The next train to Ealing Broadway is four minutes away. Commuters are milling at the edge of the platform, glancing at the electronic display.

'What's Ray Garza got to do with this?' Sami asks.

Dessie talks out the side of his mouth like he's in a prison yard. 'His boy got picked up with a shooter and eight kilos of charlie. He took a pot shot at one of the rozzers. They charged him with possession and attempted murder.'

Sami pauses to let the information sink in. The entire robbery was about perverting the course of justice. How many years do you get for that, he wonders.

Dessie is looking up and down the platform. His wet hair is stuck to his scalp like duck feathers.

'Hey, how's this for an idea?' asks Sami. 'Since I did my bit – opening the strong room and stuff – how about I split and you can deliver the gear to Mr Murphy.'

'Job's not over.'

154

'Yeah, but a deal's a deal. You got your stuff. Mission accomplished. Now Murphy can let Nadia go.'

'We started together, we finish together.'

Two transport policemen wander onto the platform, glancing up and down, trying to look like real bobbies instead of rejects from the Met. They're heading towards Dessie and Sami, who move further along, trying to be inconspicuous.

A train comes roaring through the tunnel, pushing air and rubbish ahead of it. The doors open. Dessie tells Sami to take a different carriage.

'If the transport cops get on, keep moving toward the back. And don't talk to a fucking soul.'

This is the Underground, thinks Sami. Nobody talks to anyone unless they're deranged or like talking to themselves. If he did strike up a conversation, what would he say?

'I'm the unwitting pawn in an evil conspiracy, which is why I have eight kilos of cocaine and a semi-automatic in my rucksack, along with a house-brick of money. And you see that guy in the next carriage? He's a complete psycho and he's carrying a can of explosives in his bag.'

That should liven up their Sunday afternoon in London.

The doors have closed. The train moves off. Sami can see Dessie take a seat and drop the holdall at his feet. Looking in the opposite direction, through the windows, he spies the transport cops, talking to passengers.

He takes a deep breath. Closes his eyes. Wishes he were somewhere else.

That's when it happens. Not right then. Three stops on, just outside Oxford Circus station. One moment Sami is standing near the door and the next he's upside down, in a dark world, full of smoke and shattered glass.

Something soft breaks his fall. A woman. He can't see her face in the dark but he hears her crying above the screams. Smoke pours through the air vents, making it hard to breathe. He can't see flames but it smells like the wiring is burning.

People are crawling on the floor, bumping into each other. Squares of light appear in the darkness. Mobile phones. Sami can see the faces of the people holding them. Fear. Disbelief. At the same time he begins hearing the dull thud of train windows being hit by dozens of fists.

The emergency lights flicker on, yellow and faint. A man staggers past him holding his head. A woman with her clothes blown into shreds has snot and tears leaking down her cheeks. Others are caked in dust and soot – a pregnant woman, her dress glued to her skin; a fat man with a mangled leg, leaking blood into his boot.

The woman Sami fell upon is holding her arm.

'What's your name?' he asks her.

'Stephanie.'

'Are you OK, Stephanie?'

'I think my arm is broken.' Her tears are black.

'Here, let me see.'

Sami squeezes her arm with his thumb and forefinger, feeling for a fracture.

'It's only sprained,' he tells her.

'What about the fire?'

'I don't think it's a fire.'

The man in a tweed jacket and matching tweed hat is staring at his leg as though it belongs to someone else. Blood is pouring across his ankle from a gaping wound.

'You should sit down,' Sami tells him. 'I'll put a tourniquet on that.'

The man looks at Sami and back at his leg. Still in shock, he follows orders, unsure of what else to do.

The smoke has cleared a little and it's easier to breathe. Most of the screams are coming from the other carriage – the one in front. That's where Dessie had been sitting.

Sami steps over people and peers through the shattered window. The roof of the carriage has been peeled open by the force of the blast. One wall is blackened and shredded and some seats have been torn from their mountings.

A man's face appears. His skin is splattered with blood. Wild-eyed, he pulls desperately at the door, which has been buckled by the blast and won't open more than a few inches. Sami can't see Dessie, which is strange because he's a big man – hard to lose. He was there only a minute ago.

157

Suddenly, he recognises Dessie's trousers and his over-sized work-boots. They're lying on the floor between two bench seats. The top half of Dessie seems to have disappeared. It must have been blown out the window by the force of the blast.

Sami wants to feel sorry for him, but can't muster any sympathy. Instead he turns away, walks back down the carriage, collecting warm coats, ties for tourniquets, anything to help.

Fifteen minutes is a long time when you're underground in a blown-up train with frightened and injured people. You keep saying things like, 'They'll be here soon', and then wondering quietly why it's taking so long. Where are the paramedics? The police? The driver must be still be alive – he should tell us what to do.

Waiting isn't the worst thing. It's listening to people pleading for help in the next carriage. He asks if anyone has any water and passes bottles through the shattered window. He wants to cry every time he looks at the carriage.

After a long time word filters through that people are leaving through a rear carriage and walking back along the tunnel to Oxford Circus. People are calm. Patient. There's no pushing or running.

Sami helps Stephanie and the man in a tweed hat get through the carriages. He has to lift them down the final step. The same two transport policemen are standing on the tracks. One of them has a torch and is telling people to start walking.

Sami asks about the live rail. It's been turned off. He hopes it stays that way.

Taking Stephanie's hand and hooking his other arm around the man in tweed, he leads them along the tunnel towards the station. Twisted metal, glass and plastic are scattered along the tracks. Sami half expects to see Dessie's torso propped against the wall.

Torches wave them forward.

Paramedics are waiting on the platform, giving oxygen, bandaging wounds; lifting people onto stretchers. Sami stands for a while, watching someone treating the man in tweed. Stephanie is talking to an Underground employee.

Without saying goodbye, Sami walks up the stairs, past the ticket barriers, across the concourse, into the daylight. It's a surreal experience to see how normal the world still looks. He moves past the waiting ambulances and fire engines, which are blocking Oxford Street. People are staring at him wordlessly, their eyes asking the questions: 'What was it like down there? What did you see?'

More sirens are coming. Sami tightens the straps on the rucksack and turns down Argyll Street, his head lowered, avoiding the stares.

He hears snatches of conversation. People are talking about a bomb, terrorists, a carriage destroyed . . . Someone

says there are more bombs. One went off at the Old
Bailey.

Pedestrians are holding mobile phones, raising them in
the air, shaking them or pressing buttons, hoping for a
signal or expecting them to ring.

Sami passes the London Palladium and heads towards
Carnaby Street.

Dessie is dead. What's he supposed to do now? Call
Murphy. He doesn't have a mobile. He has to find a
phone.

Right now he's in Carnaby Street. He once had a girlfriend who worked in a clothing shop on the corner. She
gave him Union Jack underwear for his birthday and said
she wanted to lower the flag. What was her name? Stacy.

He turns into Broadwick Street. Remembers his
mother bringing him here to get orthotics fitted. Then he
jumps to a different memory. Her funeral. The December
skies like darkness exhaled from the grave. The mourners
in overcoats, black suits, dark stockings, holding black
umbrellas: his mother's friends surrounding Nadia.

Scaffolding covered the crematorium, which looked as
though it was being dismantled rather than renovated.
Sami wondered why it was so cold inside. Surely they'd
heat the place.

The priest said a few words, making out that he knew
Sami's mother, which was unlikely, because to the best of
Sami's recollection, his mother had never set foot in a
church.

160

When the coffin disappeared, Nadia broke down and sobbed. Sami wanted to pick her up. Carry her away. Wipe away the hurt. Instead he held her and said nothing. The silence was so fragile he felt it could shatter.

Sami didn't cry. Crying was something he stopped doing years ago. He had to be strong for Nadia. It wasn't his turn to surrender to sorrow.

He's in Berwick Street and then Peter Street, where the sex shops masquerade as bookstores and the strip clubs masquerade as nightclubs. There are 'Live Nude Shows', peep shows, tattoo parlours and basement cinemas screening delights such as *Further Confessions of a Sixth Form Girl*.

Prostitutes have plastered phone boxes with glossy business cards. Wearing scanty lingerie and come-hither smiles, they have as much sex appeal as blow up mattresses.

Maybe Sami should get a girl and hide out for a few hours. She'd want to be paid by the quarter hour. How much would it cost?

He's puffing now. Lactic acid is building in his legs and the rucksack feels heavier. He's carrying eight kilos of cocaine and a semi-automatic pistol. That's worth about twelve years or ten grand a kilo, depending upon whether you're a glass half-full or glass half-empty kind of person. The explosion on the Underground is something different; a whole new ball game, a different league. Life imprisonment. Throw away the key.

He's in Leicester Square, opposite the Odeon. A busker is dancing on stilts, wearing a clown outfit. Another is dressed up as a cowboy, painted bronze, posing like a gunslinger ready to draw.

There are four cops standing near a statue. Two of them are talking to tourists, but the others seem to be looking for someone. Sami joins a queue waiting for discount theatre tickets. Head down. Trying to become invisible.

Then he remembers a pub in Lisle Street, the Crooked Surgeon. It's less than a hundred yards away. There'll be a phone. He can call Murphy.

Stepping out of the queue, he ducks down Leicester Place and pushes open the pub door. A dozen people are standing at the bar with their faces raised to a television set. Maybe there's a game on. Sami drops the rucksack at his feet. He's sweating. Out of breath. Then he glances up at the screen and sees fire engines, ambulances, paramedics and people on stretchers.

Nobody notices Sami. They're too interested in the bombing.

'You got a payphone?' he asks the barman.

'Take a number,' he replies, without taking his eyes off the screen.

He points. Three people are waiting to use the payphone, which is wedged under the stairs next to a slot machine. The woman at the back of the queue smiles at Sami. She has sticking plasters on her heels and is pulling one of those trolley bags that airline hostesses use.

'You want a drink?' the barman asks him.

Sami orders a beer. Upends the glass, his throat working rhythmically. Lowering the pint glass, he spies himself in the mirror behind the bar. Most of the soot on his face has rubbed off but he still has plasterboard and glass in his hair.

'Get caught in the bombings?' asks the barman.

Sami nods.

'This one's on me.' The barman pushes another pint into his hands. Then he motions to the TV. 'You were lucky. They're telling everyone to sit tight. Not much else we can do. Trains and buses aren't running.'

Sami glances at the payphone. It's almost his turn. The woman ahead of him fumbles for change. 'You can go first,' she says. 'I've talked to my husband already.'

Sami nods in thanks. Turns his back. Punches the number Dessie gave him. The call gets diverted. Someone picks up. Doesn't talk.

'Is that Mr Murphy?'

'He's busy.'

'Tell him this is Sami Macbeth and there's been a problem.'

'What sort of problem?'

'Dessie didn't make it.'

'He got caught?'

'He got blown up.'

Silence. Sami waits.

163

Murphy answers. 'Is this a secure line?'

'Yeah.'

'What happened?'

'Dessie blew himself up on the Tube.'

'How?'

'He must have dropped the bag or kicked it.'

'Where are you now?'

'A pub in Soho, the Crooked Surgeon.' Sami looks over his shoulder. 'The streets are crawling with cops.'

'Get out of there.'

'I can't. I think they're looking for me.'

Sami races through the story in an urgent whisper. When he finishes there's a long pause. Murphy is trying to think.

'I'm sorry about Dessie,' says Sami. 'He was very loyal to you.'

'Yes he was,' says Murphy. 'Loyalty is an admirable quality, but it doesn't help me now.'

How can he be so blasé and cold, thinks Sami.

'What about the stuff?'

'I got it.'

'The shooter?'

'Yeah.'

Murphy begins asking questions, talking very slowly and seriously like every answer is for a million quid, only Sami doesn't have any friends to phone.

'Get rid of the shooter.'

'What do you mean?'

'Get rid of the fucking thing. Make sure it's never found.'

'How?'

'Dump it in the river . . . down a drain. Better still, take it apart and ditch the pieces separately.'

'It's a courtroom exhibit.'

'So what?'

'You didn't say anything about Ray Garza being involved.'

'Forget about Garza. Just get rid of the shooter.'

'Then what do I do? You got to help me.'

Murphy ponders this for a moment.

'All right. All right. Keep your head down. I'm sending Sinbad.'

Yeah, right, thinks Sami, the same bastard that abandoned us in the first place. He doesn't say it out loud.

Murphy hangs up.

I got to sit tight, thinks Sami. Take my pulse. Take a deep breath. Help is on the way.

22

The head of Scotland Yard's Counter Terrorism Command, Commander Bob Piper, has always been self-conscious about his height. Five foot five simply isn't tall enough for a man of his achievements and ambition. He deserves another seven inches, maybe more.

Opening his locker, he pauses for a moment to appreciate its neatness and order. His eyes rest on his boots, which have been buffed and polished to a black sheen that catches light on the curves. The toes are steel reinforced, the soles fire-retardant rubber. They are tough boots. Working boots.

Carefully, Piper lifts his overalls from the top shelf and places them on a bench seat near his knees. Next comes his belt and toiletry bag. The boots are left till last. Once they're laced – pulled tight with a double knot – he rocks over the balls of his feet testing the snugness of the fit.

Two bombs have exploded in the West End – one at the Old Bailey and another on the Central Line near

Oxford Circus. The second was almost certainly triggered by a suicide bomber.

Although Bob Piper doesn't wish for terrorist acts (not like some firemen he knows who get a hard-on when they see a blazing building), he is a man who rises to an occasion; cometh the hour, cometh the man. A full-scale terror alert has been called in London. Code Red.

This is what he's trained for – in the field, on the firing range, in dress rehearsals and simulations. He spent four months at Quantico, the FBI headquarters in Virginia. Another two months with Mossad in Israel.

Bob Piper winks at himself in the mirror and plants a peaked cap firmly on his head, smoothing the brim in a boyish salute to his reflection. He closes the locker and turns for the door. He's ready.

23

Bones McGee has a bad feeling in his guts, which started in his stomach and seems to have shifted lower to his colon and his bowels. Now he feels as though his insides will flood unless he keeps clamping down on his sphincter.

Events have taken on a surreal, almost comic book sensibility. They're being played out on TV. Reported live from the scene. A banner rolls across the bottom of the screen declaring: LONDON UNDER ATTACK.

Another bomb has gone off – this time on the Underground. One person is dead and scores are injured. What are the chances of a bomb going off so close to the first explosion? Remote. Infinitesimal.

Forensics teams are vacuuming, dusting and bagging debris on the records floor of the Central Criminal Court. They're putting together a jigsaw or at least collecting the pieces in the hope they fit together. Meanwhile, detectives are interviewing the security guards and studying footage from the CCTV cameras.

Already a picture is emerging. The bombers had inside information and assistance. They knew the location of the security cameras. They had a cover story. The 'out-of-order' lift must have been sabotaged some time on Saturday evening. The building manager called the regular lift repair company, which promised to send a repair crew on Monday morning. That call was intercepted and a repair van stolen from outside a house in Ealing some time on Saturday night.

Bones calls Murphy. He can hear laughter and music. London is under attack and Murphy is throwing a party.

'Tony, mate, what are you doing to me? I'm feeling pretty vulnerable here.'

'You worry too much. It's under control.'

'Is that what you call it?'

'It's not your concern, Bones.'

'But I am concerned, Tony. I got MI5, Special Branch and the Counter-Terrorism boys rattling cages and putting a bug up people's arses. Your boys fucked up big-time.'

'My boys aren't your concern. This is just a squall. It's going to blow over.'

'A squall? This is a force ten gale, Tony, and we just hit the sodding iceberg.'

'Relax. Come over? Have a drink. I got a band.'

'Yeah, I can hear it. They had a band on the Titanic, which kept playing all the way down.'

Murphy loses his temper. 'You got a smart mouth,

Bones. You think you're funny. You think you can ring me and tell me what to do. You've taken my readies. You've eaten free at my restaurants. You've grown rich on my fucking largesse. So don't you start talking to me about icebergs or start eyeing the life-boats. I own you, Bones. I've owned you ever since you took that first free fuck at my club. I could have saved myself a lot of money and blackmailed you after that, but I kept being generous.'

'I don't think you should talk to me like that, Tony.'

'I'll fucking talk to you any way I please. Everything you have is down to me. The Italian kitchen, the season tickets to Stamford Bridge, that state-of-the-art, whatsit plasma TV you got in your front room.'

'You've never been to my house.'

'I know all about you and your little peccadillos, Bones, like that bird next door you're banging behind her husband's back and your bit of property speculation in Ibiza – the apartment in your brother's name. I funded that fucking thing as well.'

Bones has stopped trying to interrupt.

'. . . so don't talk to me about icebergs and force ten gales. This is a squall. They happen. That's why I take out insurance. You're my insurance policy, Bones. I paid my premium. I got you. That's why you're going to keep your mouth shut, your head down and your ear to the ground. You're my man on the inside. You can dictate events.'

Yeah, right, thinks Bones. Just like a fish in a whale.

24

Sami has washed his face, shaken the glass from his hair and tried to scrub the bloodstains from his shirt. Back in the bar he takes a seat and rests the rucksack between his knees, looping the strap around his left hand.

Sinbad is going to be here soon. That's got to be a good thing.

He glances at the TV. Footage from the Underground shows a twisted metal carriage and passengers emerging with blackened faces, covering their mouths with handkerchiefs and pieces of cloth.

Some survivors took mobile phone images in the seconds after the explosion. Sami spies himself in the background putting a tourniquet around a man's leg.

A blonde reporter appears on screen, nodding at the camera knowingly, as though she has seen it all before.

Someone turns up the volume.

'. . . television pictures don't really give a sense of what it's like to be standing here, Dean, knowing that less than forty feet below me a train carriage has been

171

destroyed by a terrorist bomb causing death and destruction.'

The camera cuts to Dean in the studio: 'Have the police been able to confirm or deny if these were suicide attacks?'

The camera cuts back to Trisha: 'At this stage police are refusing to confirm or deny the nature of the attacks, Dean, but with multiple bombsites, one underground and the other at the Central Criminal Court, this will obviously be a very complex and difficult investigation. Forensic teams are sifting through the wreckage at each scene and detectives are examining thousands of hours of CCTV footage in a bid to identify the bombers.'

Cut to Dean: 'Have the police indicated who might be behind these attacks?'

Trisha nods. 'Not at this stage, Dean, but there is speculation that the Old Bailey blast could have been aimed at disrupting the trial of Pakistani-born brothers, Hammed and Mani Yousef, who face charges of plotting to blow up a British Airways flight from Qatar during the summer. That trial was due to begin on Tuesday.'

Dean nods: 'Some news outlets are reporting the possibility of more devices.'

Trisha nods: 'Yes, Dean, this is a major concern for police. Central London has been effectively locked down. All buses and trains have been stopped and are being searched. Police are also manning checkpoints on roads in and out of the West End. I have never seen such a large police presence on the streets of London.'

172

Dean seems to have run out of questions. Trisha doesn't want to go.

'There is a real sense of defiance among survivors and rescuers,' she says. 'Sadly, all too often, Londoners have experienced events like this before and refuse to be cowed or to submit.'

Dean adds, 'I guess the best description of it would be bloody but unbowed.'

'Absolutely, Dean,' says Trisha.

Who are these people, thinks Sami.

Back in the studio a professor of Middle Eastern Studies says the bombings are most likely the work of home-grown Islamic extremists. His Adam's apple is bobbing up and down beneath his skin as if trying to break out.

Sami has heard enough. He turns away from the screen. Orders another beer. Sami has fourteen pounds and fifty-five pence left – not counting the brick of money in the rucksack, which is not really his. Possession is nine-tenths. If he gets out of this, he'll give nine-tenths of the money to the victims of the bombing and the other tenth can go back.

If he gets out? Sinbad isn't coming. They've blocked the roads. They're going to search vehicles.

'Hey, listen to this,' says a guy at the bar, pointing to the TV.

A different reporter is standing outside New Scotland Yard. Wind rattles his microphone and his tie keeps blowing up into his face.

'. . . police have in the past few minutes released security camera footage of a suspected bomber seen fleeing the scene of the Underground blast.'

Video images replace the reporter – a street scene, shot from above in grainy colour. The flashing blue lights of a police car draw Sami's gaze and then something else – a figure moving towards the camera. Someone familiar.

It's a surreal experience to see himself depicted on TV running down Oxford Street. Only it it's not a depiction. Sami is playing himself. See Sami run. See Sami jump. See Sami knock over pedestrians.

There is a new banner rolling along the bottom of the screen: BOMB SUSPECT EVADES POLICE

The reporter is still talking: 'The suspect is described as being of medium height, slim build, wearing jeans, a sweatshirt and carrying a black rucksack . . .' At that moment the footage freezes and zooms in on Sami's face. Is he really that pale? It's the prison suntan.

Nervously, he glances around the bar. Everyone is still watching the TV. Staring at it. Contemplating the man. The mind. What possesses somebody to set off a bomb?

Another banner is running along the bottom of the screen: BUSES AND TRAINS SUSPENDED UNTIL FURTHER NOTICE.

A man next to Sami groans. 'I was supposed to be at Heathrow an hour ago. I got caught on the Piccadilly line.' He has a New Zealand accent. That must be his luggage near the door.

Sami nudges the rucksack further under his feet, but the Kiwi spies it anyway.

'Same boat, eh? Where were you heading?'

'Nowhere,' says Sami.

'On your way home, eh? Where you been?'

'Here and there.'

Suddenly, a woman's voice cuts across the conversation. 'He's got a rucksack!'

Sami's head jerks around as though tied to a string. The woman is wearing a business suit and pointing at him accusingly, her mouth preparing to scream. Her eyes meet Sami's. There is a tingling in his throat, like a taut wire vibrating against his neck.

Everyone in the bar has turned to stare. Even the reporter on screen appears captivated by the moment.

Sami straightens his legs and plants them on the floor. His hand is still wrapped around the strap on the rucksack.

'What you got in the bag?' asks the barman.

'Clothes and stuff.'

'Show us,' says the Kiwi.

'Why?'

''Cause you're making everyone nervous.'

Sami glances from face to face.

'I'm not the guy they're looking for.'

'That's cool.'

'I'm not dangerous.'

'Nobody is saying you are.'

A door behind Sami opens and closes. Someone has

175

slipped out. They'll probably stop the first policeman they see.

Sami slings the rucksack onto his back. A dozen people collectively crouch and swallow wetly.

Sami is at the door. Outside. Turning right. Right again. Where is he going? There are two police officers on the corner. He turns back heading down Whitcomb Street towards Trafalgar Square. A police van is on a slow circuit of Leicester Fields. He ducks into a laneway. Leans his back against a wall. Trying to outrun them on foot is a loser's game. They'll corner him and wait for reinforcements.

Sami has to go off the radar. Disappear. He has money now – the stash from the safe – but first he has to get out of the West End; out of London.

There's a church across the square. He can hide inside. Stash the rucksack in a dark corner. Say a prayer. It's a good plan.

He comes out of the alley and finds three policemen in front of him. One of them has a gun and is crouching, holding it in two hands, like he knows how to use it.

'Don't move,' he yells at Sami. 'Put the bag down.'

Sami looks behind him . . . looks ahead. Holds his fist in the air. His thumb cocked. Empty, but they don't know that.

'I got a fucking bomb,' he yells, not recognising his own voice. 'Get back or I'll flatten this place.'

The rozzers melt away. Sami runs past them. The one

176

with the gun is lying on the ground, on his elbows, trying to get a shot. Sami keeps moving, zigzagging from side to side like he's seen in the war movies.

A bomb! He told them he had a bomb. What a joke! What a prize fuck-up. Sami isn't just unlucky, he's a walking jinx, a Jonah; he's the one-legged man in an arse-kicking competition; he's the Irishman who burnt his lips trying to blow up a bus. Forget master criminal – Sami isn't even a minor one. He doesn't open safes. He doesn't threaten police. He doesn't blow up trains. He plays guitar and wants to be a rock god.

Fifty-four hours ago he got out of prison. Thirty-six hours ago he bedded Kate Tierney on Egyptian cotton sheets at the Savoy. Life was good. Life had promise. Now he's the most wanted terrorist in London.

25

Mid-morning. Bright and clear. Ruiz heads out of
London towards Blackheath, staying south of the river
and avoiding the congestion charge. His Mercedes 280E
is forty years old but lovingly restored with two-tone
wheels and a racing green paint job.

People look twice at a car like that. They wonder who's
driving it. They envy him. They want to trade places.

Just after midday he pulls up at a house on Shooter's
Hill Road, overlooking the heath. Tony Murphy has
come a long way from a two-up, two-down in Kilburn.
Now he lives in a mansion with columned porticos and
oak trees shedding leaves into his swimming pool.

There's some sort of party in progress and cars are
parked along the driveway and in front of the garages.
A marquee has been set up on the lawn attached to the
conservatory via a white tunnel of canvas. A buffet is
laid out on long tables and waitresses in short black
skirts and white blouses are carrying silver trays with
champagne flutes.

Ruiz recognises some of the guests, but can't put names to their faces. Murphy's friends are a mix of bar-owners, licensing lawyers, union officials, bookmakers, porn stars and celebrity chefs.

A valet offers to park Ruiz's Merc. He tosses him the keys and walks across the grass.

Dressed in a beige suit and a cream turtleneck sweater, Murphy is holding court, telling a joke about three nuns and a blind man. Ruiz fills a plate with roast pork, venison, salad and a bread roll. Picks up a Corona, wanders over and joins the group.

' . . . So the air conditioning at the convent isn't working and the nuns are sweltering. They take off their clothes to cool down, but there's a knock on the door. The youngest nun yells from inside, "Who is it?" And a voice replies, "It's the blind man."

'The nuns look at each other, relieved, and let him in. This big burly fucker in overalls comes through the door and says, "Holy shit, sisters, great tits. Where do you want me to hang the blinds?"'

Laughs all round, too loud and too long.

Ruiz takes a mouthful of potato salad. 'You can't beat an old joke, can you, Tony?'

The gangster turns slowly with a fixed smile that might break into pieces if he moved too quickly. Violence flashes momentarily in his eyes. He touches his upper lip and examines his finger as if looking for blood.

'We haven't met.'

'Vincent Ruiz. Great party.'

The name means nothing to Murphy. He transfers his champagne glass to his left hand and raises a cigar to his lips.

'I know most people here, Mr Ruiz, since I invited them. I don't recall your name being on the guest list.'

Ruiz nods and rolls a strip of venison into a bread roll, making a sandwich. 'Nadia invited me.'

Murphy doesn't react. 'I don't know anyone called Nadia.'

'Sure you do. Nadia Macbeth. You paid a thousand quid for her. Toby Streak told me. Then you had her delivered to an address in Whitechapel where a sociopath called Puffa shot her full of brown and got her hooked on crack.' Ruiz takes a sip of his beer. 'Ring any bells yet?'

Murphy's nostrils dilate and his eyes are suddenly glazed. The guests are almost imperceptibly edging away from him in a slow motion social version of moonwalking, without the Michael Jackson music.

'You must have me confused with someone else, Mr Ruiz.'

'I'm just telling you what people told me.'

'They were lying.'

Ruiz plucks at a morsel of torn venison hanging from his lips and pops it inside his mouth. 'People tend not to lie to me.'

'Why's that?'

180

'They respect me too much.' His eyes are dancing.

'Are you a police officer, Mr Ruiz?'

'Used to be.'

'What's your interest in Nadia Macbeth?'

'I'm doing a favour for a friend.'

'Your friend's name?'

'She doesn't like the limelight. Shy, you know. Not like me. I love a good party.' Ruiz smiles at a waitress. 'Can you get me another beer, please, love?'

He turns back to Murphy. 'Hey, I just realised, we have a mutual acquaintance.'

'Who might that be?'

'Sami Macbeth.'

Murphy raises his meaty hand and sucks on the cigar. 'I don't think I know him.'

'That's strange. One of your waiters remembers him dining with you on Thursday. You had oysters to start and a crème brûlée to finish. Ordered specially.'

Murphy is looking over Ruiz's shoulder as if exchanging glances with someone. 'You're quite the detective.'

Murphy's gaze now drifts across his party, watching his guests enjoy themselves, but all traces of avuncular warmth have gone. It's almost as though he despises them as freeloaders and hangers-on, scoffing his food, drinking his booze.

'Maybe we can discuss this another time, Mr Ruiz – as you can see I'm rather busy.'

A bouncer has arrived, a body builder in Nike running

shoes and a dinner jacket with the sleeves pushed up over his gym-thickened arms.

'Gabriel, here, will make sure you find your way out.'

The bouncer grabs Ruiz by the arm, digging his fingers into his shoulder. Ruiz doesn't flinch. Instead, he leans down as though he's dropped something. He straightens suddenly, catching the bouncer under the chin with the back of his head.

Gabriel goes down like a two hundred pound bag of spuds on legs of jelly.

Ruiz looks at Murphy. 'Give me the girl, Tony. I'll owe you one.'

Murphy smiles at him, his teeth like yellowing tombstones. 'You got no juice any more, Mr Ruiz. There's nothing you can give me. Nothing I need.'

Gabriel is getting up. Holding his jaw. Tasting the blood. Someone crashes into Ruiz from behind and drives a fist into his back. A second fist hooks him across the jaw and strong hands wrestle him down. He can taste the vomit and beer rising from his stomach and settling again.

They haul him upright. Pin his arms.

'You're trespassing, Mr Ruiz. You have damaged my property and upset my guests. I don't know who your friend is, but she's sent you on a fool's errand. Sami Macbeth came to see me looking for a job. Offered his services. I told him I am a legitimate businessman. I don't associate with criminals and ex-cons. Now if you'll excuse me . . .'

Ruiz is marched across the lawn. His Mercedes is waiting. A side mirror has been torn off and the aerial is twisted into a modern sculpture. He looks at the damage and glances back towards Murphy, who is lighting another cigar, clicking his lighter shut.

OK, pal, now it's personal.

Ruiz gets behind the wheel. Heads down the drive. As he reaches the road he has to brake hard to avoid a Porsche 911 that cuts the corner and tries to spear through the gates before him. The plates say: RAY JNR.

The cars are nose to nose.

The Porsche driver leans on his horn. Ruiz doesn't move. A window glides down and Ray Garza's boy pops his head out.

'Move your fucking heap.'

Ruiz takes his foot off the clutch. Jerks forward. Nudges the Porsche.

The kid's eyes go wide. 'Are you fucking crazy?'

He's starting to get out. Ruiz nudges the Porsche again, pushing it towards the road. A car has to swerve.

Ray Jnr retreats. Reversing. The gates are clear. Ruiz gives him a wave as he passes. What is Ray Garza's boy doing at a Tony Murphy party?

Across the road he notices a van parked on the footpath. A plastic tent has been placed over missing pavestones and a workman in a hard hat is perched on the edge of the hole. Something strikes Ruiz as odd about the scene. It's not just the newness of his overalls or the paleness of the man's skin. They're working on a Sunday and the van has silver windows at the back. It's just the sort of vehicle used in surveillance operations.

Reaching the intersection, Ruiz turns south towards the city and ponders whether anything has been achieved by confronting Murphy. Not a lot, he suspects, but subtlety was never one of his strengths as a detective. Subtlety can serve a purpose, but sometimes you have to rattle a cage to wake a Norwegian Blue.

26

The Red Emperor Restaurant has ducks the colour of dog turds hanging in the window alongside some weird-looking sea creature that might be inside out or might be entrails.

The restaurant fronts Macclesfield Street on the corner of Horse and Dolphin Yard, near the pagoda-style gates of Chinatown. The front window is partly covered by the menu and sign advertising a hot buffet for £4.95, all you can eat.

A white Mercedes delivery van is parked at the entrance to the yard with a foot or so spare on either side. Sami tries the back door. Locked. He moves along the side and tries the driver's door. It opens. A real criminal would know how to hotwire a car. That's what he should have been learning in the Scrubs. Something useful. A life skill.

Maybe the van driver is inside the restaurant, thinks Sami.

A bell jangles above the door as he pushes it open. The

place is almost empty. The lunchtime rush is over. A couple are paying their bill at the cash register. A girl in a wheelchair is sitting with her mother. The van driver is at a table alone, hunched so low over a bowl of wonton soup that the spoon barely has to leave his lips.

He looks like a skinhead with close-cropped hair and scabby knuckles. Maybe he drives a van during the day and spends his nights kicking the shit out of gays, Pakis and Man United fans.

Sami takes a seat at a table nearby. The waitress is Chinese and barely out of her teens, with shiny black hair cut straight across her forehead. Everything about her is small except her almond shaped eyes, which are the colour of burnt toast.

Her nametag says *Lucy*. That's probably her mother at the front counter – an older version, shorter, plainer, with an unapologetic face and tiny rimless glasses. And that could be her father dressed in chef's whites, holding open the swinging half doors of the kitchen. His head is shaved and his legs are bowed.

Sami remembers his grandfather, who survived a Japanese POW camp in Burma, getting the cold sweats whenever he saw an Asian face. More than once he'd look at Japanese tourists and react as though he'd come face to face with Emperor Tojo himself.

Lucy brings the van driver a pot of green tea.

'I didn't order that,' he says.

'It's complimentary.'

186

'What else is complimentary?' His hand brushes her knee and slides up her leg until it touches the hem of her skirt.

Lucy steps back.

The driver winks at Sami. 'I just love chink women. They're like chink food – you fill up and an hour later you're hungry again.'

The nasal accent says he's a northerner.

'Ever been to Thailand?' he asks.

'No.'

'They got bar girls there who can fire ping pong balls out of their poongtangs.' He provides the sound effects. 'And I'll tell you something else for nothing. They might have slanty eyes but their pussies are straight up and down, know what I'm saying? Tight and sweet.'

He's not even bothering to whisper. That's the thing about a lot of northerners. They think they're droll but mostly they're gobby and annoying.

The keys to the van are clipped to his belt. Maybe Sami should just deck the guy and take the keys. How far would he get?

'The thing about Bangkok girls is this, right?' The van driver is leaning across the table. 'They might look like virgins but they fuck like demons, know what I'm saying? And if you like 'em young, Thailand's the place. I'm not talking about jailbait. I'm no ped. But the chinks just look younger, you know.'

187

At some point Sami finds himself switching off. Maybe it's the smell of the food or the less than riveting conversation. He hasn't eaten since yesterday.

The van driver has switched to a new subject. 'We should kick all the fuckers out, either that or hang them on the wall, know what I'm saying?'

Lucy brings him a plate of spare ribs and another of fried rice. He picks up a rib and chews it to the bone, sucking the sauce off his fingers.

'Is that your van parked in the lane?' asks Sami.

'Yeah.'

'You on a delivery run?'

'I was until them bombs went off.'

'Where you heading?'

'Shoreditch and then home.'

'Could you give me a lift?'

'Yeah, sure, where you heading?'

'Anywhere away from here.'

The driver attacks another rib. 'Might take a while.'

Lucy has come back with an order book. Sami asks for the soft shell crab and fried rice.

'You want anything to drink?'

'Just water, thank you.'

'Still or sparkling.'

'Still, please.'

'OK.'

The van driver watches her leave. 'Great little arse.'

Sami leans back in his chair. Takes a deep breath. His

heart has stopped racing. If he can stay off the street, he can give himself time to think.

He looks up and notices the girl in the wheelchair is staring at him. She must be going for the Goth look – blue lipstick, blue eye shadow and dyed black hair cut straight around her head like someone put a pudding bowl on her head and traced the edges.

Sami nods. She looks away.

Sami glances out the front windows. Between the hanging ducks he can see a police car pull up outside. They're stopping people and talking to them.

An old guy in six different layers of clothes is wandering back and forth along the footpath carrying a sandwich board that says, *Judgement Day is coming*. On the back it says, *Be ready to burn*.

People step off the pavement to avoid him.

Suddenly, he stops and peers at Sami through the window. Sami tries to look away but it's too late. The old guy bends his knees and sets down his sandwich board. He pushes open the restaurant door, walks past the cash register.

'You need saving,' he yells in a battered voice. 'You're a sinner, but there's still time.'

Sami has a helpless hollow feeling. Everyone in the restaurant is staring at him. The sandwich board guy leans over him with his hands outstretched, palms upward, like some American evangelist drawing out the evil spirits.

'This is a city of sin and sodomy. That's why God is punishing it today. This man has been down to the gates of hell. He has looked in Satan's eyes.'

'No, I haven't,' says Sami. 'You got it wrong. I'm just here for lunch.'

The sandwich board guy's voice grows louder. 'This man is a sinner, but he wants to repent.'

The doorbell jangles. A young bobby steps inside and stands at the front counter, holding a peaked hat in his hands.

'What does he have to repent for?' he asks the old guy.

'Nothing,' blurts Sami, squeezing his knees into the rucksack.

The bobby looks at him apologetically. 'Is this gentleman bothering you, sir?'

'A little.'

'I'll move him on directly.' He unfolds a piece of paper. 'I just wanted to ask if any of you have seen a man carrying a dark coloured rucksack? He's aged from 25 to 35, slim build, light brown hair, wearing jeans and a sweatshirt. If you do see someone matching this description, notify the police immediately. Please don't approach him.'

He folds the paper and puts it into his pocket.

The van driver looks at Sami. 'The guy sounds just like you.'

'Think so?'

'Yeah.'

Sami tries to laugh.

'Do you have a rucksack, sir?' asks the constable.

'It's a different colour.'

'Can I see it?'

Sami's hand is beneath the table, edging between his thighs, feeling for the rucksack. The zipper.

'What's this guy supposed to have done?' he asks, trying to sound relaxed.

'He's wanted in connection with a police investigation.'

'So he's not dangerous.'

'We're asking people not to approach him.'

Sami's right hand has found the main pocket of the rucksack. His fingers close around the semi-automatic, which is still in a plastic evidence bag. Labelled. Catalogued. Exhibit A.

The constable hasn't moved. He's looking for something in Sami's eyes. Guilt. Fear. Madness. At the same time he's edging towards the door, reaching for the handle.

He knows, he knows, thinks Sami. The only sound in his head is a dull rumbling like a bowling ball hitting the gutter and heading for oblivion.

The sandwich board guy is still standing over him, mouth open, as if trying to rediscover his train of thought. Outside, the constable reaches for his radio. Sami stands, swings the rucksack over his shoulder and heads for the kitchen.

Lucy's father is standing at the doorway. He says something in Chinese and holds up a meat cleaver like some

191

mad Ninja warrior. Sami pulls out the gun. The cleaver clatters to the tiles. Hands come together. He bows apologetically.

Sami bursts out the side door of the kitchen into Horse and Dolphin Yard. Right is a dead end. Left takes him back to Macclesfield Street where the bobby is waiting. He has no choice.

Suddenly, a police car pulls up, blocking his only exit. Sami tries the nearest door. Locked. Looks for a fire escape. Nothing.

The kitchen door is still open. He throws himself inside. Slams the door. Bolts it shut. Topples a metal shelf. Braces it across the doorframe.

Lucy and her father are staring at him.

'What's upstairs?'

'Our flat,' says Lucy.

'Anyone else home?'

She shakes her head.

'Is there another way out?'

'No.'

'You got a phone?'

She points behind the counter, but doesn't take her eyes off Sami's hand. He's still holding the gun.

'I want you to lock the front door. Can you do that for me?'

Lucy nods.

'Are you going to hurt us?'

'No.'

192

Sami walks into the main restaurant. Nobody has moved. It's as if they've been zapped by some sort of freeze-ray like you see in cartoons and old episodes of *Star Trek*.

Lucy's mother is at the cash register.

'I need to make a phone call,' Sami tells her. She says something back to him in Chinese.

'My mother doesn't speak English,' explains Lucy. 'She wants you to pay for the call.'

Sami roots for change in his pockets and finds a handful of coins. They spin and rattle on the counter top.

He calls Tony Murphy. Tries to speak. The words are like barbed wire in his throat.

'There's a problem.'

'I told you not to call me again.'

'The police think I have a bomb.'

'How did they get that idea?'

'I might have mentioned it.'

'You must be the world's biggest moron.'

'You got to get me out of here.'

'And how do you suggest I do that, son?'

'You must have contacts.'

'Sure. I'll call the good fairy. She owes me a wish.'

Sami doesn't appreciate the sarcasm. 'You can't leave me here. I still have the shooter.'

Murphy curses. 'I told you to get rid of it.'

'Must have slipped my mind.'

'Listen, you muggy toerag, don't fuck with me. Don't

you *ever* fuck with me.' He's screaming down the phone. 'Destroy the gun. Get rid of it. You hearing me?'

Sami doesn't answer. He's too busy watching events outside. People are hurrying along the street, looking over their shoulders. They're leaving shops, restaurants and the supermarket. Mr Wu's Noodle Bar, the Golden Gate Cake shop, the Pagoda restaurant . . . Police are evacuating the area. Sealing it off.

Tony Murphy is still yelling down the line. 'You get pulled, you keep your mouth shut. Understand? You mention my name and you're dead. Your sister is dead. Your entire family are dead. Am I making myself clear?'

'You got to help me,' pleads Sami.

'I am helping you, son. I'm telling you the truth. Don't call me again. Forget this number. Forget you ever met me.'

'What about Nadia?'

'Yeah. Exactly. You think about your sister.'

Sami tries to protest but the line is silent. He's talking to dead air.

27

Commander Bob Piper surveys the empty streets and the abandoned shops and offices. The perimeter has been secured and civilians evacuated. Two cordons. Concentric circles. It's textbook stuff.

The only people allowed through the outer ring are police and emergency services. The inner ring is for the counter-terrorist squad, CO19 (Specialist Firearms Command) and the bomb squad. Now the only civilians within the cordon are the hostages and the hostage taker.

Piper hates sieges. In the old days they were easy. You gave the guy a few hours to cool down (or sober up) and then issued a final warning. If he didn't surrender you went in. Breaking down doors. Firing teargas. Shooting the bad guys. Restoring order.

But ever since the Jean de Menezes debacle at Stockwell Tube, procedures have been changed. Not so much procedures as public sentiment. Two firearms officers put seven bullets into the head of a Brazilian electrician they mistook for a suicide bomber. Who knew that people would take it so badly? Turned out that shoot to kill is only acceptable if you smoke the right suspect.

There were public inquiries, internal reviews, an inquest and calls for the Commissioner's head on a spike. De Menezes became a poster boy for the civil liberties whingers and bleeding hearts who delight in portraying law enforcement agencies as totalitarian storm troopers.

After the war on terror and the war on drugs there should be a war on irritating people, thinks Piper, on the Marxists, the moaners and the greenies.

Last year a siege in North London went six days. Everyone praised the police for their patience and tolerance – except for local residents, unable to sleep in their own beds or get a change of clothes.

This one can't go on for six days. Tomorrow morning a million people are going to be catching trains and buses into Central London. What then? Chaos.

Piper glances at a TV monitor. The front of the Red Emperor is bathed in light that reflects off the silver and gold letters painted above the main window.

A dozen firearms officers are positioned on the rooftops around the restaurant. Sharpshooters. Trained professionals. One clear shot and they can all go home. In the meantime Piper is supposed to negotiate. Confer. Reach a deal.

That's his dilemma. Piper is a conservative and a believer in law and order, but not in lawyers or judges or in a judicial system which has too many flaws; too many gaps for criminals to slip through.

Piper is also a realist, who has accepted the fact that in all probability his decisions will cause irreparable harm to innocent individuals. That's the nature of policing. No matter how much training you do or how sharp your skills or how modern your armoury, sometimes the most efficient weapon is a broad axe.

The Commissioner has called a media conference. He wants Piper by his side. He will doubtless express full faith in his Commander, thereby ensuring that if the operation goes south, he can blame someone else for the debacle.

28

Tony Murphy is being 'schmeissed'. A giant-sized loofah slaps against his naked body, smearing soap over his large expanse of skin while geysers of steam billowing from pipes condenses on the marble walls and ceiling.

He over-imbibed at the garden party and now he's sweating out the toxins in a Russian steam room at Porchester Spa, an art deco building on Queensway.

The giant loofah smears across his shoulders and down his back. Peter, his masseur, offers him a cold towel.

Normally being 'schmeissed' relaxes Murphy – refreshes the parts other saunas don't reach. Not today. Sami Macbeth is on his mind.

Leaving the steam room, he takes a breathtaking dip in the plunge pool, shrinking his testicles to marbles. Peter is waiting for him at the slab. Lying face down, Murphy closes his eyes and feels the perspiration prickling on his flesh again as strong fingers go to work, breaking down knots of tension in his shoulders and neck.

Peter's hands leave his skin. Maybe he's getting more oil. The door opens. Cool air brushes his flesh.

A moment later comes a different sensation. Murphy rears up, roaring, naked as the day as he was born, only bigger, fatter and whiter. A scalding hot towel drops from his back, leaving an angry red burn.

'Hello, fat man, how's the restaurant business. You look like you've been eating all the fookin' profits.'

Murphy is looking at a familiar face in unfamiliar surroundings – Jimmy Ferris, better known as Ferret.

Irish, Catholic and Scouse, Jimmy has a chip on both shoulders and a nest of angry bees buzzing in his head. Rumour has it he once trained to be a priest. He spent three years in a seminary: up before dawn, mass every morning, vows of silence. Then one day he had a religious epiphany in reverse. He stopped believing in God. This had nothing to do with atheism or humanism or moral relativism. Ferret still believed in a higher divine, supernatural power but it wasn't Jesus or Mohammed or Buddha. The power lay within him. Behold, a nihilist was born.

Ferret approached his new career with the same single-minded fervour that he once gave to God and the Catholic Church. He became an IRA fixer. Nobody ever discovered the exact role he played in the organisation, but his phone number kept appearing on the call sheets whenever they picked up a terror suspect.

Murphy wraps a blue gingham towel around his body,

tucking it under his armpits. Ferret is also wearing a towel, but his body is lean and sinewy, covered in tattoos. He has a gold crown on one of his front teeth, making him appear even more rat-like.

'I always wondered if fat men are fat all over, you know, but you must have trouble finding that thing to piss. Now fat chicks are different. Everyone knows they got tight pussies.'

'What are you doing here, Jimmy?' asks Murphy.

'I've come to check on my supply chain. I hear from our buyer that one of the samples I sent him didn't arrive.'

'There's been a delay.'

'Nobody told me about any fookin' delay.'

'Unforseen circumstances.'

'Do I look like a fookin' eejit, Murphy? You had one fookin' job. You had to take the fookin' guns, retool the fookin' barrels and transport the fookin' things. Now I have buyers questioning my fookin' ability to deliver on my promises.' Ferret brings a whole new meaning to expletive-laden conversation. 'Why was the consignment short?'

'I kept one of the guns.'

'Why?'

'I took a liking to it.'

'That wasn't the fookin' deal. The fookin' guns are supposed to be in fookin' Africa.'

Murphy gets defensive. 'Don't try to heavy me, Jimmy. I was doing you a favour.'

200

'No,' says Ferret shaking his head. 'You were *repaying* a favour. That's a very fookin' different thing. You owe fookin' people and those fookin' people owe me. That's how the fookin' system works.'

Murphy's throat has gone dry. He can't tell him about Ray Jnr taking the Beretta and getting arrested, or Sami Macbeth stealing it back. Macbeth should have destroyed it by now. What if he hasn't? It doesn't bear thinking about.

Ferret wets one end of a towel and twirls it into a cord, flicking it like a whip. It snaps against Murphy's thigh and he dances away. Ferret moves him around the marble slab, laughing. Then he tosses the towel into the plunge pool and pushes through the misted doors to the changing rooms.

Murphy is panting and pink, but not because of the steam. He gets himself a drink of water from a fountain and spills some of it down his chest.

Maybe it's time to walk away, he thinks. Sail into the sunset or at least fly there first class. Bermuda is nice this time of year. The condo is waiting. But first he has to do something about Sami Macbeth.

29

It should be getting dark outside, but the colour of the light is unnatural. Spotlights are bathing the cobblestones in a brightness that makes them look like the centre of a stage. We're in the right place for drama – the West End. This one is unfolding in three acts.

The front door of the Red Emperor is barricaded with tables turned on their sides and stacked on top of each other. The kitchen door is also sealed and Sami has locked everyone in the storeroom where they're sitting on sacks of rice and cans of cooking oil.

Sami takes the semi-automatic from the plastic evidence bag. Weighs it in his hand. Marvels at the raw power it seems to hold. He likes the way it fits into his hand and the delicate lines his fingertips leave when he strokes the freshly oiled metal.

Taking out the ammunition clip, he counts eighteen slug-like bullets. Hollow points. The magazine takes twenty. Two bullets are missing. Dessie said Ray Garza's boy fired on two rozzers when they tried to arrest him.

A chopper sounds overhead. The whump, whump of the blades seems to shake the air. Sami heads upstairs. Walks through the flat. It has a small kitchen, a bathroom, two bedrooms and a lounge.

Lucy's room has a desk tucked under the window and books piled on either side of her chair. She's studying business or management. Her handwriting is neat and precise.

From the third floor window he can see more police cars and ambulances, parked in Wardour Street. A truck is unloading barricades, lifting them with a portable crane and dropping them across the road. Police in black body armour are crouching behind vehicles.

Sami opens a window. Leans out. He's looking for external stairs or a fire escape. Nothing. The uppermost window leads to a small flat roof overlooking Horse and Dolphin Yard. It's about fourteen foot across to another flat roof on the far side. Even with a run-up he'd struggle to make a jump like that. And even if he could get to the other side, where would he go?

A dark shadow moves at the very edge of his vision. He turns. Someone is watching him. They're crouched behind a brick wall on the opposite side of the yard. A policeman? A sharpshooter?

Fuck. Shit. Fuck.

Sami pulls back from the window and presses his body against the wall, fear sucking at his chest. Tugging a cord he lowers the blind and turns off the lamp on Lucy's

203

desk. Staying low, he moves through the flat, locking windows. Lowering blinds. In darkness, he searches the drawers and cupboards for anything that might be useful – masking tape, a ski mask, scissors, pliers and a pocket knife.

He can hear someone beating on the storeroom door downstairs. Sami takes the shooter from the waistband of his jeans. Unlocks the door.

'It's about fucking time,' says the van driver. 'There ain't enough air. We're suffocating in here.'

'There's plenty of air.'

'And the place is filthy.'

'What are you, the food inspector?'

Lucy protests. 'It's not dirty. I clean it every week.'

Lucy's mother and father are sitting on rice sacks, arm in arm. The girl in the wheelchair and her mother are at the centre of the storeroom. The wheelchair is barely wide enough for the space. Her mother is soft spoken. Modestly dressed.

'Excuse me, sir. It's very dark in here and I get quite claustrophobic.'

'You can come out now,' says Sami. 'Stay away from the windows.' He directs them to sit at tables closest to the kitchen. The van driver sits alone, tilting back his chair and propping his feet on the wall.

Lucy is translating Sami's instructions to her parents, who nod at Sami gratefully. Asians are so polite, he thinks.

'Are you still hungry?' Lucy asks him.

'Pardon?'

'You ordered food. Do you still want it?'

'I can pay,' says Sami, peeling a fifty-pound note from the bundle in the rucksack.

'Is it stolen money?' she asks.

'Would it matter?'

Lucy folds the note three times and puts it into a jar above the sink next to a picture of her grandparents in a formal pose dressed in their finest clothes.

Sami watches her prepare, a knife blade blurring with speed as she dices celery, bamboo shoots and broccoli. She heats a wok and the kitchen fills with the hissing of vegetables hitting hot oil.

'Why are you doing this?' she asks.

Sami can't answer her.

'Do you really have a bomb?'

Her eyes look incredibly wise yet she doesn't look older than fourteen.

'Why?' Lucy asks.

'Pardon?'

'Why do you have a bomb?'

It's an obvious question. Sami doesn't have an answer.

'What are you fighting for? What are you protesting against? What do you hate – Western imperialism, decadent bourgeois attitudes? Do you want independence or freedom? Are you an anarchist? Has Britain betrayed the Arab world?'

205

Sami just wants her to shut up.

'What do you hate about us?' asks Lucy.

'I don't know who "us" is.'

'Western civilisation,' says Lucy. 'Do you know what Gandhi said when he was asked about Western civilisation? He said he thought it was a good idea.'

'He was a lot cleverer than me,' replies Sami.

'I don't think you do have a bomb.' She makes him sound like a failure.

'I have a gun,' he says defensively.

A mobile phone is ringing on the counter beside the cash register. Lucy's phone. She stares at it as though expecting it to do something else, like answer itself.

Lucy picks it up. Presses green. Listens. Hands the phone to Sami.

A deep resonant male voice booms down the line: 'This is London News Radio. Am I speaking to a terrorist?'

Sami doesn't answer.

'Are you a hostage?'

'No.'

'Can you talk? Are you being held at gunpoint?'

'Sorry, who are you?'

'London News Radio.'

'Who did you want to speak to?'

'A terrorist or a hostage.'

Sami looks around the restaurant.

'I'm not a terrorist.'

'So what do you call yourself – a freedom fighter, a

206

martyr, an insurgent? What group do you represent? Are you affiliated with Osama Bin Laden? We're live to air. Do you have a message for the British people?'

'No.'

'The police are saying you might be Algerian or Moroccan.'

'I was born in Glasgow.'

'But you're Moslem, right?'

'No.'

'Can you explain why you're doing this?'

'Doing what?'

'Holding people hostage. Why didn't you detonate your bomb?'

'Pardon?'

'Your colleague blew himself up. Were you meant to die together?'

He's talking about Dessie.

'Have you harmed any of the hostages? How many are there? What are your demands?'

Sami hangs up. Looks at Lucy, who shrugs.

The van driver has turned on the TV. A policeman is being interviewed. Top brass. Chin out, shoulders back, he's facing a firing squad of cameras and microphones.

'This was a brutal, callous and horrifying act,' he says. 'One of the worst atrocities I have witnessed in my twenty-three years as a police officer . . .'

Sounding more righteous by the sentence, he bristles with intent and stresses his determination to bring the perpetrators to justice . . . no stone unturned . . . all available resources brought to bear . . . blah, blah, blah.

Reporters are shouting questions. They want to know about the second bomber, 'the one who ran away'.

The policeman avoids answering the question. Tries to move on. The reporters won't let him go.

'Why have police evacuated parts of Soho?'

'For operational reasons.'

'Is it true you've cornered a suicide bomber?'

'We hope to arrest a suspect shortly.'

'Does the suspect have a bomb?'

'We have no intelligence to confirm the existence of more devices.'

'Or rule it out?'

'By their very nature people callous enough to kill innocent civilians are hard to stop, but our services and police are doing a heroic job.'

'Is the suspect holding hostages?'

'No comment.'

'Have you made contact with him? What are his demands?'

Sami blinks at the screen. His stomach spasms like he's going to be sick. The brass is asking for public patience and co-operation. Central London will be locked down for a while longer.

The media conference ends. Next they interview the cabbie that kicked Sami out of his cab. He's talking about how he came face to face with the devil.

'He had this crazed look in his eyes, like he was obsessed, you know, and I thought I could hear the bag ticking. He could have blown me up but I kept my cool, know what I'm sayin'? I saved myself and other people.'

Hold the phones, thinks Sami. Get this guy an agent and put him on Oprah.

Next comes the woman from the Crooked Surgeon who let Sami use the phone.

'He had these cold blue piercing eyes. They were looking right through me. It was like he was undressing me, you know, like he wanted to do things to me, obscene things. Clearly he has a very twisted misogynistic view of Western women.'

Everyone is getting their fifteen minutes of fame, thinks Sami, except in the new digital age fifteen minutes is condensed into a sound-bite and should come with an extra large coke and fries.

They're calling it a siege. Nobody ever gets away from a siege. Look what happened at Waco and that school in Russia where all those kids died.

Sami lets his forehead drop onto his forearms and closes his eyes, listening to his heart thudding and smelling sweat rising from his armpits. Even if he destroys the shooter and flushes the drugs, he's guilty of tampering with evidence, perverting the course of justice, breaking and entering, blowing up a train and holding people hostage.

How many years do you get for robbing the Old Bailey

or for taking hostages in a restaurant? Fifteen years? Twenty? They're calling him a terrorist. It'll be high security, category A, Parkhurst or Belmarsh.

Twenty years. That's seven thousand and something days. Nadia won't be waiting when he gets out. Neither will Kate Tierney. She'll be long gone, twice married with three kids and thunderous thighs.

They say you only think about escaping for the first five years. After ten you stop thinking about women and by fifteen you're looking forward to a hot cocoa and lights out at ten.

Maybe they won't even bother arresting him. They'll shoot him Butch and Sundance style the moment he sets foot outside. Exclamate him. Full stop. End of story.

30

On the day Nadia started primary school Sami was supposed to walk her to the school gates and hold her hand when she crossed the road. He got as far as the skateboard park where a mate of his was trying a fifty-fifty grind on a handrail. Sami told Nadia to wait for him because he wanted a turn.

She waited for a while but then grew tired of watching the skateboarders. She saw a girl wearing the same school uniform and thought about following her across the road. The lights changed as she stepped out. Tyres screeched. The car couldn't stop. Nadia fell under the front wheels.

Sami saw her lying on the road. He started running; calling for help. Then he kept running, convinced that he'd killed her. Sure she was dead. He was to blame.

Nadia wasn't dead. The nearside tyre had run over one of her school shoes, which was so stiff and new that it didn't give way. It tore all the ligaments in her left foot and she spent two months in a cast.

Sami took his punishment like a man. His skateboard was broken into pieces.

Why does he remember that now, he wonders. Staring at the window, he tries to force Nadia to appear in front of him. He has tried to do it for three days but it hasn't worked.

Outside the restaurant it's gone quiet. Nothing seems to be moving except the Chinese lanterns rocking in the breeze. When Sami presses his left cheek against the glass and looks sideways he can make out the barricades blocking Shaftesbury Avenue. Pressing his opposite cheek to the window, he can see the twin stone dragons outside the Exchange Bar and the fruit stand at the Lucky House Mini Market. Boxes of apples, oranges and bananas are neatly stacked with prices written in coloured markers on white squares of cardboard. The doors are closed. The windows are dark.

'Why are you doing this to us?' demands a voice behind him.

Sami turns. The girl in the wheelchair has broad shoulders and strong arms. Her face might be pretty if her eyes weren't so narrow and hard. Anger seems to be trapped inside her, filling her like a reservoir.

'Doing what?'

'Keeping us prisoner.'

Sami can't answer her.

'When are you going to let us go?'

'Soon.'

212

'I have to be home.'

'Why?'

The question is so unexpected that she doesn't have an answer.

'I have things to do. I have a life.'

'What's your name?' Sami asks.

Her hands leave her wheels and are pressed into her lap.

'Persephone.'

'How long you been in a wheelchair?'

'Since I was nine.'

'What happened?'

'I got an infection.'

Sami can't think of any more questions, but his silence infuriates her.

'Is that all you got?'

'Pardon?'

'The only question you got? When you look at me is that all you see – a wheelchair? A cripple?'

'No.'

'You didn't ask where I live or what I do. You're not interested in my opinions or my pastimes; what music I like, my favourite films, what I'm reading, it's just the wheelchair. Well let me tell you: I drive a car. I go to the gym four nights a week. I have a boyfriend. I'm a dynamite fuck. Want to know more?'

Not really, thinks Sami. 'I'm sorry if I offended you.'

'You're too transparent to offend me,' she says, rocking

213

back in her chair, raising the small front wheels and spinning away from him.

Now there is a girl with serious issues, thinks Sami, as he watches her depart. It's not just her anger or her bitterness that creates a force field around her. It's as though she uses her disability to selectively embarrass people or socially bludgeon them.

The van driver is still leaning against the wall with his eyes closed.

'You don't look like a Paki or an Arab,' he says.

Sami doesn't answer.

'I suppose you figure you're going to blow a few people up and go straight to heaven; get to sleep with the vestal virgins. How do you Moslems find enough virgins to go round? Maybe they'll run out and you'll end up shagging camels instead.'

Sami's molars are clenched. Hurting.

'I suppose you think 9/11 was a triumph,' continues the van driver. 'But you dumb bastards just made the West stronger. You shoved a pointy stick into the biggest bloody wasp's nest in history and now the Yanks are gonna eat you for breakfast and shit you out before lunch like you're extra-strength All-Bran.'

Sami tells him to shut up. He's not listening.

'Look what happened in Iraq. Saddam bragged that the Republican Guard would lay waste to the infidels. He said they were gonna stain the sand red with American blood. Bollocks! They folded. They fled like frightened rabbits.

214

'Now you got insurgents instead of soldiers. Proper cowards. They bomb schools and mosques. They dress up as women. Booby-trap cripples and retards. Run away. If Gordon Brown had any balls he'd kick every last sand nigger out of this country.'

Sami spins around and kicks at the rear legs of the driver's chair, which are taking his weight. Gravity does the rest. He goes down, landing hard on his back. Winded. Sucking in air.

'I said shut the fuck up,' mutters Sami, pressing the barrel of the shooter into the driver's forehead. Leaving a mark. He pulls away suddenly. Shaking. Frightened of how much he wants to pull the trigger.

Dragging himself up, Sami slumps in a chair, arms hanging between his knees, the gun loose in his fingers. A hand brushes his shoulder. Persephone's mother has crossed the restaurant. She's one of those women who seem to have been beaten down by life, worn smooth like a pebble in a fast moving stream.

'Do you have a headache? I have some paracetamol in my handbag.'

'Thank you, but I'm OK.'

She lowers herself, perching on the edge of a chair, hands clasped in her lap. Enclosed. Bird-like.

'You'll have to forgive Persephone. She can be quite . . . acid-tongued. You see she's very independent and strong-willed. People sometimes mistake it for rudeness.'

'She has her reasons.'

215

'I used to think it was the accident, but she was always rather demanding.'

'The accident?'

'My husband was driving, God rest his soul. Persephone was thrown out of the car. I was pinned inside.' She pulls back her fringe and Sami sees the scar running across the top of her scalp, just below her hairline.

'When was it?'

'Six years ago.'

'Persephone said it was an infection.'

'She doesn't like talking about what happened. People always want details.'

Her voice drops. She glances behind her.

'I was just wondering . . . hoping really . . . that you might consider letting Persephone go – because of her disability. She wouldn't say bad things about you. You've treated us very well.'

The van driver interrupts.

'You can't let one of us go and not the others. That's fucking discrimination.'

'She's in a wheelchair,' says her mother.

'So what? We give her ramps. We build her lifts. She gets a special fucking pension. It's a rip-off.'

They're shouting at each other.

Sami tells them to be quiet.

Persephone joins the argument. 'I don't want any favours.'

216

'I bet that's what you say when the Government gives you hand-outs,' says the driver.

'You're an arsehole.'

'And you're in a wheelchair.'

Sami snaps and drives his fist into the driver's stomach. He follows up, hooking him just below the right eye with the butt of the semi-automatic, knocking him across a table.

'I told you to shut up,' he yells, waving the gun like he's conducting an orchestra. Sami balls up a serviette and shoves it in the driver's mouth, sealing it with a length of masking tape ripped from a spool.

'You don't know me,' he says, pressing his face close, squeezing the words out through his teeth. 'I'm not a Moslem and I'm not a terrorist. I'm as British as you are but arseholes like you make me wonder if I should be proud of that.'

The driver's eyes are brimming. Sami has seen guys like him before – fearless on his own turf but a coward in a confrontation.

Rolling him to one side then the other, he pulls back his arms and tapes his wrists together, behind his back. Then he pulls him up onto a chair and loops tape over the curved wooden backrest.

Nobody in the restaurant has spoken. Sami puts the gun away. Wipes his hands.

'Who wants a drink? I'm thirsty.'

31

Bones McGee is considering his position and calculating the odds. Maybe he could cut a deal with vice and roll on Tony Murphy. He could cop a plea to something minor, blame his lack of judgement on work stress, which allowed him to be compromised by a gangster.

He could wear a wire. Set Murphy up. Seek redemption. His police career would be over, of course, but he'd stay out of prison. A man with his background should avoid jail at all costs: a detective, a veteran of the serious crime squad. Dozens of his former collars would be waiting for him inside and they wouldn't be baking cakes and bringing cell-warming presents.

Tony Murphy would turn on Bones like a ballerina in a jewellery box, but that still doesn't mean Bones should do the same. Murphy has a family tree like a parasitic vine. Lop off one branch and a dozen more come looking to strangle you.

And what about Ray Garza? A person couldn't travel far enough or dig a hole deep enough to hide from

Garza. The guy has contacts in the security services, the Home Office and the Met. He plays golf with the Assistant Commissioner for fuck's sake.

None of the options are panning out for Bones. Everything depends on some kid who's holed up in a restaurant in Chinatown. An amateur. A fish. He's probably going to sing like Fat Pav the moment they prise him out of that restaurant. Not the dead Fat Pav but the one who turned 'Nessun Dorma' into an anthem and made a white hankie into a fashion accessory.

Best for all concerned if the kid doesn't make it out alive. Best if he blows himself up. Best if someone puts a bullet in his head.

Leaving his office, Bones steps outside and lets a cold breeze slap him in the face. The sun is a dying orange smudge above the rooftops and traffic is moving again.

He catches a cab to Kings Cross, keeping his head turned to the window so the driver doesn't see his face. Twenty minutes later he catches a second cab back to Piccadilly Circus and takes the stairs to the Underground.

The station is closed, but shops on the concourse have reopened and people are milling around chalk board signs announcing the line closures.

Bones has changed his clothes. He's swapped his wool and cashmere jacket for a vomit-stained overcoat and a woollen hat that belonged to a tramp at Kings Cross. It wasn't a straight swap. The tramp wanted a tenner to close the deal.

A dozen payphones are lined up along one wall. A phone is free. Bones punches in the number for the counter-terrorism hotline. Muffles his voice. Tries to put on a Middle Eastern accent but sounds more like the char wallah in *It Ain't Half Hot Mum*.

'Today is just the beginning,' he says, 'a small illustration of what we can do. Next time the Al Qaeda Martyrs Brigade will kill thousands. We will stain the streets of London with the blood of infidels, the Jews and the Jew lovers, the true terrorists. Praise Allah or prepare to die. We will not negotiate. We will not surrender.'

Bones hangs up. Wipes his fingerprints from the phone. Pulls the woollen hat low over his eyes and exits the station. He ducks into a narrow lane and puts the overcoat and hat in a plastic shopping bag. Later, he'll toss them into a clothing bin in Bayswater. Within a fortnight they'll be on sale in Romania or Albania. Recycling is a wonderful thing.

32

Lucy's mobile rattles on the table. Sami picks it up and listens. A hostage negotiator has found the number. He has one of those matey, avuncular voices that makes him sound like he wants to take Sami under his wing and teach him the ways of the world.

'My name is Bob, what's yours?'

'Is that important?' asks Sami.

'It makes it easier to communicate.'

'We're doing pretty well so far.'

'Just give me a name.'

'David Beckham.'

'A proper name.'

'I'm sure David Beckham thinks it's a proper name.'

'I don't think you're in a position to be glib,' says the negotiator, who seems to lose his place on the page for a moment. 'Can you tell me how many hostages you're holding?'

Hostages? Sami hadn't really thought of them as being hostages.

'They have families,' says Bob. 'I'd like to be able to reassure them that everything is okay.'

Sami can see he has a point. 'There are six of us counting me,' he says.

'Are any of them injured?'

'They're fine.'

'Why are you doing this?'

'Doing what?'

'Holding people hostage?'

Sami doesn't know the answer. It just sort of happened. It's not what the negotiator expects.

'Would you consider giving yourself up?'

'Would you consider letting me go?'

'I can't do that.'

'Well, it looks like a stand-off,' says Sami.

'Listen, I don't know your name, but my job is to make sure that nobody gets hurt and that includes you. I'd be lying if I said I wasn't nervous. There are people out here who aren't very patient.'

'Tell them patience is a virtue.'

'The people you are holding have families and jobs and friends. They've done nothing wrong. I promise you, you have my word, if you let them go, if you walk out of there, hands in the air, unarmed, I'll guarantee your safety. Nobody has to get hurt.'

'And I'll live happily ever after.'

'I'm giving you a chance. We can do this the easy way or—'

'The hard way,' says Sami, finishing the sentence for him.

'I'm just saying you'll make things easier for yourself in the long run.'

Bob is beginning to irritate Sami. He's treating him like an amateur or some wet-behind-the-ears wannabe. Sami isn't a terrorist at all but if he were going to be one, he'd be bloody good at it.

'Maybe we could send in some food,' suggests Bob. 'Are you hungry?'

Sami glances at the stack of takeaway menus on the counter, wondering what sort of IQ a person needs to get a job as a hostage negotiator.

'I'm in a restaurant, Bob. I could send something out if you're feeling peckish.'

'I thought you might want something else . . . other than Chinese.'

'Like what?'

'Pizza. Indian.'

'Chinese is fine.'

Next Bob suggests he send in a two-way radio so they can talk whenever they want.

'Why can't we keep talking on the phone?'

'Two-ways are better. I could send someone in with one.'

'I don't think that's a good idea.'

Sami hears a low rumble from outside. Crouching behind an upturned table, he peers through the window and sees a bulldozer manoeuvre through the gates of Gerrard Street and swing to face the doors of the restaurant. The bucket is raised, shielding the driver.

Sami is still holding the mobile.

'What's happening out there, Bob?'

'Nothing.'

'Are you pissing on my Wheaties, Bob?'

'I don't know what you mean.'

Sami kicks a chair aside and pulls a ski mask over his face. Then he forces the van driver to his feet and opens the front door, using him as a shield. Two steps. He's on the pavement, pressing the semi-automatic to the back of the driver's head.

'You see me, Bob?' he shouts. 'You get that bulldozer out of here or I shoot someone, you understand? Pull a stunt like that again and I'll turn this place into a crater.'

Sami walks backwards through the door, pulling the driver with him. Within a minute the bulldozer has started moving, spinning on wide metal treads and withdrawing.

The van driver's knees buckle. He might have pissed his pants. Sami helps him to a chair.

Bob is still on the phone. 'That wasn't necessary.' He sounds like a schoolmaster.

'Shut up, Bob.' Sami hangs up.

A dripping tap in the kitchen sounds like a clock ticking. Nobody in the restaurant has said anything. Lucy's parents are holding hands. They could be praying. They might be planning their escape.

Persephone is drawing at a table as if trying to ignore what's happening. She has a portfolio in a zip-up folder. Sami glances over her shoulder and sees an image of a half-woman and half-bird, with a hooded beak and a naked body.

'Can I look at some more?' he asks.

She nods.

Sami leafs through the portfolio. Mostly the images are of dark angels and goddesses, who are semi-naked with powerful bodies and demonic eyes. There's nothing pornographic about their nudity.

Persephone tells him her idea for a fantasy comic: a girl in a wheelchair who turns into a crime fighter, a half mythical creature who can't be killed. The idea embarrasses her a little, but she doesn't seem so angry any more. If anything, Sami senses she might be coming on to him. Maybe she's one of those women who get turned on by outlaws and rebels. Kate Tierney is a bit like that, but Sami would forgive Kate anything.

'I need to go to the toilet,' Persephone tells him.

There is no disabled bathroom and her wheelchair won't fit in the cubicle.

'I can do it myself. I just need someone to take me to the door.'

'What then?'

'I crawl.'

'I can't let you crawl. I'll lift you.'

'I don't want you there.'

'I won't stay.'

Sami expects her to say no, but Persephone accepts. He tucks the shooter into the back of his jeans and slips one arm behind her back and another beneath her knees. She doesn't weigh much.

She rests her head against his chest. It's a different girl, he thinks.

The toilets are beside the kitchen. There are two cubicles and a small washroom in between with a basin and mirror.

Sami nudges the washroom door with his hip. Slides sideways, carrying Persephone with her feet first. Making sure he doesn't bump her head.

'You're good at this,' she says. 'I have so many bruises.'

He doesn't feel her hand on his back. She snatches the gun from his waistband and holds it under his chin with both hands. Her eyes are wide.

He pauses. 'Do you still want to go?'

'No. Take me back.'

'I could drop you here.'

'I could shoot you in the head.'

'You won't shoot me.'

'Try me.'

Sami squeezes his eyes shut. 'Go on, then. Do it. Shoot me.'

Her finger closes on the trigger.

'Let everyone go and I'll let you stay here.'

'I can't do that.'

Consternation clouds her eyes. 'Do you want to die?'

'No.'

'I will shoot.'

'No you won't.'

Sami takes his arm from under her knees, letting her legs drape but holding her against him with his face close to hers. The gun is still pressed beneath his chin. He reaches up and closes his fingers around hers, pointing the barrel away from his face and then takes the gun from her hand. He can feel her heart fluttering against his chest, her warm breath against his neck.

She grows soft in his arms. Deflating. He carries her back to her chair.

'For future reference,' he says. 'This switch here is the safety. The gun won't fire unless you take it off.'

33

Ruiz is in a pub on Fleet Street, one of those dark bolt-holes panelled in wood, with leather benches that are scuffed and nicked with age. Clocks don't matter in a place like this. It's a location for serious drinking and romantic meetings and for people who want to know what it feels like to be living back in a cave.

He spent the afternoon ringing hospitals and drug rehab centres, hoping he might find Nadia Macbeth. Fruitless. Thankless. Now a bomb has gone off on the Underground and put things back into perspective.

The barman has a bullet-shaped head, polished until it catches light like the bottles suspended above the bar. He glances up at a TV, which is tuned to the siege in Soho. A message is being broadcast. People are being told to 'Go in, Stay in and Tune in'. Nobody in the bar is listening to the warning except the barman.

'Makes you want to kill a raghead, don't it,' he says.

'Not really,' answers Ruiz, who takes his Guinness and finds a table as far away as possible.

He was supposed to take Darcy for a curry tonight but it's going to take him hours to get home. Most Sundays they go to Brick Lane and she orders a proper thali and a mango lassi.

It's the only time Darcy seems to eat a proper meal, thinks Ruiz, who likes watching her spoon the dhal, pickles and curry sauces onto her rice and fashion it into balls with her fingers before scooping them into her mouth.

A woman shrieks with laughter on the far side of the bar. Ruiz raises his eyes reluctantly and wonders what anyone could find to laugh about on such a day.

What's he doing here? He's not getting paid. He's not on a promise. Miranda isn't suddenly going to invite him into her bed as a thank you if he finds Nadia Macbeth. Although he wouldn't admit it to Miranda, a part of him is quite pleased to be working on a case again. Retirement has never sat particularly well with him, despite his dislike for modern policing and most of the people who populate the Metropolitan Police.

Ruiz doesn't need a reason to get out of bed every morning and he doesn't need to be surrounded by people, not like some who are never certain of exactly who they are until they see themselves reflected in the eyes of others.

His mind is dragged back to Nadia Macbeth. In the past two days she and her brother – two people he knows only from a photograph – have snagged his thoughts and haunted his waking hours. They remind him of a vine that grows in the jungles of Belize that the locals call 'the one

229

way tree'. The tendrils have barbed hooks that are almost invisible until you stumble into them. Then it's too late. You can't go back without tearing your skin to pieces. The only way out is to go forward, deeper into the vines.

A police siren passes outside, growing louder and then softer. Ten or twenty years ago a police siren could increase Ruiz's heart rate and set adrenalin coursing through his system. Not any more. The behaviour of stupid, violent people no longer interests him. Their motives are not his concern. The behaviour of clever, driven, dangerous people is a different story. People like Ray Garza and Tony Murphy.

Just before the terrorist bombings in London on July 7, 2005, a CCTV camera picked up images of a dark-haired man in a light blue shirt, carrying a rucksack. He was filmed entering a pharmacy in Kings Cross where he bought indigestion pills and nail-clippers. Less than fifty minutes later he detonated a bomb that killed twenty-three people and injured more than a hundred.

That's the sort of fact that snags in Ruiz's mind, point-less perhaps, but captivating. When they found the bomber's body parts spread across the carriage, did they come across a finger? Was the nail neatly trimmed?

He calls Fiona Taylor and asks her for another favour – a background check on a Rastafarian junkie and dealer called Puffa.

'You really know how to pick your times,' she tells him. 'We have a live operation in Soho.'

'I can see that,' says Ruiz, glancing at the TV. 'There's no hurry.'

Fiona promises to get back to him. In the meantime Ruiz returns to his Guinness, keeping one eye on the TV screen.

They're broadcasting CCTV footage of a suspect seen running from Oxford Circus Underground. The first part of the video is grainy and blurred. Side-on. A second camera picks up the man as he crosses the street. He stops at a street corner. Looks both ways. Adjusts a rucksack on his back.

The image freezes and zooms in on the suspect's face. There's something familiar about him. Ruiz yells at the barman to turn up the volume. He can't find the remote. He searches. Finds the unit. Amplifies the sound.

Half the story is enough. It's a word association game: siege . . . terrorist . . . hostages . . . Soho.

Another image flashes on screen – a photograph of Sami Macbeth, with long hair, a Nirvana T-shirt and skinny-leg jeans. He's pouting at the camera, going for the angry don't-fuck-with-me look, as though he's posing for publicity pictures instead of a police mug shot.

Ruiz swallows his beer and walks out onto Fleet Street, turns right and strolls past the double-decker buses and black cabs.

Sami Macbeth has been out of jail for fifty-six hours and in that time he has turned himself into a human headline. The kid has a talent for trouble.

34

The street is a no go area. Paper coffee cups and wrappers spin across the pavement, getting trapped against lamp-posts and the tyres of chained bicycles.

Sami tells Lucy to watch the front window. 'Tell me what you can see?'

'Nothing.'

'There must be something.'

'Which part of nothing would you like me to describe?'

A breaking news banner flashes on TV: SOHO SIEGE.

The streets have been cordoned off. Police in black body armour are spilling from buses and taking up positions, as though ready to fight a small war.

'Eyewitnesses say a man claiming to have a bomb took over a restaurant in Chinatown at two o'clock this afternoon. We believe that hostage negotiators have made contact with the hostage taker but as yet his demands are unknown . . .'

A photograph of Sami flashes onto the screen. His police mugshot. He had longer hair, fewer lines and not a care in the world because he knew it was all a misunderstanding and the jewels in Andy Palmer's van had nothing to do with him. He was innocent. The truth would out.

Only it didn't. Sami took the fall. He didn't fall under the wheels of a truck like Andy Palmer. He fell onto the wrong side of the tracks. He fell through the cracks. He fell out of favour.

'. . . The suspect's name is Sami Robert Macbeth, born in Glasgow, raised in south London, to an Algerian mother and a Scottish father. Macbeth was released from prison only days ago having served less than three years for possession of stolen goods. Counter-terrorism experts believe he converted to Islam in prison, influenced by the gangs . . .'

Gangs? Radical Islam? The only prayers Sami said in prison were directed to the parole board.

'An organisation calling itself the Al Qaeda Martyrs Brigade has claimed responsibility for the bombings. It is likely to be one of the loose splinter groups that have flourished since the War on Terror began, with only tenuous links to Al Qaeda, but funded through Middle Eastern banks and sympathisers . . .'

Sami shakes his head in disbelief. Who are these experts?

'Counter-terrorism authorities are also speculating on why the suspect failed to detonate his device. Some believe the device may have misfired or he could have had second thoughts about committing suicide.'

So not only am I an Islamic extremist, I'm also a coward, thinks Sami. How much worse can it get. They know his name. They have his photograph. What hope has he got of finding Nadia now or leading a normal life?

Some time soon they're going to make a decision and 'neutralise the threat'. They'll use SWAT teams or maybe even the SAS, who'll swing from the roof and crash through the doors. Teargas. Flash bangs. Explosions. They'll come in wearing body armour with enough fire-power to blow him into next year.

Sami's mind is fraying, his body aching, his batteries on empty. Whichever way he looks at the situation, he's screwed. If he walks out the front door they're going to kill him or put him away for twenty years in a high secu-rity wing. He blew up a strong room. Stole evidence. They'll blame him for what happened to the train. How many people are dead?

Sami can already smell the boiled cabbage and septic stench of the showers; and feel the scum-coloured water back up around his ankles. The prison sisters will wel-come him with open arms this time. They'll kick his legs apart. Brace him against the wall. Take turns. Nothing is going to protect him if he goes inside again. He'll be a skidmark on the bowl.

If he tells the truth, Murphy will kill Nadia. If he keeps schtum he might survive for a few months inside until Murphy takes out extra insurance and has him killed. It won't matter how long he stays in solitary, eventually he'll be on his own. That's when someone will lift him over a third-floor railing or jam a homemade knife under his ribs.

Sami lowers his eyes and stares at his hands, tightening them into fists, kneading his thumbs against his forefingers. Then he pushes them beneath his thighs to stop them shaking.

The phone rattles on the table.

'Hello, Sami.' It's Bob. 'I know your name now. We don't have to pretend any more.'

'I haven't been pretending.'

'I know but there won't be any mix-ups or confusion. We can have a better dialogue.'

Bob makes it sound like they're on a corporate training weekend.

There is another long pause. Sami considers hanging up, but Bob jumps in with a question.

'Where are you from, Sami?'

'You know where I'm from.'

'You've had a tough few years. Prison and now this . . .'

No shit, thinks Sami, as Bob continues, getting dangerously close to commiserating. He's sounding so affable at any moment he's going invite Sami out for a pint and a kebab.

'You got a family?'

'A sister.'

'What's her name?'

'Nadia.'

'Where is she now?'

That's a good question, thinks Sami. Maybe the police can find her. He could make it a demand.

'I don't know where she is.'

'You lost touch.'

'You could say that.'

Bob Piper covers the mouthpiece. 'Find his sister. We need to talk to her.' He's back with Sami again. 'Tell me what you want and I'll try to help.'

'I want a miracle.'

'I don't do miracles.'

'I want to be somewhere else.'

Sami presses the red button. Ends the call. He's squatting in the corner of the restaurant, his arms crossed over his knees, his chin resting on his arms. The others are watching, waiting for him to do something.

Persephone has packed away her drawings. Her mother is clutching a set of wooden rosary beads, worn smooth by her fingers. Lucy's eyes flit from her parents and back to Sami, somehow concentrating on both.

Sami's guts are churning. When he gets scared it goes straight to his bowels. He's shaking. Strung out. Devoid of hope. Something has broken inside him and he can't go on.

Slowly opening his fists, he touches his face with his fingers. He needs a shave. A shower.

That's when it happens. An idea clicks into place. It's huge. It's risky. It's something he can only fuck up once.

He picks up the mobile.

'Bob, I want the van.'

The negotiator is taken by surprise.

'What van?'

'The one parked outside, next to the restaurant – the white Mercedes.'

'What about the hostages?'

'I'm taking them with me.'

'I can't let you do that.'

'Don't disappoint me, Bob.'

'I mean it, Sami. I can't let you take them.'

'Yes you can. You don't want blood on your hands.'

Bob is asking Sami to stay calm, but that's the thing – he's already calm. This is a calmness he hasn't experienced before.

'Listen to me. You're not taking the van and you're not leaving with the hostages.'

'No, you listen, Bob. You're a negotiator, am I right?'

'Yes.'

'Well how come this isn't a negotiation? In a proper negotiation you'd give me something and I'd give you something in return. We'd barter. We'd agree. So far you don't seem to understand the rules.'

Bob gets annoyed. 'I've been very reasonable.'

'So far you've told me if I give myself up you won't shoot me. That's a threat, not an offer. The way I see it, I'm either going to die today or rot in prison. That's not much of a choice, is it?'

Bob doesn't say anything for a moment.

'I might be able to arrange the van. I need some time.'

'Oh, come on, Bob. The humble servant routine is wearing thin. I saw you on TV. You're in charge. You're the main man.'

'I can't let you leave with the hostages.'

'That's something we can negotiate about. Each time you do something nice for me, Bob, I'll let one of the hostages go.'

'Just one?'

'Maths wasn't your strongest subject, was it Bob?'

35

Bones McGee is pacing his office, stopping occasionally to glance at the TV. The situation isn't improving. He calls Murphy.

'That little problem we discussed earlier – it hasn't gone away.'

Murphy doesn't say a word.

'We got a kid holed up in a restaurant who says he has a bomb. He looks remarkably like the same kid we caught on a CCTV outside the Old Bailey.'

Still there's no reply.

'Are you listening to me, Tony? This kid could tear the arse out of everything.'

'He knows to keep his mouth shut.'

'I appreciate you showing faith in the boy but if he sings we all go down.'

'He won't say a word. I got leverage.'

'Yeah, well I'm pulling the plug, Tony. I'm out. I'm walking away.'

'It doesn't work that way, Bones.'

'Yeah it does. You don't call me. I don't call you. It's that simple.'

'Don't tell me what's simple. I'm not some shit-for-brains Mick just off the ferry at Holyhead. Maybe you think you can play both sides of the fence and get your rozzer mates round my joint knocking on my door with a battering ram, carrying a warrant signed by whats-his-face, the Lord Chancellor.

'Well, don't go getting any ideas. You're not Frank fucking Serpico. You mess with me and I'll start a war with your body parts. I'll cut them off one at a time. I'll dig a hole and bury you so deep not even your arse-sniffing mates in the dog squad will ever find you. You hear what I'm saying, Bones? That's the blood, the guts and the feathers of it. The whole story.'

Silence.

'Are you reading me, you arsehole?'

'Yeah.'

Tony Murphy slams down the phone and grimaces. His ulcer is playing up. What with his gout, high blood pressure and haemorrhoids, he should have bought shares in Boots.

Bones is getting nervous. He has no idea how nervous he should be. If Old Bill gets hold of that shooter Macbeth is carrying, he can forget about his Ibiza apartment and his well-funded retirement.

They're going to test the gun, match the bullet and

then the shit is gonna hit the proverbial. MI5, MI6, Special Branch, SOCA, the CIA and the Mormon Tabernacle Choir, for all Murphy knows, will come looking for them. And they're the good guys, as opposed to Jimmy Ferris and his mates who won't bother with warrants and due process and the Police and Criminal Evidence Act.

Instead Jimmy will take them out onto a deserted beach and put a bullet in their heads. One shot. No tears.

Murphy has always regarded himself as a thinker. Someone interested in exit strategies and contingencies, which are things most villains forget. They plan for an operation going right and ignore the possibilities of fuckups or bad luck. These same villains will gladly accept happy accidents as being a bonus but spend a dozen years in prison whinging about how they got screwed by an unfortunate happenstance.

Murphy glances out the patio doors into his garden. The marquee has been packed up and trucked away. A catering van is being loaded with the last of the tables.

Whatever happens he has to distance himself from what happened today, from the robbery, the bombing, from Sami Macbeth. His alibi is secure. A hundred people can vouch for his whereabouts.

How long before they identify Dessie's body? Then they'll come asking questions because everybody knows the Dobermann worked for him. The answer is to distance himself from his old mucker. He could spread a rumour that he and Dessie had fallen out. Tell people Dessie had been skimming the till.

Nobody who knew Dessie is going to seriously believe something like that, but Plod might suck on the worm if Murphy baited the hook the right way.

Suddenly, he sees a new possibility. Sooner or later the rozzers are going to link the Old Bailey job with the bombing. And when they realise what's missing from the evidence room, they'll think Ray Garza hired someone to get his son acquitted. Enter Dessie Fraser, more useful dead than alive.

Sami Macbeth is the only problem. The kid could screw up a one-car funeral.

A decision works its way into Murphy's eyes and he lets out a deep breath through his nose. Stubbing out his cigar, he carries his Scotch through the patio doors and across the lawn. Gabriel is jacketless, sleeves rolled up, polishing the Jag.

'We're taking a drive.'

'Where to, boss?'

'If you knew that you'd be as clever as me.'

36

Bob Piper is sitting in a mobile control room, a Winnebago parked in Wardour Street opposite an Angus Steak House. Spread across a table, weighted down with coffee mugs, are building plans for the Red Emperor restaurant and adjoining buildings, along with satellite images of the surrounding streets. The clarity is remarkable showing individual trees, vehicles and TV aerials.

A few years back a woman in the Netherlands spent an afternoon sunbathing topless on her secluded rooftop patio and then discovered images of herself, near-naked, posted all over the internet because a Google satellite 300 miles above the earth captured the moment.

Piper is studying the satellite images with the head of SO19, the specialist firearms command, and a major who heads the army bomb disposal unit.

Thermal imaging cameras trained on the restaurant show six people inside. Each appears as a white shadow on a dark background. Individuals have been given code-names based on his or her location. Sami Macbeth is

243

Target Alpha. Right now he's located near the connecting door to the kitchen. Four hostages are located in the body of the dining area, well away from the front windows. One hostage is in the storeroom, a troublemaker perhaps, separated from the others.

Listening devices will be in place within twenty minutes. Technicians are slowly drilling through the walls from the adjoining cake shop threading microphones into position.

Piper tilts back his swivel chair and stretches his arms above his head, making his shirt pull tightly across his chest.

What is Macbeth hoping to achieve? If he does have a bomb, why hasn't he detonated it? Maybe he's bluffing. Maybe the bomb failed to go off or he bottled out.

Now he wants to take a van. It won't happen. Piper can't let a possible suicide bomber go on a joyride through the West End with hostages. No chase scenes. No slapstick.

Piper has to stall him. Make excuses. Give in to the small demands. Sound reasonable.

Normally, the longer the siege goes on, the better it is. Not this time. In the next twelve hours a decision has to be made, Piper's decision. They have to find a way of isolating Macbeth from the others. Then they could detonate a water bomb against the joint wall and blow a man-sized hole into the Red Emperor. One team could go through the front door, another through the hole.

244

They could reach the hostages in fifteen seconds, all except the one in the storeroom.

The biggest question mark concerns the possibility of booby-traps. If Macbeth does have a bomb, he could have rigged it to explode if there is any attempt to free the hostages. The explosive used in the Tube bombing was TATP, homemade and volatile. Any percussion blast from a water bomb could trigger a chain reaction.

The hotline is ringing. It's the Commissioner. Piper makes eye contact with his senior men, who watch and listen.

'With all due respect, sir, we don't need the SAS.'

Piper sucks in his cheeks. His mouth has gone small.

'Yes, sir.'

'No, sir.'

'My full co-operation, sir.'

Fucking SAS! So what if they abseil off rooftops and swing through windows? They're glory hounds. Headline hunters. They're like piranhas – they only attack when they smell blood in the water.

This is all because of de Menezes, thinks Piper. One dead Brazilian and the Commissioner heads for the tall grass.

The others are waiting for instructions.

'How do you want to proceed, sir?'

'We let him have the van.'

37

Sami feels like it's the first day of his life and not the last one. It's a fluttering deep in his diaphragm, a feverish excitement mixed with fear. He's pacing the dining room, trying to picture what he has to do.

They think he's a terrorist. They're frightened of him. He's frightened of them. He has to use these facts rather than run away from them.

Lucy moves across the restaurant, her footsteps so small and light they barely make a sound.

'Did you really blow up that train?'

'No.'

'But you *are* a terrorist?'

Sami shakes his head.

Lucy looks at him incredulously. She wants an explanation.

Sami shrugs. 'I was in the wrong place at the wrong time with the wrong people.'

'Today?'

'Today . . . three years ago . . . it's the story of my life.'

Lucy waits for more. Sami struggles to explain.

'Have you ever been blamed for something you didn't do and no matter how many times you deny it, nobody will believe you?'

Lucy nods. 'I had a teacher who said I plagiarised an essay. She failed me. I tried to argue with her, but she wouldn't look at the paper again.'

Sami can see how this might be upsetting. 'How long ago did it happen?'

'Four years.'

'That was unfair, but if you look back and be brutally honest, maybe there were times when you got away with stuff. You either didn't get caught or maybe someone else got the blame for something you did.'

'What are you trying to say?'

'I'm saying that for years I've been waiting for things to rebalance, to even up. I'm just plain unlucky.'

'You're making excuses.'

'Think so? I've been over it a lot of times, a lot of nights. I spent nearly three years inside, staring at the walls of a prison cell, thinking maybe there was something I did wrong that I can't remember – some fuck-up or careless mistake like selling a dodgy car or not dipping my headlights at night. Did I kill someone accidentally? Is someone like Persephone riding around in a wheelchair or missing a father because of something I did. Because if there's not – if I've done nothing to deserve this life; if I'm getting kicked from Camden to Christmas for no fucking reason, I'd become a very bitter bastard. Unforgiving. I might even want to kill someone or to kill myself.'

Lucy raises her chin slightly and narrows her eyes. 'You don't punish innocent people just because you're unlucky. Sounds like you're trying to correct yesterday's mistakes. It can't be done. Mark them off. Make a new start.'

'You're a pretty smart cookie for someone your age.'

'I'm twenty-one.'

'You look younger.'

Her hair is cut short and trimmed across her neck in a straight line. Sami wants to reach out and touch it. Lucy moves first, taking his hand. Squeezing it.

'They're going to kill you.'

'I'll be all right.'

'They'll shoot first and do the numbers later.'

'You watch too many films.'

'You could negotiate – give yourself up to someone famous.'

'Like who?'

'Glenda Jackson.'

Sami laughs. 'They'd shoot both of us.'

'You don't have to die.'

Sami looks into her eyes and away. Then he opens his palm as though releasing an invisible bird and watches it flutter away.

38

It takes Ruiz twenty minutes to get from Fleet Street to Covent Garden. He walks with a limping gait, straightening his left leg and swinging his right leg through. If he concentrates really hard he can almost walk normally, but why bother? The limp doesn't embarrass him or make him feel self-conscious.

His mobile vibrates in his pocket.

'Have you seen the news?' asks Miranda. 'They're saying Sami Macbeth has a bomb.'

'I know.'

'Should I do something?'

'Nothing you can do.'

'Something must have happened. I talked to him. He was adamant about not going back inside.'

'Sit tight. I'm here now.'

Chinatown is sealed off, wrapped up in police tape and barricaded with concrete blocks that can thwart a vehicle packed with explosives. Police are guarding the perimeter, keeping sightseers and onlookers at bay.

TV crews have set up cameras on top of broadcast vans and telephoto lenses point from the windows of upstairs flats. Reporters are complaining about being kept so far away from the siege. They want access. Footage. Drama.

Ruiz pushes his way through.

'I need to see the boss,' he says to a senior sergeant.

'Who are you?

'Vincent Ruiz. I'm a former DI.'

'You picked a bad time, sir.'

'I got some information.'

The sergeant ducks under the police tape and talks into his shoulder blade, pressing the button on a radio. He nods. Nods again. He motions Ruiz to follow him.

They walk along Shaftesbury Avenue and pass through a second checkpoint. A mobile control room has been parked in Wardour Street. Commander Bob Piper is bent at the waist, studying a TV screen. He straightens, turns, taking a moment to study Ruiz over the top of a coffee cup.

The introductions are short. He's a busy man, under pressure, and he isn't going to invite Ruiz to sit down or offer him a coffee.

'The guy inside is called Sami Macbeth?'

'Tell me something I don't know.'

'He was released on parole three days ago. Now he's looking for his sister.'

'How do you know that?'

'He called me. He wanted my help.'

'You know anything about a bomb?'

Ruiz shakes his head. He tells Piper about the drug den in Whitechapel and Sami's meeting with Tony Murphy. Piper isn't taking notes. He's not interested in what happened yesterday or the day before.

'Where would Macbeth get a bomb?'

'I don't know. Maybe he's bluffing.'

'Tell that to the people on that train.'

'My ex-wife is Macbeth's parole officer. She says he wants to go straight. Maybe he's caught up in something and can't get out.'

'And your ex-wife is a good judge of character, is she?'

He's being sarcastic. Ruiz doesn't bite.

Piper is getting tired of the conversation. 'No offence, Mr Ruiz, but I can't rely on your ex-wife's intuition. I have CCTV footage of this guy running from the scene of a bombing. I have his admissions. I have a call from an Al Qaeda splinter group claiming responsibility. And I have five hostages inside with families and friends and the rest of their lives to live.'

'Let me talk to him.'

'Go home, Mr Ruiz. It's not your concern.'

Ruiz is a civilian now. That's why Piper is calling him 'mister'. He's letting him know that he has no authority any more.

Piper signals a DC. 'Escort this gentleman back to the perimeter.'

251

The phone is ringing. The Commander picks it up. Ruiz can only hear one side of the conversation.

'You can have the van . . . one hostage . . . give me time to clear the roads.'

252

39

Bones McGee is dressed in dark clothes, carrying a black zip-up holdall, which looks as though it might contain his gym gear. Instead it holds a Blaser R93 single shot, straight pull, bolt action rifle, with a ten shot magazine packed with soft nosed 308s.

It's a sniper's rifle with a vibration absorbing aluminium stock and a two-stage trigger. The 600mm barrel is made of thermally distressed, fluted steel. It's black. It's beautiful. It can blow a big fucking hole in things.

Bones has been five times full bore rifle champion in the Met's annual shoot-off. It would have been six times if the organisers hadn't allowed a ring-in from the FBI to enter. He was so full of Beta Blockers he rattled. Said he had a heart condition. Bullshit.

He reaches the police cordon and flips open his badge. Makes a joke. Keeps walking. The Shaftesbury Hotel has been evacuated and the foyer is forlornly empty. He presses the intercom. A security guard answers. 'The place been searched?' asks Bones.

'It's empty. Everybody's cleared out.'

'I'm here to make sure. Open up.'

The guard appears, studies his badge and unlocks the door. Bones asks about rooms overlooking Shaftesbury Avenue.

'You want to see one?'

'I want to use one.'

The guard shows him a floor plan on the computer. 'How's it going out there?' he asks.

'We'll get the guy.'

Bones takes the lift to the fourth floor and follows a corridor, counting down the room numbers. He swipes an entry card and a green light blinks.

Tossing the holdall onto the bed, he stands at the window and gently parts the curtains by an inch. The Winnebago below him must be the control room. Raising his gaze, he has a view down Macclesfield Street to the heart of Chinatown.

The Red Emperor restaurant is bathed in light, which reflects off the gold lettering above the awning. The street outside is empty except for a white van parked in the adjacent lane.

Bones takes a set of binoculars from the bag and puts an ear jack into the shell of his ear so he can hear the police chatter. Scanning the skyline, he can pick out a handful of dark shadows lying prone on the rooftops or crouching behind walls and chimney pots.

The poor bastards must be freezing, lying in the open

254

with one eye glued to the scope and a finger curled inside the trigger guard. It's only going to take a shot over their heads and they'll all hit their triggers.

He unzips the holdall from stem to stern and assembles the rifle, something he can do in the dark or blindfolded. Running his forefinger along the barrel, he dips his head so he can sniff the metal and gun oil. Then he clips the barrel onto a bipod and aims it through the window, which is open a crack.

Tucking the stock against his shoulder, he lowers his cheek to brush against the smooth aluminium. Slowly the front of the restaurant swims into focus in the telescopic sight. He adjusts it, making sure the magnified image is sharp within the cross hairs.

One shot to the head will cut Macbeth's kite string. The soft nose bullet will core a plug out of his head and shut down his brain and nervous system. He'll be dead before he hears the shot, before he hits the ground, before he takes another breath.

Bones opens the mini-bar and chooses a soft drink and a can of macadamias. He sits in an armchair, propping his feet on the windowsill. When he finishes the drink, he puts the cans in a plastic bag tied to his waist. He doesn't want to leave any telltale clues behind, which is why he's wearing latex gloves on his hands and a hairnet beneath his cap. He'll burn his clothes afterwards and bury the boots. The rifle will join the fishes.

He's getting too old for this, but he's worked too hard to surrender it all now. One shot is all he wants. With Macbeth out of the way he can ride the storm of questions. Take early retirement. Buy himself a boat.

40

Sami has to choose a hostage. He could ask for a volunteer but that's shirking his responsibilities. None of the people in the restaurant deserve to be involved but Sami can't change what's happened or turn back the clock.

He goes to the storeroom to check on the driver, who is sitting on rice sacks with his legs stretched out like he's trying to sleep.

'Hold your head still,' says Sami, gripping a corner of the masking tape between his thumb and forefinger and ripping it off suddenly.

The driver curses in pain and gingerly touches his lips as if surveying the damage. His wrists are still bound. Meanwhile, Sami squats on his haunches near the door.

'What are you looking at me like that for?' asks the driver.

Sami smiles apologetically. 'You ever been inside?'

'No.'

'You ever done something you regret?'

'What is this – twenty questions?'

'Something really bad.'

The driver shrugs.

'You got a family?'

'My mum and dad.'

'A girlfriend?'

'You're a weird prick.'

Sami is silent for a moment. 'Those things you said to me earlier, my father used to talk to me like that. Treat me like shit. Maybe he felt threatened. Maybe he was just an arsehole.'

'Listen, pal, I'm sorry if I offended you. Family values didn't make a big splash where I came from either.'

'I'm not a terrorist.'

'Whatever.'

'I want you to understand that.'

'It's understood.'

Sami rises from his haunches and closes the storeroom door. Lucy is waiting for him outside.

'Are you going out there?'

'I can't stay in here. I'm getting sick of Chinese food.'

'They're going to kill you.'

'I'll be fine. I need you to come. They won't shoot me if I have you.'

Lucy searches Sami's eyes. 'I don't want to.'

'I know.'

'My mother and father?'

'They'll be safe. I'm leaving them behind.'

'Promise me.'

'My promises aren't really legal tender any more.'

Her voice hardens. 'Promise me.'

'OK.'

Sami begins by taping Lucy's hands behind her back and strapping bags of flour around her waist.

'This doesn't look much like a bomb,' she says.

'Do you know what a bomb looks like?'

'I've seen them on TV.'

'I'm going to put this hood over your head.'

'Why?'

'It's a pillowcase. It's clean. It came from your bed.'

'You've been in my bedroom?'

'It's the only thing I took.'

'I'm scared. Don't make me do this.'

'You'll be fine. It's going to be over soon.'

'Where are you going to take me?'

'I don't think you'll have to go anywhere.'

Sami tears tape from the spool.

'What are you doing now?' she asks.

'I'm taping the barrel of the gun to your head.'

'Why?'

'So they know I'm serious.'

'Does that mean you'll shoot me?'

'If anyone shoots, it won't be me.'

'But if you do . . .'

'I won't.'

Sami calls the negotiator.

'My watch has stopped Bob. Time's up.'

'I'm working as fast as I can.'

'You're trying to delay me. I'm coming out in ten minutes. And listen to me, Bob. I don't want to see a police car, or a van, or a helicopter, or a bike. And I don't want any of your men-in-black taking me out JFK style with a bullet from the grassy fucking knoll. Any sign of Old Bill and she dies. I've got a bomb strapped to her waist that will cut her in two if you try to take me down.'

'You don't need her.'

'Sure I do.'

'What about the others?'

'I'm leaving the rest behind. And I know what you're thinking, Bob. You think I won't risk blowing myself up because I bottled it the first time. Well let me tell you something for nothing. I don't give a shit any more. I'm not a terrorist. Never have been. To me an intifada sounds like an all-you-can eat Mexican meal. So this has nothing to do with religion or politics. I'm a musician, for fuck's sake. I play guitar. My name is Sami Macbeth and I've had a shitty day.'

'I hear you,' says Bob. 'I know you don't want to hurt anyone. Give it up. Surrender to me.'

'I've still got a shot.'

'You'll never get away.'

'Sure I will. I just opened a fortune cookie. It said I'm going to lead a long and fruitful life.'

41

Ruiz drops back beside the bomb squad truck where blast barricades fan out from the chassis, forming a protective shield around the vehicle. A robot with a mechanical arm is poised at the top of a metal ramp.

Elsewhere Wardour Street is strangely empty. Mesh screens are pulled down over shop windows, which are criss-crossed with blast tape. It's like a scene from *Day of the Triffids* or one of those end-of-the-world films where Will Smith or Clive Owen get to be heroes.

The Red Emperor is less than a hundred yards south, partly obscured by the red, gold and black painted gates of Chinatown.

A police radio hacks out static as if clearing its throat. Bob Piper is instructing all units to be in position.

'Target Alpha is coming out. He's taking a hostage.'

The restaurant door opens a crack. A small figure with a pillowcase covering her head and shoulders comes first. Her hands are bound behind her back and her feet are

261

hobbled like a geisha in training. She stumbles down the lone step.

Macbeth is behind her, dressed in a blue boiler suit and a ski mask. He's a foot taller and has to crouch to shield his body behind her. The barrel of a gun is pressed to the back of her head.

Bob Piper is watching the same scene on a closed circuit TV with adrenalin singing in his veins. Macbeth has stepped onto the pavement. His hostage is probably the daughter, Lucy, the smallest and easiest to handle.

Piper hears a voice in his earpiece.

'Sierra one – I have visual contact. A head shot . . .'

'Does the hostage have anything around her waist?'

'Affirmative.'

Piper studies the screen. Macbeth's right hand is holding the gun, but his left is behind Lucy. He could be holding her belt or a pressure trigger.

'Sierra two – I have visual contact. I can take down target.'

'Is Macbeth holding anything in his left hand?'

'It's behind the hostage, sir.'

They're nearing the van. Edging sideways. Macbeth is jumpy. Nervous. Every time he jerks his right arm, Lucy's head moves. The barrel of the gun must be taped to her head. He's making sure he doesn't miss.

Macbeth will likely want Lucy to drive. He'll have to undo her hands and feet and take off her hood. He also has to open the van door, which will mean taking one hand off the gun or the detonator. That's the moment.

'Sierra units: look for the target's left hand. If he takes it away from the hostage, neutralise him with all necessary force.'

They have reached the van. Macbeth stops suddenly and seems to be shaking his head. He drops to his knees dragging Lucy with him because the gun is taped to her head. Kneeling on the pavement, he begins yanking his right arm, jerking Lucy's head from side to side like she's a ventriloquist's dummy.

It could be an epileptic fit or some sort of seizure. Maybe he's trying to surrender.

Piper is out of his chair. He leaps from the steps of the Winnebago, landing on heavy boots, and charges towards the restaurant.

'Hold fire. Hold fire,' he bellows, almost crushing a two-way radio in his fist.

Macbeth is still on his knees. Lucy is trying to pull herself free.

'It's over, Sami,' yells Piper. 'Let her go and put your hands in the air.'

Macbeth shakes his head and tries to regain his feet. He's a stubborn bastard.

Pffft! Pffft! Two rounds zoom over Piper's head and there is a hollow *throp* like a watermelon being dropped from a window. Blood sprays across the side of the van and the top of Macbeth's head seems smaller. Half the ski mask has disappeared. He topples sideways, taking Lucy with him. Her body lands across his chest and her legs kick helplessly at the air.

Piper stops dead, holding his breath. Nothing happens. There is no explosion.

'Move! Move! Move!' he yells into the radio. SWAT teams sprint past him, bursting through the doors of the restaurant.

Piper lurches forward towards Lucy. She's hysterical, twisting and squirming on the ground, trying to get away. He tells her to stay calm, worried about the gun, which is still taped to her neck. The barrel is encased in masking tape, which is wrapped around Macbeth's fist. Why would he tape his hand to the gun?

Piper pulls the pillowcase from Lucy's head. Her eyes are wide. She's terrified. The tape is looped around her neck and across her mouth.

'You're safe. It's over. Try not to move.'

A pair of scissors is found. He reaches under the corner of the tape, carefully snipping it away. 'Just lie still until the paramedics take a look at you.'

Lucy isn't listening. She fights to get up. Her clothes are covered in blood and brain and a dark stain has leaked along a crack in the pavement and soaked the knees of her jeans.

'My parents,' she blurts out.

Piper looks up. The hostages are being shepherded out of the restaurant. Lucy's mother and father are clutching each other. Piper lifts Lucy easily and she runs to her parents, hugging them. They huddle together on the footpath with their heads bowed.

A sense of relief floods through Piper. He told his men to hold fire. He told them not to take the shot, but things have worked out OK. Minimal damage, minimal disruption, minimal loss of life; he might even get a commendation.

A voice interrupts this thought.

'You shot the wrong guy.'

Vincent Ruiz is looking down at the body.

'We got the bastard holding the gun.'

'He's not holding a gun.'

Piper follows his gaze. He wants to tell him it's bullshit but a buzz-saw blade of uncertainly is already spinning in his chest. Reaching out he begins to unravel the blood-soaked tape, fighting the dead weight of Macbeth's arms. He peels off the tape, loop by loop, until it lies curled at his feet like the shed skin of a snake.

Even before he finishes, he knows the truth. It's not a sawn off shotgun or a semi-automatic. It's a sealant gun used for fixing leaks around windows and shower screens.

Ignoring the brain matter, Piper peels the ski mask over the dead man's chin and taped mouth.

Why would he tape his own mouth shut?

He uncovers the nostrils and the remaining eye, which is locked open in a vacuous star as though some terrible revelation had been whispered into the dead man's ear just as a bullet tore through his brain.

A voice shouts from the door of the restaurant. 'Hey, boss, we got four hostages inside. Where's the other one?'

Piper rocks back on his heels, unable to focus, staring at the blood on his hands. Right now it feels as though someone has pulled a pin and dropped a grenade down his throat. The loud dull thud is his heart exploding.

42

Perched on the crest of the rooftop, holding onto a chimneypot, Sami Macbeth watches the scene below with a weird sense that he's having an out of body experience except it's not his body lying on the pavement.

The bastards shot me, he thinks. I was on my knees, trying to surrender and they blew my head off.

To be more precise they blew the van driver's head off, but they thought he was Sami so it's almost the same as being shot except Sami isn't the one who's dead.

And even if the van driver was a complete wanker, which he was, he didn't deserve to take one in the canister and have his brains decorating the pavement.

Up until this point, Sami's plan had been perfect. To begin with he made the jump, which was never a certainty. He had climbed out of Lucy's window and scaled the drainpipe onto a narrow bitumen terrace three storeys above Horse and Dolphin Yard. Below him lay a yawning gap. He told himself it was only fourteen feet, but it looked further. It always does when you're three storeys above the ground.

Sami waited until he heard the yelling, when he knew everyone's attention was focused on the front door of the restaurant. Then he took a deep breath, made a sign of the cross, and hurled his body across the gap, his arms wheeling like propellers.

For an age he thought he was going to make it easily because he seemed to be going up, instead of down. And then he realised he might not make it at all. He was falling short.

He reached out as he crashed into the wall, hooking his right arm around the bracket of a satellite dish. His hip and shoulder crashed into the bricks and air punched from his lungs. Somehow he managed to cling on through the pain until his head cleared and his chest filled. He scrambled up onto the tiled roof, avoiding the flimsy gutter.

That's when Sami looked back and saw the van driver lying on the pavement. A black stain leaked from beneath his head and his right arm seemed to be reaching out, pointing to a real target, the one the rozzers *should* have shot.

Dragging his eyes away, Sami tries to think straight. They're going to blame him for this as well. Another death. Add it to the list.

Forcing himself to move, he heads across the rooftops, keeping to the shadows and trying to avoid creating silhouettes against the sky. He walks on the brickwork and steps around the skylights so he doesn't drop in on some spotty Herbert and his missus.

A chopper suddenly sweeps overhead. Sami dives onto his stomach behind a trio of chimney pots. A searchlight turns the rooftop into a brightly lit stage. The chopper seems to hover for a moment and then swings away.

Sami keeps moving. Not looking back. He crosses another half dozen roofs and comes to the next corner, where he shimmies down a drainpipe, hand over hand, jumping the final six feet. The semi-automatic is tucked into the waistband of his jeans, nestled against his back. He heads towards Charing Cross Road and into Long Acre, looking for a park. Parks have trees and shrubs. Parks have hiding places. Parks are good news.

That's when he remembers Kate Tierney. Blonde. Sexy. Darling Kate. Why sleep in a park when he could stay at the Savoy?

43

Bones disassembles his rifle and packs it away, wrapping each component into squares of cloth. He vacuums the carpet with a mini-vac, wipes surfaces clean and washes gun residue from his hands. Satisfied, he takes the lift downstairs and finds the security guard at a console with a dozen TV screens showing footage from cameras inside and outside the hotel.

'I heard shooting,' says the guard.

'We got him.'

'Good for you.'

'I'm going to need your security footage.'

'Which cameras?'

'All of them.'

Bones takes the DVDs from the machines and slides them into the holdall.

'Will I get those back?' asks the guard.

'In due course.'

He swings the bag over his shoulder and waits for the front door to unlock. Outside, he turns right and follows

Shaftesbury Avenue towards Piccadilly Circus. The police cordon is stopping people getting in, not out of the area.

As he passes the Trocadero, he doesn't notice a short, thick-necked man with a shaved head, who is standing in a doorway, watching the police cars pass. Sinbad has both hands cupped around the phone, which looks like a child's toy against his ear.

'Mission accomplished,' Sinbad whispers, 'the kid's no longer a problem.'

Tony Murphy sounds relieved. 'How did you do it?'

'Not me. I couldn't get within a mile of the joint. Must have been the rozzers.'

'Chalk one up for Old Bill.'

'One of 'em must of learned to shoot straight.'

Bones takes a bus from Piccadilly as far as Hyde Park Corner and then walks north to Marble Arch. Then he hails a cab along the Edgware Road as far as Maida Vale and drops the barrel of the rifle into the Grand Union Canal. Other pieces will be disposed of separately, bagged, buried or melted down.

A shame, but you can't be too careful in this day and age. Guns tell stories.

hands cupped around the phone, which looks like a
and the

44

The fire door opens. Kate grabs Sami's jacket and
throws him against the wall, pressing her body against
his like she's trying to flatten her curves. Her tongue
traces across his lips.

She pulls back, holds him at arm's length. 'They're
saying you're dead . . . on the news . . . you were shot.'

'Someone else.'

'What about the bomb?'

'I never had a bomb. It's a misunderstanding.'

'So you're not a terrorist.'

'No.'

'And you're not hurt?'

'No.'

She slaps him hard across the face. 'That's for scaring
the crap out of me.'

Sami holds his cheek. Kate tugs down her blouse
which has ridden up and straightens her skirt. 'You can't
stay here. I think you're sweet, Sami, but I need this job
and I could get into a lot of trouble if someone finds you.'

'Put me in a broom cupboard, a storeroom. I won't tell anyone.'

'You don't understand.'

Sami begs. 'The police are looking for me. I have to find Nadia.'

'How did this happen?'

'It's a long story. Nadia's in trouble.'

Kate reaches out and touches Sami's cheek. 'She's not the one in trouble.'

Sami kisses her fingers.

'If you weren't so adorable . . .' Kate doesn't finish the statement. Instead, she takes him upstairs in her service lift; checks the passageway; opens a suite, closes the curtains.

'I'll register you as a guest on the computer. Housekeeping won't clean the room until midday. Don't answer the door if anyone knocks. Don't touch the phone. I'll try to come back later, but it might be difficult. I'm working a double shift. Please be careful. I'm trusting you.'

Kate kisses him on the lips; wrinkles her nose at his smell. She gently closes the door behind her.

Sami doesn't take a shower. He doesn't have the energy. Instead he collapses on the bed and listens to his heart pounding. How many people died today? They're going to blame him.

He has to sleep. Sleep is good. Sleep will stop him turning paranoid. Right now his head is his own worst enemy. This isn't about thinking straight; it's about thinking around corners.

45

A dozen firearms officers are assembled at Scotland Yard, still wearing dark overalls and bootblack on their faces. Rifles and ammunition are lined up on a table like they're preparing to invade a small African country.

Commander Bob Piper paces back and forth, trying to stop himself from exploding in anger. He wants an explanation. He wants to know which one of these men disobeyed his direct orders and pulled the trigger.

The officers look at each other, waiting for someone else to own up. Nobody does.

Piper's blood pressure is topping out. 'What is this, primary school? I want the officer who discharged his firearm to step forward and explain his actions.'

Still nobody moves.

Piper picks up the nearest rifle, unclips the magazine and begins counting the shells. Slamming it down on the table, he picks up the next one.

'You think I'm some shit-for-brains moron who earned this rank by sniffing arse-cracks? That man you shot today was a decent hard-working delivery driver from Essex who lived with his mother and father and had a dog called Bitzy. I told you to hold fire. Is there anyone in this room who did not hear my command?'

He looks from face to face.

'Are you smiling at me, son?'

'No, sir.'

'You look like you're smiling.'

'I'm nervous, sir.'

'Well, I'll give you something to be nervous about. Do you know what happens when police shoot innocent people? There are inquiries, internal ones and public ones and political ones. Police officers get suspended, careers get ruined, bosses get blamed and newspaper columnists have a field day calling us Keystone Cops who can't be trusted to carry firearms.'

Piper is breathing hard through his nostrils. The last of the weapons has been checked. He turns to his second in charge.

'Have any of these weapons been switched or tampered with?'

'No, sir, they were collected at the scene.'

For a fleeting moment he feels a sense of relief but just as quickly his eyes frame a question. If none of his firearms officers discharged their weapons, who shot the van driver?

Piper looks at his watch. It has just gone 2.00 a.m. The Commissioner wants a report on his desk by seven. What is Piper going to tell him? A security operation that cost a million pounds and shut down the West End for eight hours has resulted in a missing terrorist (who may or may not have a bomb) and a murdered hostage shot by some person or persons unknown.

Then there's the other problem. Radio stations are reporting that the terror suspect was shot dead by police. Sooner or later they're going to discover it was a hostage. If Piper denies police involvement in the shooting they'll call it a cover up and put a blowtorch to his balls. The truth is equally uncomfortable. In the middle of a massive security operation involving a hundred of Scotland Yard's finest, a sniper infiltrated a police cordon and shot a suspected terrorist who turned out to be a delivery driver who stopped off at the restaurant for lunch.

Oh, yeah, they'll just love that.

It's going to be a long day.

46

Sami opens the curtains and examines the morning. The sun is shining, joggers are jogging and the Thames is flowing, sluggish and brown. He watches a lone rower skim across the surface like a water beetle, sliding beneath a bridge. How can a day look so normal?

First he showers and shaves. Then he turns on the TV and watches a media conference at Scotland Yard. A senior policeman is answering questions. The voice is unmistakeable. It's the negotiator.

Bob doesn't sound so confident any more. His eyes are bloodshot and the collar of his shirt is bent upwards at one side. Reaching for a glass of water, he doesn't get a chance to drink. The questions are coming too quickly, shouted by reporters who are up, out of their seats, refusing to sit down.

'I want to reiterate that police firearms officers did not discharge their weapons. A homicide investigation has been launched and we are confident . . .'

'How did a gunman get through the cordon?'

'We're not sure at this—'

'How did he get away?'

'We'll know more when—'

'So the terrorist and the gunman both escaped? Could they be the same person?'

Bob doesn't understand the question.

'Could Macbeth have shot the hostage?'

'Nothing has been ruled out.'

'How did he escape?'

Bob rubs his mouth with the flat of his hand. The microphones pick up the sandpaper-like scratching of his unshaven chin. 'We believe he may have had help of some sort.'

'Are you saying he may have had an accomplice?'

'We haven't ruled it out. We are interested in knowing why Macbeth chose this particular restaurant. Was it planned? Had he arranged to meet someone?'

'Could the victim have been his accomplice?'

Bob blinks at the cameras.

'I couldn't possibly comment at this stage.'

Oh, that's clever, thinks Sami. Shoot the wrong guy and then deflect the blame. Drop an inference, a vague suggestion: we didn't get the right geezer but we got a bad 'un anyway.

Bob is trying to ward off more questions. 'I want you to understand that we're dealing with a very clever, well-trained terrorist operative, perhaps the most dangerous criminal I've come across in twenty years of service. He is utterly ruthless and hell-bent on causing maximum destruction and loss of life.'

A reporter interrupts the speech.

'One of the hostages, Lucy Ho Fook, says she doesn't think he's a terrorist and that he didn't have a bomb.'

Bob's composure is shaken. He stares at the reporter, his mouth locked in a fixed grimace. An aide steps close and whispers in his ear. Bob's mouth moves again.

'Stockholm Syndrome – it's a well-documented phenomenon.'

Sami stares at the TV screen, not knowing whether to laugh or cry. Any moment now they're going to blame him for global warming and Diana's death in the tunnel.

He turns off the TV and stares at the blank screen. Bob said the police didn't shoot the van driver. Surely he must have been lying – covering his arse.

Sami takes out the Beretta and lays it on the bed. It's a monster, a hand cannon, oiled and gleaming. He flicks a switch, the magazine drops into his hands. Eighteen plump bullets fill the clip. Two are missing.

Sami can understand how a person might appreciate the engineering of a weapon like this, but guns aren't something you get sentimental about. Yet this one means something to Murphy. It's the only thing he cared about when Sami called him – not Dessie or the explosion on the Tube, just the gun. He wanted it destroyed.

Sami repacks the magazine and turns the shooter in his hands, looking for a serial number. There isn't one. It's

279

been filed off. The semi-automatic must have a history. Maybe it was used in another crime – something Ray Garza or Tony Murphy don't want known.

Murphy wanted the gun destroyed, which means that Sami has leverage. He turns on Lucy's mobile and makes a call.

'Who's this?'

'Sami Macbeth.'

There is a long pause. Sami wonders if this is what they mean by a pregnant pause: pregnant with possibilities, pregnant with import, fucked-up pregnant?

Tony Murphy finally answers. 'You're supposed to be dead, son, said so on the news.'

'Not me. I'm bullet-proof and bombproof.'

'That you are.'

'You sound disappointed to hear from me.'

'Not at all, son, I'm pleased as punch. It's not every day I get to talk to someone who's dead. My ex-wife comes close. If you don't mind me asking, how did you get out of that restaurant?'

'I took a rooftop stroll.'

'Very impressive.'

'Like you said, Mr Murphy, I have a talent. How's Nadia?'

'She's a bit under the weather today.'

'You better be looking after her.'

'She'll be right as rain when I tell her the good news.'

'I have the package you wanted.'

280

'A package?'

'We had a deal.'

'I don't make deals with wanted terrorists.'

'Right then, I'll be off. I'll offer the semi-automatic to the cops instead. Tell them the whole story.'

'I'll give Ray Garza the good news.'

Sami's heart flip flops in his chest. 'What's Garza got to do with it?'

'Everything, you cocky little gobshite,' says Murphy, spitting down the phone. 'You think you know the whole story. You don't know a fucking thing. You're wasting your time trying to threaten me, son. Nobody died and made you king of the castle.'

'I just want my sister. I'll swap her for the gun.'

'What makes you think I want it back?'

'You don't. You want it destroyed.'

Murphy doesn't answer. Sami's hunch was right.

'I'll be in touch, Mr Murphy.'

He hangs up. His hands are shaking.

He hears an entry card being skimmed. The door opens. Sami slides the semi-automatic under the pillow and pretends to be asleep. Kate Tierney tiptoes around the bed and wakes him with a kiss.

She notices the gun peeking out from under the pillow.

'Can I hold it? Please. I've never held a gun.'

'It isn't a toy.'

'I know.'

Sami lets her.

'Where is the safety catch?'

'There.'

She flicks the switch; points the gun at his head. 'I could call the police right now and have you arrested. I'd sell my story to the *News of the World* for fifty grand: "My night with the Tube bomber".'

'I didn't bomb the Tube.'

'They're not going to care. I'll say you had your evil way with me at gunpoint, six times.'

'Nobody's going to believe that.'

'Four times then.'

Sami reaches out to retrieve the gun. Kate knocks his hand away.

'You think I'm joking? I'm serious.'

For a fleeting moment the mad light in her eyes almost convinces him. Then she laughs and points the barrel of the Beretta at the knot on his bathrobe.

'I'll drop mine if you drop yours. I'm horny.'

47

Monday morning. Ruiz walks along a metal landing with prison cells along one side and a two-storey drop on the other. Every thirty yards a warder unlocks a heavy metal gate. Ruiz steps through, continues walking. Hand mirrors extend from hatches as he passes; disembodied eyes, watching him.

He climbs another set of metal stairs. Nets are strung between the railings to discourage heavy objects such as bodies being thrown from above.

This is the isolation wing where the sex offenders, ponces, prison snitches and the incorrigibly violent are separated from the general prison population.

The interview room has bare walls, three folding chairs and a scarred wooden table bolted to the floor. One of the chairs is already taken. Derek Raynor looks like an Irish navvy with a crop of ginger hair and a long beard reaching down his chest. His top lip is shaved, which makes the beard look like a ginger hammock slung between his ears.

'I'd like to be alone with him,' says Ruiz. 'You can take off the cuffs.'

The older guard shrugs and unshackles the prisoner.

Raynor has made violence his vocation. Banged up at sixteen on a burglary conviction, he was sent to juvenile detention where he attacked a youth-worker, crushing his thorax and cracking open his skull. It was the first of three murders committed in prison. Now he's never getting out.

'Hello, Derek.'

'My name is Abdul Mohammad.'

'Is that right? How is Allah these days? He's getting a higher profile.'

'Are you mocking the Prophet, Mr Ruiz?'

'Me? No. I've seen what happens to people who mock the Prophet. Writers. Cartoonists. Women. Allah isn't famous for his sense of humour.'

Ruiz pulls up a chair opposite, rests his elbows on the table. He fixes Raynor with an ambivalent stare.

'Tell me something, Derek. Does Allah think a murdering scumbag like you turning religious is taking the piss?'

Raynor doesn't respond immediately. Behind the reinforced glass, Ruiz can see the screws at a table. One of them is doing a crossword, while the other is drinking coffee.

'I wasn't a violent man when I entered prison,' says Raynor, his eyes flat and dry. 'The system took a troubled teenage boy and turned him into a monster. Allah has forgiven me and he's taught me to forgive.'

'Who have you forgiven?'

'All those who have wronged me.'

'The youth worker you killed had a widow. I'll be sure to tell her that you've forgiven her husband.'

Raynor stares hard at Ruiz. Small dark flecks are floating in his irises like dead flies caught in amber.

Ruiz changes the subject. 'Ever had anything to do with a con called Sami Macbeth?'

Raynor shakes his head.

'You don't remember him coming to any prayer meetings or asking about joining the Brotherhood?'

'The truth grows in men's souls. I can't see inside all of them.'

'Is that so? Tell me, Derek, how far would you go for the faith? Would you blow up a train?'

Raynor smiles benignly. 'I'd tear down the world so God could rebuild it again in six days.'

'I thought that was the Bible.'

'Read the Koran sometime.'

Ruiz leans across the table, keeping his palms flat on the scarred wood. 'I don't have a problem with you finding God, Derek, and I don't even have an issue with you playing the downtrodden religious martyr, I just want to know if Macbeth mixed with the brothers while he was inside.'

'Not that I can remember. What's he done?'

'The police say he's an Islamic terrorist.'

Raynor smiles to himself. 'Like I said, I can't look into a man's soul.'

The assistant governor turns sideways on a swivel chair, blinking at Ruiz from behind rimless glasses that seem to make his eyes float an inch from his face.

On the windowsill behind him there are dozens of small origami birds, flowers and animals, a white menagerie seemingly frozen in a blizzard.

Ruiz takes a seat. The assistant governor is folding a piece of paper into some sort of antelope, hardly bothering to look at his fingers.

'You released a parolee on Thursday. Sami Macbeth. Name mean anything?'

'Not since yesterday when I turned on the box.'

'They say he's a terrorist.'

'Human beings do bad things sometimes.'

'You normally keep track on the Islamists?'

'Where possible.'

'Did Macbeth ever attend a meeting or ask for a copy of the Koran or a prayer mat?'

'Nope.'

'Didn't mingle with the Brotherhood?'

'Kept pretty much to himself.'

'He ever kick off about anything?'

'Nope.'

'He get hassled by any of the prison sisters?'

286

'Didn't complain.'

So we got a fresh fish, mid-twenties, good-looking and nobody touches him in nearly three years. All of which means he either had a benefactor or a reputation that kept him safe.

'What did you hear about the Hampstead jewellery job?'

'I heard Macbeth did it.'

'He only got done for possession.'

'Everyone knew he did it.'

'Why?'

'He played up to it.'

That's not an argument, thinks Ruiz, as he pops a boiled sweet into his mouth. He offers one to the assistant governor, who shakes his head and pats his waistline.

The lolly rattles against Ruiz's teeth. 'Did Macbeth have any regular visitors?'

'His sister.'

'Anybody else?'

The assistant governor swings in his chair; opens a filing cabinet; licks his thumb; pulls out a file. The cover sheet is a history. The second sheet is a log.

'Nobody visited him more than twice.'

'What about letters?'

He raises an eyebrow. 'We're on dangerous ground here, Mr Ruiz. Normally I'd want to see a warrant.'

'Or we could save time and I could look over your shoulder.'

The assistant governor blinks his magnified eyes and rolls back on his chair.

'Have you seen the view from this side of the desk?'

48

The morning papers are tucked under Sami's door. His face is on every front page.

TUBE BOMBER SLAIN, declares the *Sun* while *The Times* gives him the benefit of the doubt and calls him a 'Terror Suspect'.

Being reported dead is an odd feeling. It's like imagining your own funeral and trying to picture those who might turn up. Sami's friends and old workmates have been contacted by reporters. Nothing positive emerges from the quotes, most of which seem to suggest that Sami's fall from grace was always on the cards.

Kate zips up her skirt. 'You can't stay. They're going to be cleaning the rooms.'

Sami knows she's right, but the streets will be crawling with police and they're all looking for him.

'You need a disguise,' says Kate.

'Like what?'

'Leave it to me.'

She disappears for ten minutes and comes back with

a set of scissors and a bottle of hair dye. Sami sits on a chair in the bathroom while Kate trims his hair, giving him a fringe. Then he leans over the sink and she applies the hair dye.

Kate talks a lot when she's nervous. It's a constant, stream of thought monologue about her job and her family and how she wants to tell her friends about Sami, but she can't because nobody can know and they probably wouldn't believe her anyway.

This whole fugitive business seems to excite her as though she imagines herself to be Bonnie to Sami's Clyde or she's Patricia Arquette and he's Christian Slater in *True Romance*.

'What do you think?'

Sami looks in the mirror. 'I look like the sixth Beatle.'

'I think black hair suits you. Now you need some new clothes.'

She takes him to a storeroom on the floor below. His hair is damp and leaving dark stains on the towel around his neck.

She unlocks the door. There are clothes racks, boxes and suitcases. Kate pulls a charcoal grey pinstriped suit from a hanger. 'These are clothes that guests have left behind,' she explains, as she finds Sami a business shirt and holds up half a dozen ties until she's satisfied.

'You can't carry that rucksack around.'

She moves boxes and pulls an attaché case from the back of the storeroom, blowing dust off the handle.

'The ensemble is complete.'

'I look like a prat.'

'You look kinda cute.'

'If you're into stockbrokers.'

'Only if they're naughty.'

It's almost midday. Sami dumps his old clothes in the rubbish-chute while Kate checks him out of the room. He ponders what to do with the semi-automatic, the drugs and the money. He doesn't want to get caught with them.

Looking around the room he spies the air-conditioning vent. Everyone always hides shit in the air-conditioning vent, he thinks, but maybe there's a reason for that. He pulls off the panel and pushes the bags of cocaine, the money and the gun inside, before replacing the panel again.

Kate knocks on the door.

'Are you ready?'

'I guess so.'

She presses a piece of paper into his hand. It's her address in Barnes. 'Don't answer the phone. Don't read my emails. Don't look at the mess.'

'When will you be home?'

'Soon.'

She kisses him on the lips. The kiss might not mean much in itself, but when she touches his cheek with her fingertip it's as though she doesn't want to let him go. Sami feels his heart turn to porridge.

The lift carries him down and the doors open. Sami walks across the hotel foyer, trying to look like he's a businessman on his way to an important meeting in the city.

'Can I get you a cab, sir?'

Sami nods.

The doorman whistles.

A black cab pulls up.

Sami slips the doorman a fiver and slides into the back seat. He used to think that suits were like straitjackets but this one feels good, expensive, well-cut. Maybe clothes do maketh the man.

49

Vincent Ruiz steps outside the inner door of Wormwood Scrubs and discovers the weather has turned. Dark clouds are tumbling across the sky and rain threatens.

He glances at the name and address in his battered notebook:

Kate Tierney
58 Brook Gardens
Barnes

It's a long shot but Sami Macbeth doesn't have many friends left. Right now he's probably gone to ground but he can't stay hidden forever. He's going to need help.

Ruiz ponders what happened last night. A hundred coppers were outside the restaurant, two helicopters hovered above it and a small army of reporters were camped less than a block away. Police searched every cupboard, every corner, every crawlspace, yet somehow Macbeth managed to slip away. He wasn't in the restaurant. He wasn't in the building. He wasn't on the rooftop. The kid is fucking Houdini.

Bob Piper is claiming police didn't shoot the van driver, which is too outrageous a declaration to be a lie. Which means someone else wanted Macbeth dead and wanted it badly enough to risk taking a shot over the heads of a dozen firearms officers.

This has nothing to do with terrorism. The notion is ridiculous. Macbeth was an unlikely jewel thief and an even less likely extremist.

Reaching his car, Ruiz slides behind the wheel and calls Fiona Taylor.

'Can you talk?'

'I have a meeting in five minutes.' She sounds amused. 'Your name came up in the morning briefing.'

'How so?'

'Bob Piper wants you investigated.'

'What did I do?'

'He says you've been in contact with Sami Macbeth.'

'The kid called me once. He's looking for his sister.'

'So you said. You might be getting a visit.'

'Thanks for the heads-up. Listen, I'm interested in the bombing at the Old Bailey. What was the target?'

'They blew up the evidence room.'

'Anything taken?'

'Eight kilos of cocaine. Cash. A semi-automatic pistol.'

'How much cash?'

'Just shy of fifty thousand pounds.'

Ruiz considers the haul. It's not big enough to warrant the risk.

'Islamic terrorists don't normally steal drugs.'

'We got a call from an Al Qaeda splinter group claiming responsibility.'

'How many other groups claimed it?'

'Six at last count.'

That's the thing about would-be bombers and terror groups: hoax callers outnumber genuine ones and without a code word there's no way of confirming their claims.

Ruiz asks about the shooter.

Fiona Taylor reads off the manifest: 'A Beretta 93R machine pistol with a twenty round magazine and eighteen bullets in the clip.'

'What was it doing in the strong room?'

'It's evidence in an attempted murder case. The perp fired a shot at police.'

'Ray Garza's kid.'

'How did you know?'

'Lucky guess.'

Ruiz is trying to get his head around the coincidences. Ray Jnr turned up at Murphy's garden party. The two must know each other. Maybe Ray Garza organised the robbery to get the boy off, although it's not Garza's style. He'd rather blackmail a judge or bribe a jury than rely on something as clumsy and outdated as blowing up a strong room.

'What did ballistics say about the shooter?'

'They haven't tested it. Some sort of paperwork problem. It should have gone straight to the lab.'

'What about the slug or a shell casing?'

'Unrecovered.'

Ruiz ponders this. 'Without the cocaine and the shooter what happens to the case against Ray Jnr?'

Fiona Taylor catches the inference in his question. 'I hope you're not suggesting that Ray Garza is behind this . . .'

'I'm just trying to make sense of it,' he replies unconvincingly. 'Were there any witnesses?'

'Dozens of them, but most of them were Garza's mates. Things turned ugly when the police tried to arrest him. The officers had to call for back-up. They couldn't secure the crime scene.'

Fiona has to go. 'Hey, one more thing, but you didn't hear it from me: we just ID'd the dead guy on the Tube. His name was Dessie Fraser, a long time associate of Tony Murphy. You know him?'

'By reputation,' says Ruiz. 'He liked writing his signature with a baseball bat.'

'According to Murphy they had a falling out a few weeks back and Dessie went to work for someone else.'

'Did he say who?'

'Ray Garza.'

50

Sami bounces on Kate's bed, checking out her mattress. It's a nice place, a bit too girly and her flat-screen TV is on the small side but at least she hasn't got stuffed toys on her bed.

Half of Kate's clothes are strewn over the dresser and an armchair while make-up and cosmetics fill every inch of the bathroom shelf and the edges of the sink. How many types of moisturiser does a woman need?

Sami looks in the kitchen. You can tell a lot about a girl from the contents of her fridge. Is she a manic dieter, a binge eater, a gourmet cook or a take-out junkie? Kate's fridge has bread, milk, an avocado, a bar of dark chocolate and half a dozen jars of Indian chutneys and pickles. Her freezer has a bottle of vodka and a packet of frozen yoghurt Popsicles. Sami could fall for a girl like this.

He makes himself a coffee and puts his feet up. Ponders how long he should let Murphy stew before calling him again. He also tries to get his head around the shooting.

What if Bob was telling the truth and the police didn't shoot the van driver? Someone else must have been there; someone who wanted Sami dead.

Tony Murphy has the wherewithal to hire a dozen hitmen – he probably has them on speed dial – but it takes more balls than a bingo caller to carry out a hit during a police siege.

The buzzer sounds. Someone is at the door downstairs. Sami presses the intercom.

'Hello?'

Nobody answers. He asks again.

A male voice replies. 'You got a package.'

'Who's it for?'

'Kate Tierney.'

'What is it?'

'Listen, mate, I just deliver 'em, I don't look inside 'em.'

'Just leave it on the steps.'

'Can't do that, someone's gotta sign.'

'Hold on.'

Sami walks to the window of the lounge and opens the curtains. He can't see a delivery van. Smells like fish.

He goes to the window in the kitchen, which overlooks the rear garden. The ground floor has an extension – a flat roof about ten feet below the window. He could lower himself down and then jump onto the grass.

A part of him thinks he's being paranoid. Another part of him says to trust nobody.

Sami returns to the intercom. 'Give me a minute, I got to get a shirt on.'

He goes back to the kitchen window. Slides it upwards. Climbs over the sink and sits on the ledge. Spinning round, he lowers himself down until hanging by his fingertips. He drops the final four feet and crosses the flat roof at a run before leaping onto the lawn.

There's a Wendy house at the back fence, closed up for the winter. A paddling pool has been stuffed inside. That's when Sami realises he isn't alone in the yard. He tries to turn but someone crash-tackles him low and a second man goes high, forcing his face into the turf. His hands are pulled behind his back and bound together with a plastic cable-tie. Tape covers his mouth. A hood slips over his head.

Sami is dragged to his knees. His head is wrenched back.

'Can you hear me, Mr Macbeth?'

Sami nods.

'Stay calm and you won't get hurt. Someone important wants a word with you.'

Sami mumbles into the gag and then shouts as he feels his sleeve forced up and a needle slide into his arm. His mind swims and he swallows the darkness.

51

Ruiz stands outside the address in Barnes, listening to a South West train rattle towards Clapham Junction. The main door is open. He climbs the stairs.

Kate Tierney's flat is on the first floor. One of the timber panels on the door has been kicked out and lies splintered on the floor. The door is open. He steps inside.

Kate Tierney is sitting on a low table at the centre of the lounge, amid the broken pieces of her life. A TV without a screen, a glass coffee table without glass, radiators ripped from walls, wallpaper in ragged strips, carpet and underlay peeled back, a mantelpiece torn from the fireplace, a sofa disembowelled . . .

Water is spilling from the bathroom where the cistern has been torn from a porcelain plinth and dumped in the bathtub. Tiles are smashed. Shards of broken crockery and glass are scattered on the floor.

Kate looks up at Ruiz. Her cheekbones are shining. She's dressed in a black skirt, dark tights and a loose white blouse. Honey-coloured hair is plaited in a French braid down her back.

'Have you called the police?' he asks.

'No.'

'Did they hurt you?'

She shakes her head. Her eyes swim with the knowledge that her life contains elements of loss and betrayal.

'Where's Sami?'

'He's not here. I just got home.'

Ruiz punches a number on his mobile. Calls it in.

'Who are you?' she asks.

'I'm a friend of Sami's.'

Kate blows her nose. Wipes it once, twice, three times. Bunches the soggy tissue in her fist.

'Will they send me to prison for helping him? I know I should have called the police.'

'If I were you, I'd leave Sami out of this. You were robbed. Keep it simple.'

She nods.

'Do you know who did this?'

She shakes her head. 'It wasn't Sami.'

'I know.'

'When did you last see him?'

'This morning.'

'He spent last night with you?'

She lowers her eyes to the Oriental rug, which has been sliced open. 'Don't tell my work. I'll lose my job.'

Water is leaking slowly across the floor. Ruiz finds the stopcock in the bathroom and turns it off.

'Did anyone else know Sami was here?'

Kate shakes her head.

'You didn't tell anyone – a girlfriend or a friend?'

'No.'

Kate takes a cigarette from a packet lying on the floor beside a broken drawer with no base. Her hand is shaking as she tries to flick the flywheel on the lighter. Ruiz does it for her. She holds the cigarette in her clenched fingers, making no attempt to smoke it. Water has reached her shoes.

Ruiz takes it from her. Sits close.

'Listen, Kate, I think you realise how much trouble Sami is in. People are looking for him – not just the police. People who want to hurt him. Did Sami tell you anything?'

'Someone has his sister. Sami is trying to get her back.'

'Did he mention any names?'

'He called someone this morning. I can't remember his name.'

'Was it Tony Murphy?'

'That's him. Sami wanted to arrange a meeting.'

'Why?'

'I don't know.'

Ruiz glances around the flat. 'Does Sami have something Murphy might want?'

'He had a gun.'

'What sort of gun?'

'A black one.'

It must be the Beretta from the Old Bailey strongroom, Ray Jnr's gun.

A police car has pulled up outside. Ruiz gives Kate his card.

'If Sami calls I want you to give him this number. I can't promise him anything, but if he tells me why he's doing this, maybe I can help.'

She takes the card in her hand, presses a soggy tissue against it.

'How are you going to help him?'

'I think Sami is caught up in something that is bigger than he is. He's trying to get out but he just keeps getting in deeper.'

The intercom sounds. Ruiz passes two constables on the stairs. Outside, he watches as another train rattles past towards Clapham Junction. Fallen leaves dance in its wake and a grey squirrel dashes up the nearest tree where it freezes, pretending to be a statue.

This all comes back to the gun, thinks Ruiz. Murphy wanted it stolen, but why? He could be working for Ray Garza or trying to blackmail him or maybe they're locked in some sort of turf war.

Murphy was jacking cars to order when still in his teens, stealing off the streets of Dublin, Manchester and London, shipping them to Eastern Europe and North Africa. Garza was in a similar business, moving looted vehicles out of Iraq and Kuwait after the first Gulf War. Maybe they used the same distribution network or bribed the same customs officers and border guards.

303

That's where the similarity ends. Wealthy and well-connected, Garza has turned himself into an establishment figure, while Murphy will always be a gangster no matter how many garden parties he throws.

In the meantime, Sami Macbeth has disappeared again – abducted violently and perhaps permanently. Maybe his luck finally ran out, thinks Ruiz, although he isn't convinced. The kid is like Lazarus with a triple heart bypass.

52

Sami wakes in a bed almost as soft as the one at the Savoy. The curtains are open. Light spills across the bedspread, lighting up dust-motes that float just out of his reach.

Sami looks down. He's naked beneath a blue bathrobe cinched at his waist. Someone has taken his clothes. Getting out of bed, he opens a wardrobe and finds a selection of jeans with a 32-inch waist, along with cotton sweaters in different colours and an oilskin jacket with a fleece lining. Six shoeboxes are stacked on the floor containing Nike trainers, Italian loafers and Oxford brogues – all in Sami's size.

Spooky. He tries not to think about it.

After getting dressed, he goes to the window and opens the curtains. Figures he must be at some sort of country house. The crushed marble driveway circles a fountain and follows a line of oak trees to a stone bridge. In the near distance he can see hedgerows, fields and the outline of farm buildings.

Double doors open onto the balcony. Sami tries the handle. It opens. He steps outside. A movement catches his eye and he notices a woman riding a horse over jumps with painted poles resting between drums. She's wearing jodhpurs, a short red jacket and riding hat. Her blonde hair bounces on her back as her buttocks rise and fall in the saddle.

There is a knock on the door behind him. A maid enters. Her skin is so black it almost has a purple sheen.

'Mr Garza wants you to join him in the library for afternoon tea.'

Sami feels his scrotum tighten as his balls crawl upwards into his body, looking for somewhere safe to hide.

As he laces up his trainers, he tries to think it through. If Ray Garza had wanted him dead, he'd be dead. Now people have seen him – the maid at least. She's a witness. And surely Garza wouldn't give him a choice of clothes if he was going to mess them up with bullet holes.

Murphy must have called him and said Sami was being difficult about handing over the shooter and the drugs. That's all right, thinks Sami. He just has to hold his ground. Insist on getting Nadia. There's no option.

Opening the bedroom door, he stands on a landing and looks down a marble staircase that is like something from *Gone With the Wind* before the fire. A chandelier the size of a Mini Cooper hangs above the entrance hall.

Sami's trainers squeak as he walks. He should have chosen the loafers.

A different maid is polishing the foyer with a machine. 'I'm looking for the library,' says Sami.

She points along a corridor and tells him to keep going as far as the ballroom and then turn right. After that it's the fourth door, just past the billiard room and home theatre.

Sami stops outside the door. Knocks. Waits. Enters. Nobody seems to be around, but a silver coffee pot is sitting on a tray with cups, saucers and paraphernalia.

The room is lined with bookshelves that stretch to the ceiling. The upper ones are reachable via a staircase leading to a walkway that skirts three walls and is draped with heraldic flags and pendants.

Ray Garza emerges from the patio outside, talking on a mobile phone and motioning Sami to take a seat. Garza must be about fifty, but looks good for his age. Tanned. Fit. Dressed in casual trousers, Gucci loafers and a cashmere sweater, he has the relaxed air of someone who knows the value of money because he has a mountain of it.

He ends the call, looks at Sami, smiles. Teenage acne scars have cratered his cheeks and removed any chance of him being handsome.

'Are you interested in politics, Mr Macbeth?'

'No, sir.'

'Neither was I at your age. I didn't read the newspapers,

307

didn't vote, didn't care what bastards were in power.'
Garza's eyes glitter. 'Now I make it my business. Politics is
like a microcosm. So is business. Every element is linked,
just like in nature.'

Sami has no idea what he's talking about.

'If this is about what I said to Mr Murphy . . .'

Garza raises a hand to dismiss the interruption. His
voice is proper and clipped, but Garza didn't go to private school. He grew up in a Bristol tenement, the son of
a meat packer at the city abattoir.

'Do you know anything about hyenas, Mr Macbeth?'

Sami wonders if it's a trick question. 'They laugh.'

'Actually, they make a whooping sound, which can't
really be mistaken for a laugh. Hyenas have the strongest
jaws in the world of mammals. They also have a pseudo
penis, which means you can't tell which one is the male or
the female when they're born.'

'You know a lot about hyenas, Mr Garza,' says Sami,
unable to think of anything else to say.

'I used to have a private zoo until the council closed it
down. I had to sell off my animals because the animal lib-
erationists spent six months camped at my front gate.
They poisoned my trout lake – I guess they don't care so
much about fish – they scared away my feed suppliers
and firebombed my vet's car. They didn't seem to appreciate the breeding programme we were running. Some
people make it hard for you to do the right thing.'

'I'm sorry.'

'Why are you sorry? It wasn't your fault. Don't ever say sorry for something you didn't do.'

'Yes, sir.'

'Do you know who I am?'

'You're a friend of Tony Murphy's.'

Garza roars with laughter. He rocks back on the Chesterfield sofa, unable to stop himself, wiping tears from his eyes.

'He told you that?'

'Not exactly,' says Sami. 'I just assumed.'

Garza has stopped laughing. It's amazing how quickly his eyes fill with violent intent. 'Why did Tony Murphy ask you to rob an evidence room at the Old Bailey?'

'Mr Murphy didn't give me a reason.'

'But you did it anyway?'

Sami can tell that he's misread the situation and there's no point in lying. He tells Garza everything, recounting what Murphy said to him at the restaurant and at the dog track. He tells him about Nadia and the drug den and Dessie blowing himself up.

'When I saw the evidence bags and your boy's name I just assumed Murphy was doing the job for you.'

Garza's turns his face to the glass doors. Light catches in the pockmarks on his cheeks and they look even more like lunar craters.

'You remember the two gentlemen who brought you here?'

'Yes, sir.'

'If I'd wanted someone to break into an evidence room and take exhibits, they could have done it in twenty minutes and left none of the fucking mess you did.'

'So you didn't want the stuff stolen?'

'Not by you, son.'

Sami feels his insides betray him. He reaches for a coffee cup but his hand is shaking too much.

'If I'm to believe you, Mr Macbeth, I owe you an apology,' says Garza. 'You've been had over by Mr Murphy. Consider it a learning experience.'

'I swear, I had no idea,' says Sami.

Garza motions him to lean closer. 'That still leaves one question. Why did Murphy want you to take the stuff? My lad got himself into trouble. I'll get him a good lawyer – the best – and I'll fund his defence, but if he goes down so be it. Might be what he needs.'

'You don't really mean that,' says Sami.

'Don't I?'

'I've been inside. Prison doesn't teach you any lessons.'

'Do you want to go back inside, Mr Macbeth?'

'No, sir.'

'Sounds like you learned something.'

Garza invites Sami to take a walk with him. Maybe this is where they go into the garden and he hands Sami a shovel to dig his own grave. They walk past the stable block and down a long path between empty enclosures. There are signs still attached to some of the gates. One of them reads: *Saltwater Crocodiles* (Crocodylus porosus).

Inside is a brackish pool, surrounded by rocks and weeds.

'The interesting thing about a saltwater croc is the teeth,' explains Garza. 'They're not razor sharp so they can cut. Instead they're like pegs. That's why a croc rolls its victim over and over, ripping the flesh. The death roll. Sometimes they'll take the carcass underwater and tuck it under a log or a ledge for a few weeks, waiting for the body to go soft before they eat it.'

Sami peers into the murky pool. 'And you're sure this one's gone?'

'Went to Whipsnade.'

Garza opens an inner gate and they walk across a large grass enclosure.

'What exactly did you take from the evidence room?'

'Drugs and a gun.' Sami doesn't mention the cash.

'Where are they now?'

'I have them.'

'Where?'

'In a safe place.'

'Are you purposely being obtuse, Mr Macbeth?'

'No, sir, I don't know what obtuse means. Murphy still has my sister. He wants the gun badly.'

'Why?'

'I don't know. It's all he seems to care about. He wants me to destroy it.'

They reach another enclosure. The sign says, *African Wild Dogs* (Lycaon pictus).

311

'It means painted wolf,' explains Garza. 'People sometimes mistake them for domestic dogs gone wild.'

'They *look* like dogs,' says Sami.

Garza points to a photograph on the sign. 'They
have round bat-like ears and only four toes. Domestic
dogs have five. African Wild Dogs are more efficient as
killers than lions or leopards or cheetahs. They hunt
together, taking turns, chasing down a buffalo or
wildebeest and ripping it apart as it runs, eating it
alive.

'That's what Tony Murphy is doing to me, tearing
chunks of flesh, spreading rumours that I'm behind the
robbery. I've had two Members of Parliament cancel
appointments in the past twenty-four hours and an old
friend from the Lords rang and told me not to bother
coming hunting.'

It's just a few knobs, thinks Sami, but doesn't say it out
loud.

'Why would Murphy do that?'

Garza's eyes are flat and expressionless. 'Good question, Mr Macbeth. Good question.'

The woman Sami saw riding earlier is talking to a
group of gardeners near a cluster of greenhouses. She
raises a hand and shades her eyes from the winter sun
and for a moment Sami thinks she might wave. Instead
she turns away and continues her conversation.

'My wife,' explains Garza. 'She comes from a
respectable family; old money. They were so fucking poor

312

when I met her, I had to bail them out and buy this place to keep it from the taxman.

'My wife says I'm cold. She can talk. That's her over there – the ice queen. Five years ago she got busted by the police for giving her personal trainer a blowjob in a car park. The newspapers got hold of the story.

'I squared the indecency charges and I got the newspaper to drop the story. I didn't divorce her. She thought I was going to forgive her. She thought I needed her name to be respectable. That shows how little she knows me. When she came home from her next exercise class, she discovered two twenty-year-old hookers in the hot tub. I told her to get us all a drink.'

Garza gazes at the trees proudly as though he planted them himself.

'I told her if she wanted to stay, she could stay, but if she ever screwed around again, I'd make sure she got nothing, not a pot to piss in. I had all the evidence I needed – substance abuse, alcoholism, psychiatric reports. She'd be lucky to see our son once a fortnight with supervision. People don't screw me twice, Mr Macbeth, do you understand?'

'Yes, sir.'

'I want you to phone Tony Murphy. Organise a meeting. Give him the shooter. Get your sister.'

'Then what?'

'Duck.'

Sami takes a moment to digest the implications.

313

Garza's lips curl upwards into a smile. 'I'm joking, Mr Macbeth. Get your sister. Make sure she's safe.'

Sami tries to enjoy the joke but can't tell if a smile ever reaches his face.

53

Murphy picks up on the second ring.

'It's me,' says Sami, clearing his throat. 'We meet tonight at midnight. Putney Bridge.'

'Where on Putney Bridge?'

'In the middle.'

'You're going to hand me a shooter in the middle of Putney Bridge? Why not take an ad in *The Times*?'

'This way I'll know you're alone. Bring Nadia. Nobody else.'

'And the rozzers will be waiting either end?'

'Only if they follow you.'

'You're a cocky little shite.'

'And you're a fat windbag, Mr Murphy. Now we've cleared that much up, we can both get down to business. Tonight. Midnight. Don't be late.'

The call ends and Murphy drums his fingers on the desk. It could be a trap. Macbeth might already be in police custody. No, Bones would have called him if that had happened. The situation can still be retrieved.

Murphy lights a cigar and tilts his face to blow smoke towards the ceiling. His fingers touch the sides of a whisky glass. The exit strategy is almost in place. It just needs one final piece for the whole jigsaw to land on Ray Garza's head. The trick is not to panic. It's all comedy. He could be dead right or dead depending on the outcome.

Murphy picks up his phone and calls Ray Jnr.

'My boy, my boy,' he says, sounding like a Jewish grandfather. 'It's been too long . . . no hard feelings . . . I got a new batch of girls in. There's one in particular I want you to try. She's sweet as a peach. Come on over.'

54

The front door opens before Ruiz can raise a knuckle. Frank Dibbs must have been watching him open the gate and walk up the path.

'It's about time,' he says, looking irritated.

'Time for what?'

'I've left dozens of phone messages . . . and I've written letters.'

Mr Dibbs is shaped like a sea elephant and is wearing a tartan sweater knitted with love but very little skill.

'Have you brought your noise thingumajig?'

'You seem to have me confused with someone else.'

'You're from the council aren't you? I said to Margaret, "This will be the noise officer from the council." Didn't I, Margaret?'

Margaret must be the woman standing behind him in the hallway wearing a dressing gown and protective glasses. Maybe it's a form of foreplay.

A burst of laughter emanates from the Anglesea Arms

across the road. Three young guys stumble out, shouting to the mates they've left behind.

Mr Dibbs can't hide his disgust. 'You hear that? Every night we have to put up with fights, vomit, drunkenness, broken bottles. Last week we had a shooting.'

'That's what I'm here to talk about,' says Ruiz, pleased to change the subject.

Mr Dibbs doesn't seem disappointed. The shooting is his next favourite subject. He describes it in graphic detail, rising to great levels of personal umbrage, pointing out where the participants were standing.

Mr Dibbs was upstairs when the fight broke out. He looked out of his bedroom window and saw two policemen arguing with a driver of a Porsche parked on the footpath outside the Anglesea Arms.

'The police had opened the boot and one of them lifted out the spare tyre. That's when this young bloke went mad, screaming at them and claiming he was being set up. One of the officers began using his radio and the next thing I saw was the gun.'

'Who had the gun?'

'The young bloke. He was waving it about, yelling at them. I had to duck.'

'Why?'

'Why what?'

'Why did you have to duck?'

'Because of the bullet.'

Mr Dibbs has managed to omit this detail from his account. Ruiz takes him back over it again.

'You saw the flash.'

He nods. 'The bullet hit the house. That's why I ducked.'

'The second sound must have been close.'

'Right below me.'

Ruiz retraces his steps and stands in front of the Dibbs' house. He studies the lilac painted brick façade, scanning the unbroken horizontal lines of mortar beneath the paint.

'Are you sure he was standing over there?'

'Absolutely.'

Ruiz moves back and forth across Wingate Road, searching the asphalt and gutters. Ray Jnr had a Beretta 93R machine pistol set on single shot rather than rapid fire. The shell casing would have been ejected from the breech – but where did it go?

Lying flat on his stomach, Ruiz looks under the parked cars. The nearest drain is eight yards away, covered by a square metal grate. He crawls beneath the chassis of a car and peers between the bars.

'Have you got a torch inside, Mr Dibbs?'

'Of course, we're always prepared.' He doesn't move.

'Perhaps I could borrow it.'

'Oh, right, yes.'

Still lying on his stomach, Ruiz watches tartan trousers with matching slippers disappear into the house

319

and re-emerge a few minutes later. Mr Dibbs hands him a torch. Ruiz nudges it between the bars and tries to peer into the blackness of the drain, which smells of sump oil and dog turds.

Four feet below him, wedged between a flattened hubcap and a broken umbrella, he spies the brass 9mm shell casing.

Ruiz slithers out and fetches a tyre lever from the boot of his Merc. He jams the tapered end beneath the edge of the grate and prises it upwards, far enough to hook his fingers underneath and prop it open.

Leaning head first into the drain, he slips the end of a ballpoint pen into the hollow case and drops it into a Ziploc bag. He's been carrying that bag around for three years, ever since he retired and even before then. Old habits die hardest.

55

Ray Jnr looks at himself in the mirror and sneers, doing his best De Niro impersonation.

'You talking to me?'

'You *talking* to me?'

'You talking to *me*?'

He looks over his shoulder. 'Then who the hell else are you talking to? I'm the only one here.'

He spins and draws his hand from his pocket, finger pointing and thumb cocked, like he's holding a gun.

'Don't mess with me, fucker.'

His eyes are twinkling. He adjusts his hair, teasing it into spikes.

For the past five days Ray Jnr has been dining out on the story of doing time in the 'Big House'. It's like he's been 'made' now. He's a proper wise guy.

There's still the issue of the attempted murder and drugs charges, but his old man will sort that out. He'll huff and puff and call Ray a fuck-up and say, 'not this time, junior', but he'll come through. He always does. Blood is thicker than mud.

Ray Jnr is at Tony Murphy's club in Bayswater, where the girls all look like wannabe models or page-three girls with big hair and bigger racks. It's one of those discreet establishments where a limo picks you up and drops you home and they provide a receipt at the end of the night, which any self-respecting accountant would put straight into a pile labelled 'business expenses'.

Not one of those clubs full of rich old codgers fixated on shagging nanny or being spanked by matron. The place is full of talent – real talent – a classy international smörgåsbord of pussy, fresh off the plane from Prague or the boat from Beijing.

Ray Jnr wouldn't mind a stake in a place like this – he should suggest it to Murphy. Free food, complimentary drinks, discretion guaranteed. So what if some of the girls are coked up, there's never a shortage. They all want to come to London and they don't mind paying the fare.

Tonight is one of Murphy's special parties. Select guests only. A new batch of girls has arrived at the club and Ray Jnr gets to sample the merchandise before it gets bruised. He might even break a girl in; some of them are so naive they're as good as virgins.

Ray Jnr peels back his lips, rubs the charlie off his teeth and takes one final look in the mirror. It's party time.

Murphy watches him leave the bathroom. The CCTV camera covers the hallway and beams images directly to

Murphy's office on the topmost floor of the large Georgian terrace, overlooking a community garden.

Secret cameras are also hidden in each of the eight bedrooms and above the spa. The footage isn't high definition or porn industry quality, but it doesn't have to be. Insurance, you see. Everyone should have insurance. Not your poxy, thirty-quid-a-month life-cover in case you drop off your perch, or income protection in case you damage your wanking hand. Real insurance. Murphy's homemade DVDs are protection against accidents and mistakes and criminal investigations. Hopefully, he'll never need to show them to a wider audience, which is probably a good thing when you see the wobble on that judge's arse as he bangs a girl dressed up like Dorothy in *The Wizard of Oz*. She'd click her heels together and think of home if she could get her legs around his arse.

Murphy puts a phone call in to Bones.

'How's it hanging, partner?'

'I told you not to call me.'

'And I told you that your sorry arse belongs to me, Bones, and you'll do as I say,' Murphy chuckles. 'Are you grinding your teeth, Bones? It's a terrible habit. My wife does it.'

'I can't think why,' says Bones.

'That's more like it. You're getting your sense of humour back.'

Murphy hears static on the line. 'Are you recording this conversation, Bones?'

'No, are you?'

'Maybe we should talk about something else,' suggests Murphy, slipping into football speak. 'Did you see the game at the weekend? That player who should have been axed is still running around. He called me today.'

'What did he want?'

'He's setting up a meeting. Wants to trade.'

'Are you going to say yes?'

'I want to know if he's talking to any other parties, know what I'm saying? Is he playing for the Blues?'

'I've heard nothing, Tony.'

'Maybe you should make a few inquiries. The lad might even have an agent. He's one of yours. A guy called Ruiz.'

'Vincent Ruiz?'

'You know him?'

'Yeah, he's retired.'

'Well, he's not playing golf. He came to see me yesterday.'

'Why?'

'Good question, Bones, find me a good answer. Your manager fucked it up last night. He took off the wrong player. Should have benched the kid permanently. There's another game tonight – a testimonial. The kid is playing his last game.'

'You need any help?'

'I've got it covered this time.'

*

Murphy leans back in his chair and peruses the CCTV monitors. Ray Jnr is stripped to the waist, propped up in bed, watching Nadia Macbeth dance. Dressed in a short black negligee and high heel shoes, her breasts stand out stiffly against the opaque fabric.

Ray Jnr looks a lot like his old man did at the same age, but their taste in women is different. Ray Snr liked them young and demure, the girl-next-door types who looked too old for Sunday school and too young to fuck. Ray Jnr prefers them horny and coked up, wearing lingerie or leather.

Back in the old days, Ray's father used to rely on Murphy to find him girls. 'Just something for the weekend,' he'd say when he organised his diary. Murphy would have the girls delivered in a limo to the hotel, telling them that Garza was a big-shot modelling agent.

Ray Snr was a real coke-hound back then. Like father like son.

Then one night some girl laughed at Ray when he was trying to seduce her and he lost it completely. Raped her. Chewed open her cheek. She topped herself before the trial. Ray dodged a bullet and he swore off drugs completely. He married, concentrated on business, made a fortune.

On screen Ray Jnr has just looped his belt around Nadia's forearm, pulling it tight. A lighted candle and spoon are on the nightstand beside them. The flame dances in Nadia's eyes.

Ray mounts the needle in her vein. Presses the plunger. Nadia sighs and tilts her head back, her mouth open and jaw slack. He pulls the syringe free and puts his hand behind her neck, pulling her towards his lap.

'Come on, baby, now look after me.'

Murphy opens the door and interrupts. Nadia raises her head. Wipes her mouth. The revulsion on her face might never leave her.

Ray Jnr is reclining on the bed, one arm casually behind his head, a joint hovering over the ashtray balanced on his stomach.

Murphy tells Nadia to go next door. Ray Jnr watches her leave.

'You were right about that one.'

'I told you not to inject her.'

'She wanted it.'

'And now she'll want it again in a few hours.'

Ray Jnr draws on the joint, taking a long deep hit. The edges of the paper glow bright red.

'We have business to discuss,' says Murphy. 'I want you *compos mentis.*'

'What's that mean?'

'Of sound mind.'

Ray tries to blow smoke rings. 'I thought it was the name of a band.'

Murphy goes to the bar in the corner and pours himself a Scotch adding a splash of soda from an old-fashioned soda stream. Then he eases back on a sofa that's so big it must have come through the windows.

'The semi-automatic you took from me – the Beretta – it was stolen from a police evidence room yesterday morning, along with the cocaine you were carrying.'

'Allegedly,' says Ray, who is suddenly paying attention. It takes him a few moments to digest the information. A smile creases his face. Goes away. Comes back again. It's like he's responding to some internal dialogue.

'Without the shooter or the drugs, I'm a free man. They'll have to drop the charges.'

'Not so fast, son,' says Murphy. 'Getting away isn't always that easy.'

'Why?'

'You see, the thief who stole this stuff is trying to blackmail your old man. He wants half a million quid or he's going to give the gun and the cocaine to Old Bill and say that *you* put him up to the robbery.'

'Did I fuck!'

'Exactly, but what are the police going to think?'

Ray Jnr stands, slips his belt through the loops, buckles it up.

'Who is this geezer, Tony, do I know him?'

'Sami Macbeth. He's an ex-con.'

Ray Jnr shakes his head. 'And he thinks he can turn me over? He's dreaming.'

'Yeah, but I'm worried,' says Murphy. 'The police already think your old man organised the robbery. They got a team of detectives working on the case. Unless we stop Macbeth, he could send us all to prison.'

'How so?'

Murphy leans forward. Elbows on knees. Scotch close to his lips.

'I should tell you something about that shooter you took from me. It has a history. Nine years ago it was used to kill a journalist in Belfast. The crime was never solved. Don't look at me like that, son, I didn't pull the trigger. Do you need a clue? Think three letters, Paddies in ski masks.'

Ray Jnr is pacing the floor, puffing air through his nostrils. 'The IRA.'

'Just so.'

'But I thought they were old news.'

'Act your fucking age, son. You think the Provos are going to take up knitting just because Gerry Adams and Martin McGuinness get plush offices at Stormont?'

Ray Jnr still can't grasp the issue. Murphy slows down and gives him a history lesson about the Northern Ireland Peace Accord and how Sinn Fein, the IRA's political wing, got a seat at the table because the Provos renounced violence and agreed to decommission weapons.

'You know what decommissioning means, son? It means out of commission. Off limits. Put beyond use. They chose a Canadian general to oversee the operation. A thousand rifles, three tonnes of Semtex, twenty-five surface-to-air missiles, flame throwers, rocket-propelled grenade launchers – you wouldn't believe the shit they decommissioned.'

'What's it got to do with me?' asks Ray.

'Now what do you think would happen if one of these weapons were to turn up somewhere?'

Ray Jnr has stopped pacing. The penny drops from the fortieth floor and lands on his head.

'The shooter you took from me was supposed to get a new barrel and a new firing pin before it was recycled, but that didn't happen. If the police discover where it came from, it's not just your sorry arse in the fire. The entire peace process goes up in flames. Are you getting this, Ray?'

'It's political.'

'Fucking right it's political. And it's going to get personal in a screaming hurry. Governments, political parties, Special Branch, MI6, Criminal Intelligence, SO11 – every one of them will do whatever it takes to save the peace process.'

Ray flinches. 'Why is it my fault? It's your gun.'

Murphy swings from the waist, holding the heavy Scotch glass wrapped in a hand towel. It strikes Ray Jnr flush on the jaw, sending him sprawling across the bed. The glass shatters and a piece is sticking out of Ray Jnr's cheek.

'What'd you do that for?' whines Ray, holding his cheek.

329

Murphy is standing over him. 'Listen, you muggy prick, you stole that gun from me. Now you're going to get it back. You're going to meet Macbeth tonight and you're going to get the shooter.'

Ray is holding his face. 'Why is he going to give it to me?'

'Because I have his sister.'

'What are you talking about?'

'Macbeth's sister – you were massaging her tonsils.'

'No shit!'

'I shit you not. I've arranged a meeting. You get the stuff. He gets the girl. Then you cut his kite string.'

'You mean I got to kill him?'

'I'm talking about saving your sorry arse and keeping Daddy out of jail.'

Murphy wets the towel and hands it to Ray, who pinches the shard of glass between his fingers and pulls it from his cheek. He holds the towel against his face. Murphy sits on the edge of the bed and turns on his avuncular charm, explaining how he's doing him a favour, contributing to his emotional development and familial ties.

'You're a fuck-up, Ray. Always have been. Well, now's your chance to make amends. You can do something for your old man. Earn his respect. Make him proud. And it's going to make you a name. You want to be a player, son. You want to be a wise guy. You have to be prepared to pull the trigger.'

330

Ray puffs out his chest. The idea is growing on him.

'I'll have you covered, son. I'm not going to leave you out there on your own. Your old man would never forgive me.'

'What about the girl?'

'What about her?'

'She'll be a witness.'

'You seem handy with the brown, Ray. Give her a little extra juice. Send her on a long trip. One way only. It's what every junkie wants.'

331

56

Ruiz is sitting on a park bench overlooking the river, watching the sun setting behind a bank of puce-coloured clouds that have brought storms all afternoon.

The air is criss-crossed with birds and, standing in the mud on the shoreline, a large white seabird seems more like a statue than it does a live creature.

Normally Ruiz has a beer at this time of day but he doesn't feel much like drinking or fishing or conversation. Today had not enriched or improved his views on human nature.

He hears his name being called. Darcy is standing at the door of the house, holding the phone.

'Take a message,' he shouts.

'She says it's important.'

Ruiz rubs the heels of his hand into his eyes until bright lights explode behind his eyelids. The colours float and fade as the world comes back into focus.

He limps across the road and takes the phone from Darcy. Fiona Taylor is calling from the Yard.

'How you doing, big man?'

'Been better.'

'The shell casing you sent over – the ballistics boys are looking at it now.'

'Good.'

She hesitates.

'You didn't call me just to tell me that,' says Ruiz.

'We have a problem.'

'What's that?'

'Your fingerprints were found in a flat at Abbey Road – Toby Streak's place. The neighbours say you kicked open the door, forced your way inside, made threats.'

'Has Streak lodged a complaint?'

'No.'

'Then what's the problem?'

'They found his body this morning. It was floating in a flooded grease pit at a garage in Finchley.'

Ruiz can feel a constriction in his throat, but strangely no other emotion. Normally he can find something to regret about any death, but Toby Streak was a skid-mark on the world and if someone laundered his sheets they were performing a public service.

Fiona is still talking. 'Someone beat him to death, Vincent. They broke every rib, both his hands and his kneecaps. Homicide and Serious Crime want to talk to you. They want to know what you were doing in Streak's flat. And they want to know why I looked up his address on the computer.'

333

Ruiz starts to apologise. Fiona cuts him short.

'Don't sweat it, big man – if arseholes could fly, this place would be an airport. Just don't ask me for any more favours for a while.'

Ruiz feels an odd sense of loss and disappointment. Not for himself. Fiona faces being hauled over the coals, disciplined and maybe even suspended. A letter would go on her file and stay there for ever. They could use it against her when she sought her next promotion.

'Who's the investigating officer?' asks Ruiz.

'DCI Baxter.'

'I didn't know Baxter had made Chief Inspector.'

'Some turds are floaters.'

Ruiz puts the phone back in the cradle and ponders the fate of Toby Streak. Unconsciously, he shivers as though he's left the front door open and the river chill has leaked inside. But this is a different sort of cold; an icy foreboding that penetrates his bones and wakes the little man sleeping at the bottom of his soul.

An hour later he signs his name in the visitor's book at Westminster Morgue and waits for a pathologist to collect him from the waiting room.

They've redecorated since he was here last but the interior design never changes. The aluminium and stainless steel has a minimalist feel and fluorescent lights reflect off every smooth surface. The troughs and drains are running with clear water and the only sound he can hear is the hum of the air conditioning.

The pathologist is wearing a white coat and has eczema on his hands. It's an allergic reaction to latex gloves, he explains, calling it an occupational hazard. Cutting open bodies is an occupational hazard, thinks Ruiz. A skin rash is a skin rash.

Phil Baxter pushes through the swing doors with an urgency that is designed to impress. He's a busy man. Don't stand in his way. Ruiz remembers Baxter as a young DC working the drug squad back in the days when good crack was conversation rather than a Class-A narcotic. Now he's a Detective Chief Inspector – a higher rank than Ruiz ever managed.

Baxter has put on weight, cut his hair shorter, but his wardrobe is the same – the black brogues, dark slacks and a sports jacket.

He offers his hand. Ruiz shakes it. The DCI grips it tightly and turns it over, examining Ruiz's knuckles. He lets him go.

'Sorry to drag you away from your hot cocoa.'

'Get to it, Phil, you're wasting my time.'

The pathologist examines the paperwork and pulls open a stainless steel drawer. The sound is like someone exhaling.

Toby Streak isn't pretty any more. Most of his teeth are broken and his right eye socket no longer has an eye.

Baxter studies Ruiz's face instead of the cadaver. Ruiz

tries not to react, but the sheer ferocity of the attack leaves a mark on his lips and in the corners of his eyes.

'Would you like to know how your friend here died?' asks Baxter.

'He wasn't my friend.'

'You were in his flat.'

'He had information I needed.'

'You beat it out of him.'

'He tripped as I came through the door.'

The pathologist is watching this exchange as though viewing a tennis match, turning back and forth as sentences are volleyed. Baxter interrupts the exchange.

'Tell us how Toby Streak met his maker.'

The pathologist picks up the autopsy report.

'Initially, it seemed as though he died when a rib punctured his heart but he was already on the way. A brain haemorrhage caused by multiple blows to the head.

'We believe they used a tyre iron or a metal bar of some sort. Both his hands and his kneecaps were broken early in the assault. They were held against a hard surface and smashed . . .'

Baxter interrupts to paraphrase. 'He went every round. They propped him up and kept hitting him. See the marks on his neck. Someone held him by the throat to stop him sliding down a wall. He had brick dust in his hair.'

Ruiz has heard enough. He pushes open the door and walks back down the long neon-lit corridor, past the autopsy suites and the dirty body room. Baxter has to jog to catch up and demands that he stop.

Ruiz spins to face him. 'You think I'm good for this? You think I broke that boy's bones in there; that I ripped out his eye, you really believe that?'

Baxter is stunned by the ferocity of Ruiz's anger.

'I think you spent too long in the job, Vincent, mixing with these people, believing they were just like us but without the same advantages or upbringing. Only you're wrong. People don't choose the world they're born into, but some escape it and some embrace it and some get buried by it. I think you know who killed Toby Streak. Maybe you even tried to warn him.'

'I was looking for a girl.'

'Oh, that's right, the sister of a terrorist.'

'Sami Macbeth is no more a terrorist than I am.'

'Is that an admission?'

'Fuck off!'

Ruiz walks down the concrete ramp and across the loading dock. It has started to rain. Exploding raindrops have misted around the security lights and turned the street outside into a neon-coloured pool.

Ruiz stands on the corner looking for a cab. Three of them pass, already occupied. Water leaks beneath the collar of his overcoat, but he's too angry to care. He's working through the details of Toby Streak's last hours like it's a Twelve-Step Programme inside his head.

A police car pulls up. Through the windshield and

beating wipers he sees Phil Baxter in the back seat. He leans over and opens the passenger door.

'I don't need a lift home,' says Ruiz.

'Oh, we're not going home,' replies Baxter.

57

Sami's suit has been dry-cleaned and his shirt pressed. He brushes his teeth, rinses his mouth and spits into the sink. His gums are bleeding. A prison diet. Stress.

Two large black Landcruisers with tinted windows are waiting downstairs. Engines idling. Occupants unknown. There is a knock on the door. It's time.

Ray Garza is standing in the foyer. Sami counts six men, dressed in black. One of them has a hand like a withered claw with the fingers compressed together and curled inward towards his wrist. He has to raise his fist above his eyes to take a cigarette from his mouth.

Car doors open. Close. Seat belts, please. The convoy moves off into a night made darker in the countryside, lit periodically by streaks of lightning that tremble in the clouds.

Sami is in the back seat of the first Landcruiser, sitting next to 'The Claw'. The driver is wearing leather gloves and dark glasses, but his most notable apparel is a shoulder holster with a machine pistol. They're going to start a war, thinks Sami.

The car doors aren't locked. Perhaps he could shove the door open and roll out. He'd bounce along the road. He might even survive. What then?

No, this has to end now. Garza had been right about that much. The rest of his spiel was a self-pitying whine about his unfaithful wife and ungrateful son, as he tried to unload his moral guilt on others, but it didn't take long for his ego to reassert itself and he became the same man. Not just the same man – worse because he was angry.

Sami had witnessed Garza's moment of weakness and become his confessor, which then made him an embarrassment. That's why Garza hadn't spoken another word to him since. Sami was persona non grata, surplus to requirements, a waste of space.

Fuck him. Murphy and Garza could kill each other a dozen times over for all Sami cared. He just wants to get Nadia and to get away; to clean her up and say he's sorry. After that he'll tell the police everything. He'll give himself up and throw himself on the mercy of the court. Unmerciful as it is.

Then his imagination really goes into overdrive. He starts fantasising about arresting Garza and Murphy and bringing down their operations. He can see the headlines spinning into focus: TERROR SUSPECT PARDONED and WANTED MAN TURNS HERO. Next he's meeting the Prime Minister at Downing Street and watching him weep with

340

gratitude. He gets a book deal, Guy Ritchie directs the movie and Sami walks Kate Tierney up the red carpet while she's wearing one of those backless evening dresses that have the paparazzi shouldering each other out of the way and screaming her name. Charlie Cox plays Sami and Sienna Miller plays Kate. (As long as they don't get Jude Law – any guy who's engaged to Sienna Miller and gets caught shagging the nanny is a complete tosser.) All of this is flashing through Sami's head like a badly cut rap video.

Meanwhile, the Landcruisers have crossed the Thames and are heading along Cheyne Walk and the Embankment. Five minutes later they pull up outside the Savoy. The door opens. Sami steps out and the coolness of the air makes him realise he's been sweating.

The hotel doorman ushers Sami inside. He crosses the foyer. The Claw is smelling distance behind him. The knot in Sami's bowels won't go away.

They enter the lift. Sami presses 9. He glances at his minder and gets nothing back. The geezer has ice in his veins and a tumour the size of a football up his arse.

It's not until they reach the corridor that Sami considers how he's going to get in the suite. They're outside the door. He doesn't have an entry card.

'I gave the key back to reception,' explains Sami. 'Should I knock?'

The Claw stares at him blankly. Maybe Sami should ask him one on sport.

341

Sami knocks. Nobody answers. A black housekeeper is further down the corridor. Shaped like a duck in a blue uniform, she gives Sami a flat stare as he explains that he's locked himself out of his room. She takes a key card from her apron pocket. Slides it into the slot. The door clicks open.

'Thank you, very much,' says Sami. 'Have a nice day.'

She's already waddling away.

The Claw is already inside, searching the room. Making sure Sami hasn't planned an ambush. He's a professional, special forces most likely, who dares wins, trained by Her Majesty and let loose on society.

Sami takes a chair from the desk and sets it down near the wall. Steps up. Unclips the air-conditioning vent and reaches inside. The Beretta is wrapped tightly in a hand-towel. He leaves the bags of cocaine and banknotes.

Sami tucks the semi-automatic into his belt, nestling against the small of his back. He checks his reflection in the mirror to make sure the bulge doesn't show.

They take the lift back down to the foyer, not saying a word. Sami wants to ask The Claw about his hand. How did it happen? Was he wounded in Crap-istan? Did they torture him with a deep fat fryer?

The lift doors slide open. Kate is standing at the reception desk, talking on a phone. She's dressed in her usual work clothes, looking every inch the hostess and hotel manager. Sami knows that body. He knows the colour of her underwear, the hollow between elastic and thigh, the small butterfly tattoo on her left ankle. He can smell her Pantene-scented hair. He can hear the mewling sound she makes when she's nearing nirvana. Please don't look up, he prays.

Kate puts down the phone. Her eyes latch on to his. She's confused. Angry. She wants to walk towards him but Sami's stare makes her hesitate. She looks past him at the minder. Sami steps through the turning door, crosses the footpath, doesn't look back.

Kate's hands are shaking. She opens her handbag and rummages through it, looking for Ruiz's business card. She can't find it. Shit. Shit. Shit.

Upending the bag, she spills the contents onto the counter – lipstick, car keys, breath mints, tissues, a compact . . .

'Are you OK?' asks her colleague.

'Get the number of that car.'

'Which car?'

'The one that's leaving now.'

Kate finds the card and scoops her belongings into her handbag. 'I have to go.'

'Where?'

'Tell Magna I'm not feeling well.'

She runs for the door, stumbling as her left heel slips on the polished marble. The four-wheel drive carrying Sami has stopped at traffic lights in Savoy Lane, fifty yards away.

'Follow that car,' Kate tells a cab driver, as she opens the car door. The driver looks at her through the glass partition, thinking it's a wind-up.

'Are you going to take me or do I get another cab?'

'No problem, love.'

She punches Ruiz's number into her mobile. He's not answering. She sends a text, using both thumbs to punch the letters.

Sami at Savoy 2nite. Fubar. Following him now. Call ASAP.

58

It's almost stopped raining. The police car splashes through puddles and Ruiz watches headlights flaring on the wet windows. Even in darkness he can recognise the location. He's been here before.

Crime scene tape bulges in the breeze as it twirls from posts on either side of a lane. A group of black teenagers are watching from a pizza place across the road, acting like they own the neighbourhood and resent any trespassers.

Ruiz gets out of the car, ducks under the tape. He can smell curry cooking. A fat woman in a pink sari is watching from a balcony. She shields her face with a veil and turns away from his eyes.

They are a few blocks from the river. The last time Ruiz was here he entered on the other side of the building. The place used to be a furniture factory, according to Baxter, until it was turned into council flats and then sold off to a developer who had plans to bulldoze the place and erect luxury flats. He ran into liquidity problems –

namely, water in the lungs. They found him floating in the river near the Thames Barrier.

Thirty yards ahead a bright pool of light has bleached the cobblestones and thrown warped shadows against the brick walls. A car is parked at the centre of the light – a Fiat Panda. As they get closer, Ruiz notices the car has no roof. Closer still he realises that the roof has been pressed in by the weight of an object falling from above.

Beside it now, the object has become a body – a Rastafarian with beaded hair, who has hit the car with such force it has turned it into a bathtub full of blood. Most people travel a good distance and take a lifetime to reach hell. Puffa managed it in seventy feet and less than five seconds.

Baxter's second in command is a Detective Sergeant Frome. Pale, tall, blade-faced, he looks like an undertaker touting for business. Tonight he's been lucky.

'Victim's name is Dwight Powell. Called himself Puffa. Two witnesses say he took a hit of Ice, climbed onto the roof and did a swan dive from the fifth floor,' he tells Baxter.

'Anyone else on the roof with him?'

'That's the only thing they agree upon – perhaps a little too strenuously.'

Ruiz glances up to the roof and back to the car. Twenty feet separate the nearside tyres from the edge of the building.

'Either Puffa was the lovechild of Bob Beaman or someone threw him,' he says.

'Bob who?' asks Frome.

'Mexico. 1968. The Olympics. Beaman set a world record for the long jump and it was twenty-three years before anybody broke it. They called it the greatest leap in history.'

'Before my time,' says Frome dismissively.

'So were the dinosaurs but it doesn't stop people digging them up. Can I talk to the witnesses?'

'You're here to answer questions, not ask them,' replies Baxter.

'You want to blame me for this as well?'

'Two men are dead. You visited both of them on Saturday. Witnesses claim you assaulted and threatened them. I'd say that makes you a suspect. And you might want to tell me why Crim Intel put your car at Tony Murphy's house yesterday; a known villain.'

Ruiz can feel his mobile vibrating and tries to ignore it.

'The problem with you, Baxter, is that you're like the blind man who touches the elephant's trunk and thinks he's holding a snake.'

'And you're the elephant.'

'I'm the big swinging dick.'

Ruiz's mobile has stopped shaking. It beeps instead. Kate Tierney has sent him a text message.

'What does "fubar" mean?' he asks Baxter.

'Fucked up beyond all recognition.'

347

59

Tony Murphy lifts his face to the sky, feeling the light drizzle cling to his eyelashes. Lately his life seems to be unravelling but tonight he gets it back on track. They say boredom is the brother of misery but after the past few weeks he'd settle for a boring life rather than a dangerous one.

He checks his watch – it's half eleven – and presses speed dial on his mobile.

'You heard anything, Bones?'

'Nothing.'

'No radio chatter?'

'None.'

'Any mention of Putney Bridge?'

'Is that where it's going down?'

'At midnight,' says Murphy.

'What about the kid?'

'He'll be joining his ancestors.'

Murphy ends the call and tucks the phone into his pocket.

348

Ray Jnr is sitting in a car with Nadia. Shadows like rivulets are running down his face. His hands are shaking. He needs another line to settle his nerves.

'You ought to stop snorting that stuff,' say Murphy.

'And you ought to go jogging.'

The windows are fogged with humidity. One of them is cracked a little to let out Sinbad's cigarette smoke.

'Let's do it,' says Murphy.

'Give it a minute,' replies Ray Jnr, 'it hasn't stopped raining.'

He looks nervous, skittish, like a child waiting for a party to begin. Nadia is beside him, sitting on her hands. Her heart-shaped face is pale, devoid of make-up. Her light cotton dress and sweater cling to her like a second skin. The past week has been a nightmarish blur of drugs, paranoia and revulsion. Now she's going home, according to Murphy. Sami is coming to get her.

She takes a cigarette from a packet on her lap; needs both hands to light it. Blinks smoke from her elongated eyes. Oily coils of her hair hang down across her cheeks as inner demons work their magic on her. Desire. Obsession. Addiction.

A bolt of lightning leaps across the western sky. The rain has eased.

'It's time,' says Murphy.

60

Sami has been waiting on the bridge for fifteen minutes, smelling the brine and feeling the cold dampness blowing off the water. A solitary boat is visible, tethered to a pylon near the boat ramp.

The traffic has thinned out. It's mainly cabs and minicabs and people coming home late. Light seems to evaporate from the surface of the asphalt as each vehicle passes.

Ray Garza and his men must be somewhere nearby, although he can't see any of them.

The number 22 bus from Piccadilly Circus to Putney Common pulls onto the north side of the bridge and pauses at a bus shelter. A passenger gets off. The double-decker pulls away. The figure disappears down stone steps on the east side of the bridge.

The bus has almost rumbled past Sami before he notices two people alone on the brightly lit upper deck. One of them is Nadia. She's sitting near the front, staring straight ahead. A man is directly behind her, head down, face hidden.

A massive flood of relief washes through Sami. Nadia's alive. She's only yards away. He yells and starts running, trying to get her attention but the bus is pulling further away, turning right into Lower Richmond Road.

There's a bus stop around the corner. There's nobody waiting. The driver carries on.

Sami cuts across the road, dodges a car and tears along the footpath past mansion blocks, a row of shops, terraces, a petrol station . . . It must be a trick; a trap. Murphy's doing. Sami's mind is telling him this but his legs are still moving; sprinting after the bus as it veers away from the river.

He's a hundred yards behind and can't see if Nadia is still on board. The Beretta is coming loose from his belt. He reaches back to stop it falling.

Brake lights flare. The bus is stopping. Somebody steps off. It's not Nadia. Still sixty yards away Sami screams at the bus to stop but the driver can't hear him. The doors are closing. Gears engage.

The disembarked passenger throws himself against a wall, holding his briefcase like a shield.

'Where does that bus go?' yells Sami, spinning to confront him.

'Putney Common.'

'How far is that?'

'About two stops.'

The double-decker is disappearing again. Sami

351

sprints after it, trying to keep the bus in sight. The shops and restaurants are closed and shuttered but he can still smell the hot oil and the rubbish bins out back. Bill posters have plastered the lamp posts and the windows of empty shops.

The bus is three hundred yards ahead, indicating left. It's turning. Sami is growing tired. His shoes weren't meant for running. The row of terraces ends suddenly but the road continues across the common, swallowed by darkness. It's as though a section of the city has collapsed into a black hole leaving only the streetlights behind.

Sami turns the corner. The double-decker has stopped. He can see the driver climbing out from behind the wheel. The bus doors are open. Sami swings inside, ignoring his protests. He runs through the lower deck; climbs the stairs; searches in vain. Nadia's not there.

'Did you see a girl? Where did she get off?'

The driver is a big guy, gut over his belt.

'She's gone.'

'Where did she go?'

He points across the road towards the common. 'They headed that way.'

Sami scans the darkness, the street, the muddy paths, the deeper shadows. Then he spies something moving a hundred yards away, barely visible against the dark walls of a building rising high above the treetops silhouetted against the faint glow of the sky.

'What's that place?' he asks.

'The old Putney Hospital.'

'Why is it dark?'

'They closed it down years ago,' says the driver. 'They can't decide what to do with it.'

He mentions something about making movies there, but Sami is already crossing the road. Slipping the Beretta from his belt, he unclips the safety. Holds it in both hands. He's not thinking any more. Logic, reason, common sense were abandoned back on the bridge when he chose to ignore his own instructions and let Tony Murphy dictate events.

A metal boom gate is padlocked in place across the entrance to the car park and weeds sprout from broken asphalt in the ambulance bays. Odd things are scattered through the weeds. Junk mostly, broken furniture, old appliances, a plastic jerry can collecting rainwater.

The red brick hospital is four storeys high and could fill a city block, but appears out of place on the edge of the common, surrounded by heath and parkland. The doors are sealed with sheets of metal and wood, bolted in place, and guarded by steel mesh fences. The lower windows are also covered, but the upper windows have been left unprotected and many have been punctured with rocks. Knotted and filthy curtains billow from inside.

Security lights are attached to the outer walls, illuminating yellow warning signs:

DANGER
Private Property
KEEP OUT
This site contains serious hazards.
All valuables have been removed.

Sami pauses and for a moment catches a glint of something revealed, a shadow in front of him, which disappears in a patter of raindrops. He listens. Nothing. Glancing up at a window on the first floor, he notices a torch beam flash across the broken glass and disappear.

A metal gate lies open ten yards to his right. A sign on the wall says *Accident & Emergency: All Enquiries to Reception.* Sami forces open an iron sheet, which is curling at one corner. Nails rip from the rotting frame. He pulls a trailing vine from his ankles and steps inside, smelling the mould and faeces.

His eyes adjust to the dark. He wants to stand still. He wants to move.

Pushing open a second door he emerges into a wide corridor. Low wattage security lights are evenly spaced along the walls, providing just enough light to see as far as a central staircase. Ceiling panels lie broken or missing with wires hanging through them and pools of water have dried and left stains on the grey linoleum floor.

There are doors along either side of the corridor and lighter squares of paintwork where paintings once hung on the walls. Discarded metal trolleys lie abandoned and covered in dust.

Sami scans the scene; listens to the drip of brown water into a sink.

A sign opposite the nursing station gives directions to the various wards. Occupational Therapy and the Rehabilitation Units are on the second floor.

Sami reaches the stairs, which are in darkness. He has to feel his way upwards, one step at a time. On the first floor is another corridor with doors down either side. The X-ray department is ahead; a strip of light leaks from beneath the door. A sign says, *Danger: Radiation.*

He pushes it open, every muscle tense. Nadia is sitting on a metal chair with her hands beneath her thighs, her red eyes like wounds. The robot-like arms of the X-ray equipment seem to be imprisoning her as part of some fearful experiment.

Her eyes meet his; pleading, fearful.

Sami does everything wrong. He steps towards her. Something moves to his left. He gets the Beretta halfway to horizontal before an object smashes hard against his arm sending the gun skittering across the floor.

In his mind's eye, he twists and swings his left fist, fighting for his life, but he doesn't have the opportunity. A second blow strikes him high across the chest and ribs break with a crack. His knees collapse. Nadia sobs.

Lying face down, Sami turns his cheek and sees someone standing next to Nadia. Wrapping her hair in his fist.

Jerking her head. Telling her to be quiet. It's a face he recognises, but not the person he expects.

It's the kid from the cell next door on Sami's last night in prison. The one who couldn't stop talking; the one who blathered and big-noted himself saying his old man was going to post bail for him and how he'd be eating dinner at the Ivy by the next night.

He's looping a belt around Nadia's forearm. Pulling it tight. He taps the end of the needle and pinches skin on her forearm, looking for a vein.

'Don't do it,' groans Sami, through clenched teeth. 'You remember me.'

Ray Jnr pauses. Recognition comes with a twisted smile as though they're sharing a joke.

'Well, fuck me!' He raises a revolver and scratches an itch on his cheek. 'What are you doing here?'

Sami glances at Nadia whose face tells a story of confusion.

'I'm here to get my sister.'

Ray Jnr jerks Nadia's head back; looks at her face and then back at Sami. He can't see the family resemblance.

'Are you sure you got the right girl?'

Sami nods, sucking in a breath.

Nadia looks at the needle almost lovingly. Her cheeks are hollow and her eyes look huge. Sweating and trembling through withdrawal, she wants another hit.

'Well, this is a turn up for the books,' says Ray Jnr,

356

pulling up a chair and straddling it backwards. 'Why are you trying to blackmail my father?'

'I'm not. He sent me here.'

Ray gives one of those prissy little laughs like there's nobody in the world who's going to believe a story like that.

'It's true. He's outside somewhere.'

'You're trying to get money out of him.'

Sami shakes his head and drags his body up. Every breath lights a fire in his chest. He closes his eyes and tries to do a re-cut on what's happened. Imagines a different outcome where he's not in pain, not in trouble, not going to die. Opening them again, he seeks out Nadia.

'How are you, Princess? I've been looking for you everywhere.'

Her mouth opens. She can't find any words. Instead she falls to her knees and wraps her arms around him. Sami can feel the furnace heat of her cheeks, the dampness of her hands. Her pupils are like pinpricks.

'I missed you,' she whispers.

'I'm here now.'

Ray Jnr is spinning the pistol around his finger. 'Why did you steal the shooter?'

'Murphy told me to do it. He had Nadia.'

'Why would he do that?'

'He needed the gun back.'

Ray Jnr blinks slowly. His thin lips seem rouged against the paleness of his face. He begins to speak in soft insinuating tones.

'You remember that night in prison? You let me talk. I didn't want to close my eyes. I wasn't scared.'

'I know.'

'You think I was scared?'

'No.'

'I've never done this before, but I'm ready, you know.'

'Ready for what?'

'I've made some mistakes but this is going to fix them. I'm going to clean up my act. I'm not going to prison. Not without the gun or the drugs.'

'We won't say anything,' says Sami.

Ray straightens his arm, aiming the pistol at Sami's head. 'Don't fucking interrupt me. Let me give you a news flash, mate, your sister is a junkie, you're a loser and I'm the shit who has to kill you both.'

'You don't have to kill us.'

'What else do you expect me to do?'

'Let us go. I had a deal with Murphy – the gun for my sister.'

Ray Jnr laughs. Still aiming the pistol at Sami, he collects the Beretta from the floor and tucks it into his belt. Then he folds an old blanket around his own pistol, holding both ends together with his left hand to muffle the sound. Ray Jnr places the pistol to Sami's head. Nadia's mouth opens to scream. Ray Jnr hesitates, lowers the pistol. Raises it again. Walks to the window. Turns.

Sami doesn't hear what he's saying. He's too busy looking down the barrel of the gun. It's huge. Gaping.

Sami closes his eyes. The hammer falls. An explosion detonates within his head.

'Don't do it. Please,' he hears himself say, but maybe the words don't come out.

61

Bones McGee has been lying prone in bushes on the eastern side of the hospital for twenty minutes, not far from where Sami Macbeth disappeared inside.

He couldn't get a clean shot on the bridge and followed Macbeth for more than a mile after the kid took off. Now he's cornered in the hospital and has to come out sooner or later.

The breeze dislodges droplets from the branches, pattering on Bones' oilskin jacket. The ground is wet, but the trees and undergrowth offer him plenty of cover. He has a different rifle tonight, his favourite – the L96 – the British Army's sniper rifle of choice.

This time Macbeth isn't getting away. And Tony Murphy's name is also pencilled on the dance card. Murphy has blackmailed Bones for the last time. No more jumping through hoops. No more belittling calls. Two clean shots and the fat lady can sing a requiem.

Murphy said he was meeting Macbeth to do the exchange. They're probably inside now. Murphy will have brought some muscle – dumb-as-dogshit ex-cons bulked up in prison weight rooms – but they won't see Bones until it's too late.

Right now he's feeling pretty relaxed, but the old excitement is growing. It's almost no challenge to take someone down from this range, but this isn't a contest, he tells himself, still smarting over yesterday when he took out the wrong target. The image of the dead van driver has been playing on his mind. He has to squeeze his eyes shut, willing the picture to change.

Opening them again, he sees a flash of torchlight cross a window and a silhouette against a broken pane. Someone is waving a gun around, either Murphy or Macbeth. One shot to the neck and they feel nothing again.

Bones tugs the hood of his rain jacket further over his head to block out any distractions. He gathers up the rifle, lowers the bipod, and tucks the high impact plastic stock against his shoulder. His bottom lip brushes the smoothness of the stock as though lingering over a kiss.

He exhales slowly, holds his breath. Smoothly tightens his finger in the trigger guard.

361

62

A cab drops Ruiz on the northern approach to Putney
Bridge. He hangs back for a few minutes, surveying the
scene, looking for anything untoward or out of place.
Then he sets off along the footpath looking for Kate
Tierney.

He calls her mobile.

'I've lost Sami,' she says, urgently. 'He was on the bridge
and then he started running. It was like he was chasing
someone.'

'Where are you now?'

'I don't know the name of the road. You have to cross
the bridge and turn right.'

'Lower Richmond Road.'

'Maybe.'

Ruiz follows her directions and finds her waiting outside a service station, her hands deep in her coat pockets
and wet hair plastered to her forehead.

'Are you OK?'

She nods, bracing her shoulders against the cold. Her

high heels make clicking sounds on the concrete. She describes Sami's sudden appearance at the Savoy. He was with someone; a man in black, who kept his left hand in his pocket.

'How did Sami look?'

'Scared. Trapped.'

'He didn't say anything?'

Kate shakes her head.

'Why would Sami come back to the hotel?'

'I don't know.' She glances along the road in the direction that he disappeared. 'What was he running from?'

Ruiz wants to answer her, but his mind is churning in a kind of underwater panic like a fish caught in a net. Puffa and Toby Streak are dead. Somebody is cleaning up, removing witnesses, tying up loose ends. Sami and his sister could well be next.

Murphy or Garza – it doesn't matter any more. When Ruiz was married to Miranda, she used to argue that the workings of the world were all connected and everything happened for a reason.

Ruiz would try to reason with her, talking himself into a spluttering, head-shaking tirade of frustration, but Miranda wouldn't concede an inch or lose her temper or change her mood. She lived in Laura Ashley-land, he told her, while never admitting that he wanted to live there too. Her world was nicer; gentler. And the sex could still be dirty.

His phone vibrates in a pocket full of coins.

363

DI Fiona Taylor has her hand cupped over the mouth-piece, trying not to be overheard. Ruiz is listening to her distractedly. Ballistics has tested the shell casing and the computer threw up a match.

'It set off some sort of internal alarm at Vauxhall Cross.' She's talking about MI6. 'Two carloads of spooks arrived at the lab and seized the shell casing. Now they're here. They want to talk to you.'

'Why is MI6 interested?'

'The shell matches one used to murder a journalist in Belfast nine years ago.'

'The same gun?'

'The weapon was supposed to be decommissioned eighteen months ago by the IRA. The destruction was independently verified. The witnesses are beyond reproach.'

'How then . . . ?'

'Exactly.'

'Are they listening to this call?'

'They are.'

'Tell them they can wipe their feet on me tomorrow.'

Ruiz is about to hang up when in the distance beyond the houses there is a bright flash in the darkness of Putney Common, too low for lightning. The sound of a shot reaches him a fraction of a second later. He's already moving.

'What was that?' asks Fiona Taylor, still on the phone.

A second flash lights up the darkness.

'Shots fired,' says Ruiz. 'Lower Richmond Road – near the Common, I need back-up.'

In the same breath he turns and yells to Kate. 'You stay here. Don't move. The police are coming.'

63

The hole in Ray Jnr's throat is no bigger than a cigarette burn, but the matching one at the back of his skull is the size of a fist. His shirt is soaked with blood, which leaks across the linoleum in a black pool that has reached the toe of Sami's left shoe.

Ray had hesitated, trying to decide if he was going to shoot Sami. Then he lowered the gun and started talking again, saying that Sami should get Nadia out and he'd try to square it with Murphy. Arrange a deal. Do his best. He was in mid-sentence, looking out the window when the high velocity bullet took out his throat.

Sami crouches next to the body, feeling for a pulse. Ray's mouth relaxes and his tongue peeks out as though he wants to say something.

Nadia is still sitting on the chair. One hand is clamped across her mouth as though trying to muffle a scream. The other kneads the front of her dress into a ball in her fist. Her body seems to spasm.

Sami scampers to the window, peers out a corner of

the watery glass. A bullet punches into the frame beside his head. He pulls away. Stays low. Crawls to the body and pulls the semi-automatic from Ray's belt. He and Nadia crouch together, breathing the same air.

'Are you hurt?' he asks.

She shakes her head.

'Can you walk?'

She nods.

'We have to get out of here.'

'I'm sorry.'

'You got nothing to be sorry about.'

She pulls at his arm, wanting him to listen. 'They did things to me.'

'I know. It's not important any more.'

Sami doesn't want to listen. He wants to pretend it never happened.

Nadia pulls away from him and crawls across the linoleum towards Ray Jnr. Kneeling beside his body, she needs both hands to lift his head and smash it on the floor. Over and over.

Sami has to unhook her fingers and hold her arms down. He can smell her snot and tears. Feel her heart beating.

'He raped me,' Nadia sobs.

Her eyes shine with tears. Sami can feel his own tears coming – the ones he didn't shed for his mother or father. In his mind he can see Ray Jnr with his pants down, between Nadia's thighs, pounding her flesh, ignoring her pain.

'It's over now,' he says. 'We have to get out of here.'

'Can you make it go away?' she asks, trembling. Flecks of charcoal seem to float in the brown of her eyes.

'No,' says Sami, his heart breaking.

Ignoring his broken ribs, Sami crushes himself against her, feeling her heart beating. It is like a clock counting the seconds for both of them.

Someone is coming along the corridor. Sami holds his finger to his lips. He motions Nadia to hide. Crouching in the shadows behind the door, he waits for it to swing open. He sees forearms and a rifle before launching his shoulder against the wood, smashing it closed. Grabbing a plank of wood, he swings it hard across the fallen figure. Sends him down, legs quivering, a strip of wood embedded in his spine with rusty nails.

Sami takes Nadia's hand and they zigzag along the main corridor to the central staircase. Descend. As he reaches the ground floor, something makes him stop.

The main entrance is to the right. Two, three, four men are moving along the passage, spreading out, sheltering in doorways. Keeping each other covered.

Shotgun pellets spray the brickwork near Sami's right arm. He hears another shell ratchet into the chamber.

A second bullet from a different angle slams into the hospital sign above Nadia's head, punctuating the name of the specialist oncologist. Suddenly gunfire is coming in bursts and rounds, dancing off the walls and floor. Murphy's men and Garza's men are shooting at each other from opposite ends of the corridor.

Sami climbs the stairs, retracing his steps, urging Nadia on. He has to wrap his arm around her waist to stop her falling. Sulphur and cordite float upwards through the stairwell. She stops. Vomits.

Maybe Sami could outrun them without Nadia, but he's not losing her again. One way or another, they're getting out of here. Heading along a different corridor, he passes the occupational therapy rooms. Opening doors, he goes to the windows, looking for a way out. Smashing glass and running the Beretta around the jagged edges, he leans out looking for a fire escape or some other way down.

Sami stops. Listens.

'What is it?' she asks.

'Nothing.'

'Tell me.'

'There's someone coming.'

'That's what I thought.'

'We can't outrun them.'

'We have to go.'

'Can't we hide here?'

'They'll find us.'

'You go,' says Nadia, leaning against a wall. Her legs are giving way.

'Not without you.'

Back in the corridor, they pass through swinging doors and Sami shoves a plank of wood between the handles to buy them more time.

369

There is some sort of gas or fuel tank lying on the floor. He pushes it against the door and they keep running.

A bullet gouges a white streak across the top of the wall above his head. Someone is firing through the barricaded door and trying to shoulder it open. The hinges give way. Sami pushes Nadia ahead of him. He turns, pivoting onto one knee, resting one buttock on his heel and holding the Beretta with both hands. He aims at the tank and squeezes the trigger. In a matter of seconds he empties the clip in a deafening roar. His hands are numb from the recoil.

The explosion is a burst of white blue flames that billows outwards as if the air itself were on fire. Men are screaming. One of them staggers through the flames, silhouetted against the fireball. His clothes are smoking. He sways from side to side, drops to one knee, falls.

Sami keeps trying doors, looking for an exit. They're locked in. Trapped. Turning left, he runs the length of another corridor, pulling Nadia with him. They reach a new flight of stairs. The gunfire is becoming more sporadic downstairs.

Sami has no plan. He isn't headed for a particular exit or gate. He's only running.

A large window fills with a flash of lightning and goes dark again. Sami looks down. The ground is clear. Beyond he can see open ground and trees with headlights winking between them. If he could get there, he could flag down a car. Get Nadia to hospital.

370

She has slumped on the stairs, resting her head against the handrail.

Sami gathers a mattress in both his arms.

'Come on, we're going to jump.'

'I can't, Sami, I'm sorry.'

'Yes, you can.'

'No.'

Sami screams at her, 'Listen, Princess, suck it in. I know they did terrible things. I know you're hurting. But we're not giving up.' He does a fireman's lift, hoisting her over his shoulder, ignoring the pain in his chest.

Holding the mattress in both arms he runs at the window, breaking glass. Falling. They land together and roll from the mattress onto their backs on muddy turf. Winded. Disorientated.

There's no time to take an inventory. Sami grabs Nadia again and drags her into thorn bushes. Turning, he catches a glimpse of someone watching from the broken window. They'll have to come down the stairs and find a door.

Nadia's body has gone limp. A flash of lightning reveals blood on her lips and beyond her a wire fence and a gate.

64

Ruiz climbs the stairs two at a time, kicking bottles and debris aside. The gunfire has stopped but he can hear shouts from distant corners of the hospital.

There were two bodies downstairs, one near the main entrance and a second further along the corridor. Both were dressed in black. Armed. He took a pistol from one of them, who was in no position to argue.

Ruiz pauses. Listens. The sound of a soft groan punctuates a roll of thunder. He moves to the left. The X-ray room has warning signs about radiation and unauthorised entry. The double doors are splintered and smeared with blood.

He raises his foot and pushes it open. A body lies in a dark pool that looks like sump oil and smells like death. Ray Jnr; shot through the neck by a high velocity round; dead where he fell.

Ruiz scans the room and notices a smeared trail of blood that disappears behind a partition used to protect radiologists from exposure during X-rays.

A rasping breath comes from the other side; someone in pain, trying not to make a sound. Moving to his right, Ruiz uses the robotic arms of the machine as cover, he crouches and peers around the bed-sized plinth beneath the X-ray camera.

Bones McGee lifts his head from the rifle, which is aiming at the other side of the partition. A question forms in his eyes.

'I see you're still trying to make the Olympic shooting team, Bones. You're a little early. Opening Ceremony isn't until 2012.'

Ruiz quickly catalogues the scene. Bones has a high velocity rifle. He also has a shattered piece of wood that appears to be stuck to his spine. Looking at the trail of blood, he must have dragged himself this far.

'So how are things going?' he asks.

'I can't feel them,' says Bones, looking at his legs, which flop at odd angles.

'You want me to call an ambulance?'

Bones shakes his head. 'You should have stayed out of this, Ruiz.'

'I'm not the one who's paralysed.'

Bones rests the rifle on his lap and brushes a non-existent fringe from his eyes. His finger is still on the trigger.

'Where's Sami Macbeth?'

'That's him over there,' says Bones.

'No it's not.'

Bones doesn't answer. Ruiz fills the silence.

373

'I figured there had to be someone on the inside. Tony Murphy needed floor plans of the Old Bailey and knowledge of the camera system. And someone had to sabotage the lift and set up a cover story to get them inside. You're the man, Bones. That's why you're here. And Murphy must be paying your rent rather than Ray Garza.' He motions to the body on the floor. 'If you were working for Garza you wouldn't have shot his boy.'

Bones seems to gag and swallow hard. His eyes are plaintive like a supplicant's.

'I'm sort of fucked,' he mumbles.

'You are.'

'You going to arrest me?'

'I am.'

'Are you armed?'

Ruiz raises the pistol.

Bones leans his head back against the wall and gazes out the window as if looking into the future and finding nothing to look forward to. In his next breath he swings the rifle across his body taking aim. The pistol jerks in Ruiz's hands. The recoil snaps his wrists in the air.

Bones looks down at the hole in his chest as if grading Ruiz on his marksmanship and giving him a C for effort. Then he slides sideways down the wall, resting his rifle gently beside his head.

65

Sami covers the first few hundred yards across open ground heading for a line of trees that is etched darker against the low clouds. For half that distance Nadia hadn't seemed so heavy, but now he's labouring. Slowing down.

Sweat dims Sami's vision and his mind is whirling like a broken fan belt in a runaway engine. Something slips through the grass ahead of him and disappears. It could be an animal. Something feral. He changes direction. The ground pitches forward. He notices a trail of silver water, a small stream surrounded by rotting trees and fallen logs. Everything seems scaled up and reeks of mould and decay.

The rain is heavier, drowning out other sounds. He has no weapon. The clip was empty. He threw the Beretta away.

Ahead he sees a chain-link fence topped with barbed wire. A building site. Turf has been peeled back and the topsoil scraped away by heavy machinery, bulldozers and earthmovers. Massive drainage pipes are stacked along the fence and silver pools of water indicate where boring machines have punched vertical holes deep into the earth.

He notices a gap beneath the fence where a ditch has been dug to let water drain away. He drops to his knees, lowering Nadia to the ground. Jumping into the ditch, he lifts her onto his back, screaming at the pain in his chest. Mud clutches at his shoes as he wades through knee-deep water, ducking beneath the fence. He falls. Gets to his feet. They give way again.

Dragging himself up the bank, he doesn't have the strength to lift Nadia. Sitting on the ground, digging his shoes into the earth, he leans back and pulls. It feels like someone has taken a branding iron to his heart.

Suddenly, a forearm drops past Sami's eyes and tightens across his throat, closing his windpipe. He can smell wet clothes and hear a rasping breath. Kicking his legs, he tries to twist free. One hand rises to his neck. The other loses grip on Nadia, who slides sideways into the ditch and comes to rest with her head just above the waterline.

Sami is being lifted and turned, held still. Tony Murphy swings a fist into his stomach. Hits him again. Gets into a rhythm.

The fat man is breathing hard. Saliva bubbles in his mouth.

'Where is the gun?'

Sinbad loosens his forearm so that Sami can speak.

'I dropped it.'

'Like fuck you did.'

'Back there – at the hospital.'

'Where?'

Sami struggles to remember.

'It was before I jumped out the window.'

He wants to reach Nadia. She's slipping further down the bank, her face almost touching the water. 'Please let me help her.'

Murphy glances back towards the hospital.

'Who did you bring?'

'Ray Garza.'

Murphy pulls a gun from a shoulder holster. Points it towards Nadia's body.

'She's done nothing wrong,' screams Sami.

'You'll watch her die and then I'll kill you.'

He walks to the edge of the ditch and lowers his foot, pushing her head beneath the surface.

Sami hurls himself towards the ditch, but Sinbad wraps a forearm around his throat again. Sami kicks his legs and twists, trying to claw his fingers beneath the crushing pressure squeezing his windpipe.

Trembling with waves of nausea and shock, he's losing consciousness. So this is how death comes. It's not a disease that takes him in sleep when he's an old man and it's not the monster that stalked his childhood dreams. Instead, in those few seconds, he glimpses the damp blackness of puddles and smells the stench of decay.

From somewhere far away he hears a hollow *popping* sound and Sinbad's head slams against his own. The forearm loosens around his throat. Sinbad collapses forward like a slaughtered beast, his brains in Sami's hair.

Murphy rears backwards in surprise and seems to hover on the edge of a flooded hole, swinging his arms in small circles, trying to regain his balance. His toes rise. The fight is lost. Gravity takes over, sending him backwards into the hole.

Murphy surfaces and claws at the muddy sides looking for a foothold or a handhold, but earth crumbles in his hands. He swallows water, coughs and takes another mouthful. The hole is too narrow for him to kick his legs and stay above the surface.

Sami reaches Nadia and rolls her over. She's alive. Conscious. He drags her out of the ditch and hears Murphy calling for help. His head looks like a sculptured clay bust, slick and shining, rearing up from the water with his mouth open, then disappearing again.

His eyes and ears are full of mud. He can't see or hear. And his hands keep reaching up, as though trying to breathe through his fingertips.

Sami doesn't stop to think. A moment ago he wanted Murphy dead. Wanted to do it close up. Would have pulled the trigger himself. Emptied an entire magazine into him. But now he crawls to the edge of the hole and grabs one of Murphy's flailing hands. The clay is so slippery and Murphy so heavy, he can't pull him out. He hunts around for something else. A plank. Drags it across the flooded hole.

Murphy reaches up and hooks his fingers over either side. He can hold his head above the water. Breathe.

'Step away,' says a voice. Sami turns slowly. Ray Garza has a gun in his outstretched hand.

'He'll drown.'

'Let him.'

Sirens are coming. The sound cuts through the rain and crosses the common.

Ray Garza walks to the edge of the flooded hole and steps onto the plank. His shoes are next to Murphy's fingers, which are struggling to get purchase on the wood.

'Hello, Murphy. I was going to dig a hole and bury you but you found one all by yourself.'

Garza raises the toe of his muddy shoe and pivots on his heel, lowering it again on Murphy's fingers. The fat man's face contorts in pain. One hand collapses from the plank.

'Do you think I'm a cunt, Murphy? Do you? Do you think I'm going to let some dumb-as-fuck Mick tear down everything I've built?'

'You got it wrong, Ray. This has nothing to do with you.'

'It has everything to do with me.'

The sirens are getting closer. Garza raises his other shoe and lowers it on Murphy's fingers.

'Just tell me why you did it.'

'It was a mistake. Your boy fucked up. He took some-thing that didn't belong . . .'

Murphy fingers slide off the plank and he disappears beneath the muddy surface, rearing up again a few moments later, more mud than flesh.

Another figure emerges from the darkness. Sami does-n't recognise him, but he's holding a pistol on Garza and looks like he knows how to use it. For a long while noth-ing changes. The stranger doesn't move. Garza doesn't move. Nobody acknowledges anyone.

Then the stranger says, 'It's over, Ray. Drop the gun.'

Garza turns slowly. Lowers his gun. 'I'm here making a citizen's arrest, what's your excuse?'

'Unfinished business.' Ruiz glances at Sami. 'Are you OK?'

Sami nods.

'How about your sister?'

He nods again. 'Who are you?'

'I'm the ex-husband of your parole officer.'

Sami tries to make the connection. It takes a while. Eventually he remembers leaving a message for an ex-detective called Vincent Ruiz.

'Sorry it took me so long.'

'That's OK,' says Sami. 'How did you find me?'

'Girl called Kate Tierney. You might want to do some-thing nice for her. Buy her flowers. Take her to dinner. Girls like stuff like that.'

66

The wind has risen, shunting the clouds away. Now the moon emerges, shining onto puddles and creating thousands of silver lights on the common.

Police cars have surrounded the old hospital, which doesn't seem abandoned any more. It was sleeping and now it's come back to life with paramedics working in the corridors and bodies being wheeled from within.

Nadia is sitting inside an ambulance with a blanket around her shoulders and an oxygen mask over her face. Sami is wearing handcuffs and is under guard, but they've let him sit with his sister. His ribs are broken. He'll need X-rays; painkillers. The adrenalin has stopped coursing through his system and exhaustion takes over. He closes his eyes.

Torches move across the common. Tony Murphy is being carried on a stretcher. It takes six men. Mud has been washed from his eyes and mouth, but his clothes make him look like a terracotta statue dug up from a swamp.

Ruiz watches two detectives climb into the back of an ambulance on either side of Murphy. Then he notices Ray Garza, arguing with Fiona Taylor and demanding to see his lawyer. Garza claims he was trying to apprehend the gang that robbed the Old Bailey and to stop Murphy framing him.

'Listen, sweetheart, you should be thanking me instead of treating me like a criminal,' he says. 'Maybe I should talk to one of your superiors.'

Fiona Taylor doesn't let her anger show but she'll find a way of taking it out on Garza.

Another body is being brought out on a trolley, wheels rattling over the broken asphalt. Fiona Taylor tells the paramedics to stop. She summons Garza over.

'Would you like to make a formal identification now or do it at the morgue?'

'What do you mean?'

Fiona unbuckles one of the straps and peels back the corner of the sheet, revealing a face; a young man, serene given the circumstances. He might even be sleeping except for the blueness around his lips and the small hole in his neck at his larynx.

Ray Garza's face says everything. Murphy sent a boy to do a man's job – *Garza's* boy; his wayward son; his only child.

Reaching out, he touches Ray Jnr, brushing the fringe from his eyes, letting his fingertips drift lower to his lips, willing him to breathe. Garza's eyes fold for just a moment before he throws back his head and howls. Devastated. Inconsolable.

Ruiz watches without any sense of triumph or satisfaction. For twenty-two years he has wanted to see Garza pay for what he did to Jane Lanfranchi, to see a cell door welded shut behind him. But revenge is a poisonous emotion. Jane Lanfranchi's parents lost a beautiful daughter. Ray Garza lost a good-for-nothing son. That doesn't make it even. It doesn't make it ironic. It certainly doesn't make it right.

Four Months Later

Sami Macbeth is back at the Old Bailey. Third time lucky. His trial begins today and the courtroom is so full they've had to close the doors and limit public access.

Emerging from the underground cells, flanked by guards, Sami feels like he's sneaking into the place when everyone else has had to queue for a seat.

He looks around the courtroom. Nadia is sitting in the front row of the public gallery. Kate Tierney is next to her. Holding hands. Keeping their fingers crossed.

Sami has everything crossed. He's not particularly religious but he prayed this morning. It was easier than he thought, like having a one-sided conversation with someone in a coma.

Sami turns. Waves. They wave back. A few other friends are also in the gallery, including some of his mates who made quick readies selling stories about Sami to the tabloids. Their looks seem to say, 'No hard feelings, mate, I was misquoted.'

Vincent Ruiz is sitting next to ex-wife Miranda, Sami's

parole officer, who looks like she's only wearing black until they invent a darker colour.

Ruiz arranged for Sami to get a decent solicitor this time, although Eddie Barrett doesn't look much like a lawyer. He has a bulldog walk and growls at people like he needs distemper shots. Sami hasn't met his silk, but Eddie has faith in the guy.

The prosecutor is a woman, who has short hair and a tailored black suit. She's going for the androgynous look that turns professional women into lovely mysteries.

Everyone rises. The judge is coming – a crusty old fart, who puts a cushion on his seat. Settles down. Reads a long letter, which might be from his mother or could be important.

He takes off his glasses. Raises his eyes.

'Am I to understand, Mrs Lascelle, that the Crown Prosecution Service has sought advice from the Attorney General and decided to alter its position on this matter?'

'Yes, your honour.'

The judge looks at Sami's QC. 'And you're satisfied with the case to proceed on this basis, Mr Gallagher?'

'Yes, your honour.'

'Has your client been made aware of the situation?'

'I haven't had an opportunity to consult with him. Perhaps I could take a few moments ... .'

'By all means.'

The judge puts his glasses back on and returns to his mum's letter. Sami's QC sweeps his black robes behind him and leaves the bar table to talk to his client. His horsehair wig seems too small for his head, or maybe his brain is too big.

In a low rumbling whisper he begins telling Sami that he no longer has to enter a plea as the charges will 'lay on file' for the foreseeable future.

From this point in the briefing Sami becomes fixated on the idea of entering a plea and becomes completely lost.

Eddie Barrett joins them. 'Trust me, kid, do as he says.'

'I did that last time.'

'This is a better deal.'

Mr Gallagher goes back to the bar. The judge folds the letter and puts it in a file. Then he begins writing notes. For the next twenty minutes the courtroom has to watch him scribbling, with nobody saying anything above a whisper.

Finally, he's ready. He blinks through his glasses at Sami, addressing him directly.

'Let me say this, Mr Macbeth. I spent last night reading the details of this case and I can only conclude that you are, without question, one of the unluckiest people to ever set foot in my courtroom. You also appear to have the unfortunate ability to turn a desperate situation into a hopeless one. Does that seem a fair thing to say?'

'Yes, your honour.'

'Armed robbery, manslaughter, grievous bodily harm, abduction, firearms charges, possession of explosives, trespassing, criminal damage . . . I could go on, but there doesn't appear much point given I've been asked to let these matters lay on file until some later, indeterminate date.

'Conceivably the Crown Prosecution Service has thought long and hard about how to proceed in this matter and has chosen to seek your co-operation in other matters before these courts.

'Based upon the recommendations of the CPS and the Attorney General and given the ordeal that you and your sister have endured, I struggle to see how society would benefit from your further incarceration.'

He bangs a polished wooden thingummy on his desk and tells the clerk of the court to dismiss prospective jurors or reassign them to a different jury pool.

Sami raises his hand as though he's still at school.

The judge pauses and looks at him quizzically.

'You have a question, Mr Macbeth?'

'Yes, your honour, I just wondered or hoped, really, that you could explain to me what just happened?'

'There will be no trial today. You're free to go.'

'Free?'

'The allegations against you, Mr Macbeth, have been set aside. They may one day be resurrected but that depends on your co-operation. What you *know*, Mr Macbeth, has become more important than what you've done.'

The judge is gathering his papers to leave.

Sami is dumbstruck. 'Thank you,' he whispers.

His voice carries to the bench. The judge stops and turns.

'Good luck, Mr Macbeth. It may well be that your sole purpose in life is to serve as a warning to others. That's for the future to decide.'

Terminal Four at Heathrow Airport is like a third world outpost with families of refugees taking up corners of the lounge and backpackers sprawled out on hard plastic chairs that will outlive civilisation.

Vincent Ruiz has been allowed airside, along with Miranda. They're watching Sami and Nadia stock up on suntan lotion and travel guides. According to the witness protection guidelines their destination is supposed to be a secret but Sami is wearing a *Save the Whales – Harpoon a Jap* T-shirt promoting Greenpeace in Australia.

'So you're ready,' says Ruiz.

'We're ready.'

Nadia is showing Miranda her purchases. Sami looks up at the departures board.

'Guess we'd better go.'

'I guess so.'

'We'll be back for the trial.'

'You will.'

'Do you think Murphy and Garza will go to prison?'

'That's not your problem. You swear on oath. You tell the truth. You walk away.'

391

'Just like that.'

'Just like that.'

'And what happens then?'

'The rest of your lives.'

Sami nods. Ruiz wants to say stuff like 'stay in touch' and 'don't be a stranger' but none of that's going to be possible. From now on Sami and Nadia will always be someone different. Someone new.

Miranda gives Sami a hug.

'Looks like I'll never be a rock god.'

'You can still have a band. Just don't get too famous.'

'I could wear make-up.'

'Too seventies.'

The goodbyes are said. The hugs are given. Sami and Nadia disappear through the gate into an aeroplane that's so huge it takes a leap of faith to imagine it could sail through the air.

The psychologist, Joe O'Loughlin, once told Ruiz about one of his patients, a commercial pilot, who believed that God picked up each plane on take-off and set it down again on landing. There was nothing that said the guy couldn't fly. He's probably still working.

Ruiz and Miranda walk back through the terminal and step outside.

'You want to come to Paris with me?' he asks.

'Why?'

'Because I've bought the tickets and I don't know if Eurostar will give me a refund?'

'You want my body?'

'Not as a temple – I want it as an adventure playground.'

Miranda laughs. 'You haven't changed.'

Ruiz looks aghast. 'You mean after all the work I've done on myself, trying to shed my bad habits and personality traits . . . and I'm still the same.'

She sighs and tucks her arm through his. 'When do we leave?'

'Saturday.'

'I choose the hotel. You pay the bill.'

He sighs happily. 'It was ever thus.'